FIVE MILE HOUSE

FIVE MILE HOUSE

KAREN NOVAK

BLOOMSBURY

Published by Bloomsbury, New York and London.
Distributed to the trade by St. Martin's Press.

Library of Congress Cataloging-in-Publication Data has been applied for

ISBN 1-58234-159-1

First published in the United States
by Bloomsbury in 2000
This paperback edition published 2001
10 9 8 7 6 5 4 3 2 1

Typeset by Palimpsest Book Production Limited
Polmont, Stirlingshire

Printed in the United States of America
by R. R. Donnelley & Sons Company,
Harrisonburg, Virginia

For Fred,

my last magician.

ACKNOWLEDGEMENTS

A novel may provide a writer with many years' worth of purpose – not to mention nightmares – but it is the people in a writer's life who provide the time, understanding, and faith necessary to see the work to completion. In the case of this novel, I would like to offer thanks and love to the participants of the Mason Writers' Group, especially Shannon Hetz, Nancy Hanner, and Norm Mitchell; to Steve Heilman; and to Deborah Morrison. Thanks go out also to everyone at the Union Institute and the Chenango Valley Writers' Conference: another alum makes good.

To my editor/manuscript shrink, Karen Rinaldi, countless thanks for the gift of your honesty and insight and handholding. Twice that to my agent, Elizabeth Sheinkman at Elaine Markson. A thousand times all of it – and a quilt – to Fred. Moon and stars to follow.

I would thank my family, my husband and daughters, but mere vocabulary would never adequately convey my gratitude. Just know that without you, it's all empty prattle.

Ghost cries out to ghost –
But who's afraid of that?
I fear those shadows most
That start from my own feet.

The Surly One, Theodore Roethke

Prologue

F IVE MILE HOUSE ANTICIPATED intrusion. Even more, it anticipated escape. The house was designed to defend against both, and I, unwilling guardian to this malignant labyrinth, have served only to improve upon Five Mile's forbidding nature. My presence keeps the curious away.

Such was the limit of my existence until Leslie Stone climbed the hill. She stood in the weedy drive and looked up into Five Mile with a defiance that could only bring her to harm. To me, however, it brought joy, for in that defiance I saw myself, more of myself than illusions of face and form might convey. Surely, the time had come. Leslie would know me as I had her. To that end, I laid my hand upon Five Mile's rotting timbers to stay them from collapse. I inhaled, and the front door inched itself ajar. More than permission, it was invitation to come closer.

Leslie laughed a bit at the sudden movement of the door. She did not hesitate. She made her way straight up the front steps. The tremor of her footfall carried along plank and beam, up to rafter, down to foundation. The house shuddered with recognition. By the time Leslie pushed through the entry, Five Mile House had taken full measure. It sensed, as did I, that second chances, at last, had arrived.

The house, of course, made its usual attempts to seduce witness away from me. Leslie wandered the odd front rooms, looking forward and back, trying to see sense in them as though the flaw lay in her perception and not the house itself. Five Mile was configured so one might spend a lifetime in such pursuits. Leslie, however, had not come for the house; she had come for me. In short order, she returned to the main hall and followed it deeper into Five Mile, toward the center of the house and the tower stairs.

I hurried in from my hiding places to meet her, seeping away from cellar and attic, trailing down corridors; I gathered form from old dust and errant light. I shaped voice from a memory of sound. I waited for Leslie in the shadows on the first landing. That is as far as I may go.

Leslie paused at the railing, considering the dim, twisted staircase spiraling up into the heights of Five Mile. She placed her foot upon the step, testing it, and steadied herself with a hand against the broken plaster of the wall. Uncertain, slow, she took one riser, then the next. She was halfway to me. I could wait no longer. I spoke.

'Leslie,' I said, and it sounded like wind in the eaves. 'Leslie.'

She stopped, her head tilted, listening. She took another step. Closer.

'Leslie.'

Her faced changed. She realized it was not the wind she heard. She tried to descend, to back away, but lost her footing and fell, catching herself on the railing. 'No,' she said, motionless for a moment before struggling to right herself. She whispered something instructive, and then she ran. Leslie ran out of Five Mile House.

I watched her slide and scramble down the hill. She did not look back. Not once. It was then my hopes deflated. She had neither heard nor seen me. Whatever frightened Leslie Stone had entered with her.

One

I AM ELEANOR, AND I, like this house, am haunted. I died when I fell from this tower, that window. It is sixty-seven feet from the sill to the stone upon which my neck was broken. All a matter of record. Not recorded, not known, is that I died with secrets: one on my lips and another in my belly. Secrets because there was no one to tell. Not until Leslie. From the moment I first saw her, I knew Leslie Stone had been sent to me as rescue; she would hear my story and in turn relay it back to the living. Truth would get told, and I would be – not forgiven but better understood.

Yet, it was apparent Leslie had brought her own ghosts to Five Mile House. Until those phantom voices quieted, Leslie could hear nothing else. I needed her to hear. And so I resolved to allow time to take her forward into destiny. What else was there to do? It had already begun.

I cannot lay claim to the exact moment that my story began, but Leslie recalls the moment of her beginning well. The memory of it runs in an endless loop of details, like the shadows of a magic lantern rotating against the wall.

It begins in a city, not far from here. It is morning, a few minutes after six. The August sun is a glare creeping up the window shades. Leslie is in the cluttered bedroom she shares with her husband, Greg. She is looking in the mirror, thinking again that she should color her hair, cover up the early gray. She straightens her cotton blouse and khaki skirt, and in her pocket the handcuffs rattle. She makes certain of her badge and the safety on her gun. She puts on the shoulder holster, and then the khaki jacket. The gun, a nine-millimeter Beretta, goes into the holster. The grip is wet because her hands are sweating. Already. They have an air conditioner in the bedroom window. It shudders and purrs like a refrigerated cat. Still, she perspires as though she has been running, full out, for a very long time.

'Hey, Greg,' she calls, 'how high is it supposed to go today?'

'You don't want to know,' he calls back. Greg is at the breakfast table with his coffee and paper, his face shaved clean and his skin menthol scented. He is dressed for his work in blue jeans and a sports shirt. He turns a page of the paper and nearly knocks his coffee mug to the floor. He catches the mug and curses, softly. He hates the tiny kitchen, the cramped apartment, and so each morning he scans the paper for an opportunity, an open call for bids on a suitable property in a country location. The ones he likes he clips out and files. He is thirty-seven and he takes medication for his blood pressure. Greg calls himself an independent contractor.

Leslie comes into the kitchen, where Molly, age ten, is pouring cereal into a bowl for Emma, age four. Greg smiles at his wife and they banter over which of them has the worst of it: he in the sun all day arguing with the subcontractors, she in the car all day rounding up the subcivilized. They laugh. Their daughters sing about Little Bunny Foo-Foo, their mouths full of rainbow-colored milk. Leslie tells them to knock it off, to finish up, to go get dressed. It is a normal morning. The last normal morning.

Molly and Emma dawdle. Leslie shoos them along so she might have a few quiet minutes to talk with her husband. She sits down at the table beside him and runs her fingers over the clippings.

'Anything interesting?'

'Nothing new. Same old invitations to subdevelopment sprawl. I'd rather stick with city work than punch out suburban boxes and strip malls.' He closes the file folder. 'The ones I'd really love to take on are always these arty historical restoration deals. A drywall and drop-ceiling guy like me would look like an idiot if I even tried to bid.'

'You took art history.'

'Art history was one of the courses I was taking when I dropped out.'

'So, fake it. Talk your way in and then prove what you can do.'

'Lie? Fine talk from a cop.'

'Okay, Mister Integrity. I'll keep my fingers crossed. I cannot believe how freaking hot it is.'

He lays his hand against her cheek. 'You feel feverish. Maybe you're coming down with something.'

'Don't think so,' she says, pulling away from his touch.

Greg packs lunches for himself and the girls. He scolds, hurries them toward the door. It's his turn to take them to day-care. There is a last minute chaos of hugs, kisses, and instructions exchanged. Leslie waves to them as they disappear down the hall. They, smiling, look back. She will remember this image of them, again and again, in the coming months. Her family looking back as they disappear. She will remember this and weep until wrung dry of tears.

At half past seven, Leslie is on the subway in the crush of the rush hour commute. Another stop and more bodies push into the train. She grips the hand rail harder. The heat lies on her skin like wet wool. A short woman in a pink linen suit smiles up at Leslie with candy pink lips and tobacco-stained teeth. A noxious swirl of body odor and perfume fills Leslie's lungs, leaving little space for air. She has a headache. Out the corner of her eye, she sees something, someone she knows. Or thought she did – for when she turns, the sense of recognition is gone. Odd. Now her head hurts even more, and she fixes her will on getting to the station house, to the bottle of aspirin in her desk drawer. What? There it is again, that feeling of awakened awareness. A 'wait a minute, don't I know you?' chill sends ice winding down her spine. Leslie begins to look about in earnest: the smiling woman in the pink suit, a pair of teenage lovers kissing violently, the various blank stares of various blank faces. Someone, someone is close, coming closer, and all Leslie knows is that she must get away. The subway brakes engage with shrill fury as the train lurches to a stop. Her stop. Hurry. She elbows, shoulders, squeezes her way toward the door. The platform is crowded and the loudspeaker is blasting unintelligible static. From behind her comes a voice, a child's voice, distinct and bright.

'Is he here?'

Leslie spins around just as the graffiti-covered doors slide shut. The train shudders, and begins moving forward. All Leslie can do is stand and watch as the passing windows gain momentum, making all those blank faces one continuous blur.

Is who here?

She watches the subway rush into the darkness, its retreating lights like the red eyes of carnival demons. She walks toward the exit and climbs the steps up toward daylight on legs that feel mechanical, detached.

Leslie makes her way against the prevailing current of pedestrian traffic. The sidewalk glitters bone bright, and the giant buildings seem hunched closer to the ground as if trying to move away from the tyrannical sun. It is day eleven of a high pressure oppression, eleven days of marking silver lines of mercury in ascent, passing ninety, ninety-five, ninety-seven, ninety-nine . . . No wonder I'm hearing voices, thinks Leslie – weather like this makes the normally sane crazy and the already crazy really determined. She lifts the placket of her blouse off her sweat-damp skin and uses it to pump a bit of a breeze on to her chest. It is not quite five blocks from the subway to the station house. Her head is pulsating with pain. She walks faster.

Leslie reaches Homicide at twenty minutes after eight and heads for the vending machines. She thinks that from the sound of it, Homicide is getting pretty damn close to becoming its own source of business. Cops are yelling at suspects. Suspects are yelling at one another. Somewhere down the hall, a woman wails grief and fury in a foreign tongue. Telephones compete for attention. The air is thick with the singed aroma of burnt coffee. Central cooling is still down. The computers are still down. The vending machines haven't been restocked in a week. SOLD OUT. SOLD OUT. EMPTY. Leslie plugs a dollar's worth of coins into a slot and opts for a forlorn-looking sweet roll. It drops like a sugar-coated hockey puck. She picks it up by one corner of the murky cellophane package and shoves the whole idea into the first waste can she sees. You are spending far too much time in Homicide, she tells herself. No kidding? What was your first clue?

She has not been reassigned so much as appropriated. What with the budget cuts and manpower shortages, her responsibilities as a mediator on the Domestic Violence Task Force had devolved into the deceptively simple task of counting up the bodies and calling in the guys at the other end of the office. Putting her in Homicide was a genius move toward efficiency.

And efficient she is. Leslie has called in seven domestic deaths in less than ten days. Five of them kids. Three shootings: one accidental, two deliberate. Number four had been kicked to death for breaking a portable air conditioner. Number five, the most recent one, just yesterday, was a six-year-old who had tried to stop his mother's boyfriend from beating her. The boyfriend, annoyed by the interruption, had picked up the woman's child and tossed him out the window. Sixteen stories. The end.

Later, at the inquiry, the department psychologist will say the death of this little boy had been the trigger. Those in attendance will nod knowingly. Of course. Of course.

Leslie says good morning to her partner, Ross. He grunts a reply. She positions herself at her beat-up old desk, turns on the little oscillating fan she brought in from home, and begins writing up her report on the six-year-old boy. The pen scrapes and drags. The shapes it forms look in no way familiar to Leslie. She keeps writing. The fan is moving its round head, back and forth, back and forth, back and forth. No. No. No. She turns it up to its highest setting because, although she doesn't feel as though she's crying, tears are dribbling down her face, and she can't seem to make them stop. The press of the fan's forced air helps to dry them before they drip from her jaw onto the blue ink of the report. She keeps trying to reread the words that have crawled from beneath her pen, but her eyes refuse to recognize any of them. She squints hard, but the blue loops and spikes are meaningless. Her hands shake. The phone rings.

Later, the doctors will tell Leslie if that call hadn't come right then, she would have most certainly shattered there at her desk. But the phone does ring, and like everyone else she works with, her response is Pavlovian. At the sound of the bell, she stops feeling and she goes to work.

Leslie takes the call. It's another one. She writes down the address.

'We've got another kid, Ross.'

Ross looks up at her from his pile of manila folders. He loosens his tie before tightening it again. She will remember that. The investigators from Internal Affairs will ask what she remembers and she'll tell them about Ross's tie. The stenographer will take it down on the transcription machine. She takes down every word Leslie says:

I know it sounds stupid, but that's what I remember, that dark blue knot moving down and then moving up. And then Ross asked me what the call was and I said the word but I didn't actually hear. There was a sound in my head, like a seashell sound, that made it hard to hear anything at all. Ross said something back that I didn't understand. He looked at me and shook his head. Then he grabbed his jacket off the back of his chair and said, 'Let's go.'

I think that's what he said. That's what he usually says. Anyway, I got up from my desk and followed him out. There was this weird sense of not being attached to myself. It was like I was following myself as I followed him down the stairs. Does that make sense? I felt dizzy, really sick inside, as if I might vomit. I blamed it on the heat. It was so goddamn hot.

When we got to the parking lot I told Ross he'd better drive.

Ross just kind of stared at me. He knows how much I love to drive. He said something like – 'Jesus, Les, you look like bleached shit' – something like that. He said that Jutzi would cover for me. But I said no, I was okay.

We got in the car. Again there was that feeling; it's so hard to describe. It was like I was still standing in the parking lot watching myself drive away. We drove and drove. I knew the address was only a couple miles from the station house, but it seemed as though we'd spent hours in the car getting nowhere at all. The heat, you remember how horrible it was. It was as if some vacuum had sucked up all the breathable air. I kept trying to inhale, but all I'd get was a mouthful of exhaust fumes. The sidewalks were full of people. One moment they looked normal, the next they were – they seemed to be staggering, just trudging along with their heads down like zombies or something. Like I was watching a movie. I kept trying to focus on details, to see one of them as separate from the others, but I couldn't. They were just this river of deaths waiting to happen. At least, that's what I remember thinking. I couldn't save them. By this time my hands were shaking so hard I had to hold them still. Ross was talking. I couldn't hear a word he said.

We pulled up to the address, a small but classy residential hotel. Prewar, my husband would say. There was an ambulance farther ahead, but the paramedics were putting things away. Too late.

We ran up the front steps anyhow. The doorman was giving a statement to a uniformed officer, and I heard how his voice shook. His face was wet, shiny wet, and his eyes were red. He pulled back the heavy glass door for us. The lobby was very – you know – anonymous looking, all polished wood and metal. It was all air-conditioned, cold and quiet. It always gets really quiet when it's a kid. I recall another uniform was speaking with the woman at the desk. She was showing him a book, and he was writing something down. I wanted to ask him what he'd found, but the elevator doors slid open and Ross said, 'Let's go,' because that's what he always says.

We went up to the third floor. The hallway was lit by fixtures on the ceilings and the walls. I remember thinking that I don't like all these lights because it either throws shadows everywhere at once or cancels shadow out completely. It's crappy for surveillance because you can never tell from which direction things are coming. Anyway, I remember getting dizzy again, but it was worse this time. I felt, for a second, as if I was going to pass out. Half a second at the most. I think the pattern on the carpet was playing tricks on my eyes. It was sort of an off-white grid over dark green . . . never mind, just an optical illusion. We passed by a lot of rooms. The doors were closed. I found myself counting ahead. 322. 324. 326. That door was open. Sunlight fell from the space where the door should be. Voices were coming from inside the light. I couldn't go in there. I had to go in there.

Ross went in first. That strange splitting sensation was back, and I ended up leaving a part of myself out in the hall – that's how it felt. We entered a sitting room with a couch and chairs and a television. The room was rigged with video equipment. There was a third officer. Young, just a baby, he had a little bandage on his chin where he'd nicked himself shaving. He introduced us to the man sitting in a chair with his face in his hands as the manager. Ross asked about the body. The officer tilted his head to the side, toward the louvered door to our left. The officer didn't want to look again.

'Let's go,' Ross said.

I went in behind him. The first thing I saw was more camera equipment. I was about to mention it to Ross, when I saw his back tense, his fists clench, as his body braced itself against the impact of discovery. 'Ah, Christ,' he said, and moved aside so that I could see. And so I saw.

She was such a little thing, about four years old. She looked like – do you have kids? Yeah, you know how the real little ones can just dive into sleep? One minute they're bouncing off the wall, the next they've disappeared into that deep, open-mouthed, end-of-the-world slumber? That's how she looked. I wanted Ross and me to just tip-toe away so we wouldn't disrupt her. Just tip-toe away. But we couldn't, of course. So much blood. So much, well, you saw the photos, didn't you? You saw what he did to her, didn't you? I was standing at the end of the bed looking down, seeing, just seeing.

My throat suddenly clamped down tight and I felt as though I were shrinking or the room was getting bigger, or both. I was seeing a little girl on a bed and the . . . and then the child became Emma. It wasn't a momentary flash like the dizzy spell or a misplaced fear. I saw Emma, my Emma, dumped there like a ruined doll. I couldn't move. Ross was talking to me. I looked over and saw his mouth moving, but I heard only this dull, snoring buzz in my head, like an alarm clock I couldn't shut off. I looked back to the bed, still seeing, until Ross pulled me away, sort of steered me out of the room. He handed me over to the officer. He literally put my arm in the young officer's hand. Ross told him that Detective Stone was not well, told him to take her back to the station house.

'Listen up.' Ross put his hand on the back of my neck and squeezed hard; it hurt. 'Listen. Les, I want you to get your stuff and go home. Go see your kids. Give 'em big hugs. Take 'em out for ice cream.' He held my neck, making me look at him, nothing but him.

I reached up and placed my hands on Ross's big, dark face. Kindness. I wanted to touch someone kind. I wanted to take that kindness with me, wear it like a cloak, carry it like a shield.

Ross glanced over at the uniform and then said, 'That's not one of yours in there, Leslie.' He took my wrists and lowered my arms back to my side. 'Not one of yours.'

'They're all mine,' I said, but I don't know if I said it out loud.

'Go home, Leslie.'

Go home? He didn't understand. I couldn't see the difference. I couldn't see anything before me except my baby ravaged and dead. Where could I go to not see any more dead children? The officer guided me out of the room and into the hallway, where I thought I would find myself waiting. No one was there. We went down in the elevator, across the lobby and out the door. God, it was hot.

The uniform led me along the path. He shouldered through the gawkers crowded along the sidewalk. He started yelling, 'It's too hot to be standing around looking at nothing! Let's get moving, people! Nothing here to see!' The stuff we usually yell. They grumbled but started to break up. The officer turned back and nodded at me.

It is good to be able to do something, I thought, anything that helps. Poor baby.

He secured me in the passenger seat of his patrol car. Once behind the wheel, he reached under his seat, brought up a can of ginger ale, and offered it to me. I took it. He logged in on the radio – very by-the-book – as he pumped the accelerator and nosed the car into traffic.

He told me his name – Rigby, I think it was. He tried to start a conversation. I said nothing, I only stared at the top of the soda, the little engraving that shows how to open the can. PULL UP. PUSH BACK. *It's funny what you remember.*

He kept looking at me. I think he expected me to say something wise or comforting. Finally, he said it for me. 'You never get used to it, do you?'

I lifted the key on the can. It opened with a crack and a pop. I'd done as I was instructed.

Then he said something like 'At least they got the sick bastard.'

I remember feeling my head turn toward his voice. That sort of spurred him on, I guess, because he told me how the woman at the desk had seen the little girl come in with the suspect. He kept the place on a long-term lease, used it when he was in the city on business. Which meant there are probably other . . . victims.

I closed my eyes, but the image wouldn't go away. Emma, brutalized, murdered, reflected back infinitely like a funhouse hall of mirrors. Except these weren't tricks of light; each and every one of them was real. They were all mine.

Officer Rigby was still talking about how they'd picked up the fucking predator on the platform, waiting for the train to take him back to his big house in the suburbs. He couldn't understand it. The guy had a wife, three kids of his own. Poor Rigby.

'Where are they taking him?' I asked him that – I think it was just as we got to the station house.

'Here,' he said. 'Detective Saunders probably wants to bring in the hotel manager and that desk clerk to ID the asshole. We'll just line 'em up, shoot him down.'

He pulled the vehicle to the curb, and said, 'I have to be getting back out there. Hope you're feeling better.'

'Yes, of course,' I said. 'And thank you,' I said.

Later, Officer Rigby will testify that yes, although she had seemed more stable at that point, the dullness of Detective Stone's voice had concerned him. If there had been time, he would have escorted her into the station house. If his own mind had not been so blunted by the murder and the heat, if he'd had more experience, he would have known to ask her to surrender her weapon.

She steps out of the car; the soda can falls from her hands. It hits the sidewalk with a thud and a gush of liquid. Leslie watches the can spin round and round like an insane little engine, until exhausted of its energy it rolls away to drop into the gutter. Suddenly cold, as though in the midst of some private winter, she hugs herself and looks up at the opening, closing, opening, closing of the station house doors. She starts up the stairs.

Her colleagues speak and she smiles. To each of their questions, comments, puzzled expressions, she says only one thing: 'Is he here?' No one understands what she is asking, so she moves on until she finds Detective Michael Jutzi, who is sitting on the edge of his desk, eyeing her in careful appraisal.

'Who you looking for, Les?'

'Is he here?'

Jutzi stands and comes over to the wooden rail that separates the detectives from the public. He runs his fingers over his mustache. 'Ross called in. I'm supposed to haul your ass out the door and drive you home.'

'Is he here?'

'Interview Two. He's awaiting the arrival of his attorney.'

'Thank you.' She turns away, heading for the back of the building.

Jutzi jumps the rail and lands in front of her. 'Let it go, Les. I called Greg. He'll be at your place before we are – '

'Have I been taken off the case?'

'Technically? No.'

'Okay, then let me have three minutes. Maybe I can get him talking before his attorney gags him.'

'Three minutes?' Jutzi grins.

'You can come in with me. Make sure I behave myself.'

He sucks on his teeth. 'I don't know.'

'Do you really think I'd do anything to jeopardize a conviction here?'

Detective Michael Jutzi never has a chance to voice his opinion. In her deposition Leslie will state that the telephone began to ring. The squad secretary was away from her desk. No one else was around.

He raises a finger in her face, indicating she is to wait for his return. Jutzi runs for his phone, leaving her alone outside Interview Two.

She can see the monster, the shape of him, behind the wire-reinforced window in the door. The precinct is so short of personnel, they've had to leave him alone. So, he's in the cage. Good. The doorknob is old, heavy. It sticks. She lifts up and turns.

Leslie shuts the door behind her, pulling to make sure the catch is set. There is a long table and three sturdy wooden chairs. He's staring at her. A big man in a plum-hued polo shirt and shorts the color of wet putty. His face is thick, his expression clouded and mistrustful. He is perspiring; great heavy drops of sweat drip down his skin.

'I want my attorney.' His voice is plaintive, almost an adolescent whine.

'Of course you do. I thought maybe you'd also want to get out of there for a minute, stretch your legs. Have something cold to drink.'

He pouts. 'So, what? You're the nice cop?'

Leslie laughs. 'Maybe. Look, I'm one of the detectives on this case. I've got to start my paperwork. I need some basic info – '

'I'm not talking to anyone without my attorney.'

'You want out of there or not? We're talking name and address, that's it. It can't hurt you any to come across as cooperative. The innocent are always cooperative, right?'

'Yeah. Okay.' He stands.

'Move back,' she says. She bangs back the latch at the top of the cage with one hand as the other dives into the pocket of her skirt. Her fingers close around the strangely cool metal teeth of handcuffs.

She has no idea what she is doing, yet it feels as though she's done it hundreds of times before. The cage door comes open. She slips inside. She whips the cuffs out of her pocket. One ring of the cuff closes through the rigid steel lattice on the door. The other closes about the frame. So fast. So slow. Click. Click.

'Hey!' he yells, and keeps yelling. Her gun is in her hand. She doesn't remember drawing it. And then Jutzi is shouting at her, and the cage door is rattling mightily. Click. Click. Jutzi is trying to get in. The monster on the floor beneath her is trying to breathe around his terror and the gun Leslie has rammed into his mouth. She's just trying to do something that makes sense. Click. Click. Nothing happens. Something's wrong.

Stupid. Stupid. Still laughing, she releases the safety as Michael Jutzi, behind her, unlocks the cuffs. The monster is cowering, pushing himself into the corner as Leslie takes aim. Aiming is difficult as she is jumping up and down. A happy little dance. It is good to be able to do something that helps.

Later, she will sign the paper stating the last thing she remembers of that morning, the very last thing, is Michael Jutzi, his voice coming toward her, his hand, so gentle, on her shoulder. He is calm and kind, saying her name, nice and low, talking her down, the way they were trained. Her arms relax. The gun lowers.

'Aw, Jesus . . . Aw, Jesus.' The guy on the floor is wiping his eyes. This is what she says she remembers.

Leslie will sit fascinated by the motion of the stenographer's fingers two-stepping over the transcription keys. The fingers will stop, pausing, waiting for Leslie to finish.

The guy on the floor, the suspect, stated his belief that my behavior was his guarantee of release; he'd be back on the street by happy hour. Happy hour, those were his words. He started to laugh. He was right. I knew he was right, so I shot him.

14

Two

S HE SITS WITH HER eyes closed, her left hand rubbing her right, trying to erase the ache the gun left when it fired. Her ears drone with a sort of infinite echo. Ross squeezes her shoulder.

'Can I get you something, Les?'

'No,' she says, and opens her eyes to see the preliminary report still on the table in front of her. Ross has brought this to the room where they are holding her. He wants her to see what they know, hard fact, before she is confronted by the already gathering speculations. He sits beside her, watching.

The victim's name was Amy. 'Amy,' Leslie says it aloud.

'Yeah,' says Ross. 'Coroner's office has already leaked cause of death as probable – how are they putting it – catastrophic cerebral event. An aneurysm, something like that.'

'The fear got her.'

'Or the pain,' Ross says. 'It happens.'

She looks at the notes again. 'And there's nothing that puts him there. Not one thing?'

'The room was leased in his name, but he let business contacts use it when they were in town. The place is covered in prints. The camera equipment belongs to his company. No film was found. The front desk clerk remembers the girl but is no longer real clear on who came in with her – she says she can't be sure.'

'Somebody got to her?'

'I think she's afraid somebody might if she gets too good with her memories.'

Leslie reads down the list of evidence gathered. 'No semen?'

'The reports indicate that trauma was inflicted with a variety of inanimate objects. Look, Les, seventeen years of this crap has given me damn sharp instincts and my instincts tell me you took out a world-class creep.'

Leslie closes her eyes again, rubs her hand harder. 'She tried to warn me, Ross. She tried to warn me to make sure.'

'Who warned you? What are you talking about?'

'Amy. This morning on the way to work. She was on the subway. She tried.'

Ross sucked in air through his teeth. 'You gotta hold it together, Les. Listen, this is going to get fucking ugly, fucking fast. The guys upstairs have all kinds of sympathy for you, but the widow is pressing charges. Crazy cops do not make appealing press. They're going to let you ride this as far down as it'll go. You gotta keep your head clear and fight. You gotta give me and Jutzi a chance to take the stand and make sure they hear all of it.'

'"Is he here?" That's what Amy said. "Is he here?"'

'Shit, Les. I'm sorry.' Ross took her elbow. 'Let's go. I gotta take you down to booking.'

I will not trouble you with all the dark matter avalanched down upon Leslie Stone in the days immediately following. Leslie was arraigned and tried. Based on the testimony of her colleagues and the public pleas for clemency from Amy's family, Leslie was found to have been not guilty for reasons of temporary insanity. The judge accepted the verdict but stated his concern for Leslie's safety, as she had been held on suicide watch for most of her detainment. He ordered her committed to an appropriate facility until doctors told him she was not a risk to herself or anyone else.

Five times each week, Greg drove Molly and Emma to visit their mother. While Greg spoke with her doctors, the girls would show Leslie pictures they had drawn for her. They'd tell her knock-knock jokes and sing songs they learned at school. Leslie might listen and nod. She might hug them tight and weep. She might doze or be so distracted as not to pay any attention to them at all. On the way back, Greg would explain that Mommy was still taking the medicine that made her seem so far away. Molly might scream that she hated Mommy and was never going back to that awful, disgusting place. Then Emma would cry because she was scared of Mommy if Molly wasn't there. Molly would hold Emma, as closely as their seatbelts allowed, and promise, cross her heart, she'd go next time. Greg would nail his mind tight to the task of driving. If the girls saw him cry, he figured they'd all be lost.

At night, while the girls slept, Greg pored over his file of clippings. Every so often, he'd choose one and dash off a letter inquiring if he might be qualified to bid. The next morning, he'd drop the letter in the mail with the sort of giddy doom he'd known bluffing a bad hand of cards; he'd lost before he'd started. The rejections came swift, and he found a sort of comfort in their bracing nothing-personal dismissals. Greg began to collect these turn-downs along with the clippings. The files lay side by side on his desk. He'd labeled them: MAYBE and NO.

And so it went, week after week, until the first Saturday morning in February when they were together at visitors' hour in the hospital's sun room. It was a cold, clear day. Sunlight gleamed off vinyl couches and sparkled the cobwebs spanning the leaves of wilting fichus trees. Speakers hidden in the ceiling sent forth a steady flow of mediocre music. It had been snowing the night before, and Emma, in dripping snow boots, was showing Leslie the list of seeds they'd ordered for their little plot in the community garden. Leslie held the ragged-edged page ripped from one of Molly's school notebooks. She nodded at the diagrams as Emma explained about the carrots and broccoli and tomatoes and zucchini. Molly paced the length of the room and corrected Emma's pronunciation. Greg alternately hushed one and encouraged the other. Leslie's expression darkened. Husband and daughters froze.

'Rhubarb?' Leslie said. 'We're planting rhubarb? No one in this family eats rhubarb. What am I going to do with all this rhubarb?' It was the first time she had spoken of herself as being a part of them, as belonging somewhere other than this bright, sterile place with its stupefying music and artificial cheer. From that moment on, the word *rhubarb* became the Stone family's private code for hope.

In mid-March, when the green fingertips of crocus leaves pushed through the dirty gray crust of old snow, Leslie's doctor, Janice Caudril, placed a call to Greg. She said that they were reaching the terminus of what help the hospital might offer his wife. Leslie had responded well to the medication. She understood her actions as destructive and accepted responsibility for them. She was the walking definition of remorse.

'But . . .' said Greg.

17

'But,' said Dr Caudril. 'She's struggling. Like most of us she finds being angry easier than being afraid. The problem is she is still very afraid.'

'Afraid of what?'

'Herself, mostly.'

'Maybe she's not ready to be released?'

'Mr Stone – Greg, we can't hold people for being human.'

Greg was quiet for a while. 'Excuse me for saying so, Doctor Caudril, but that's not exactly what I'd call reassuring. Is the judge just going to let her walk away?'

'Leslie has served her sentence as it was defined. She's depressed, Greg, not psychotic. Dealing with the violent death of children is a tremendous burden to the psyche, a burden that, for one moment, was more than Leslie could carry. That's what *temporarily insane* means.'

'But what happens if she's overwhelmed again? Even temporarily. It seems too big a risk.'

Janice Caudril half laughed. 'Getting out of bed every morning is too big a risk. If it were you, Greg, what would you want?'

'I'd want to know my kids were safe.'

'Of course your daughters are safe. It was your daughters Leslie believed she was protecting when she pulled that trigger.'

He hung up the phone, clasped his hands together to stop their trembling, and then went into the living room that served as his office. On his desk sat a pile of bills and the MAYBE and No files. The No file had grown thick, and it took Greg a few minutes to sift out the envelope he'd received a few weeks ago, the one that had spurred genuine optimism until he realized it must be a bad joke. It was a short, handwritten note:

Dear Greg Stone,

You were referred to me through your correspondence with a former client. I am told you are looking for a supervisory position in a restoration project. I am the historical consultant on a project that is in need of someone who recognizes the business end of a hammer. Perhaps we might prove of help to each other. If you are interested in obtaining further information, please contact me at the address below.

Gwendolyn Garrett
c/o Five Mile House
Wellington

Attached to the note was a photocopy of an open call for bids on something called the Five Mile restoration. The project was a gut and reconstruction of an old mansion in the lake region to the north. No photograph was provided, only a rundown of very basic information about the house and its current condition. It was the note that had made Greg suspicious. Gwendolyn Garrett had used letterhead from Mansfield Custom Builders, a concern that Greg in his wildest flights of ambition would never dream to approach. Mansfield Custom were high-profile artisans who never hired from outside. He had been almost entirely certain whoever sent this had connected his name to the press coverage Leslie had received. Ha, ha. Very funny. Better to assume that humiliation than concede the faint possibility that it was indeed a sincere offer made out of pity for his family's fortunes. Still on this day, at this moment, Greg Stone knew that their future rested on his success at erecting some sort of barrier between Leslie and her monsters.

He studied the rudimentary Five Mile specifications, scribbling notes on a legal pad and punching numbers into a calculator. When he had some preliminary figures, he dialed the phone number written on the note. Gwen Garrett answered on the third ring. She was saying that she was happy and relieved that he had called. He interrupted her before she'd finished her first sentence.

'First, I need to know why me.'

She paused. 'If you don't like my answer, will you still take the job?'

'I don't have the job. I don't even know if I want to bid yet.'

'Bids aren't really necessary, Greg. We don't really have much of a budget to consider here.'

Then he understood. 'I'm going to have to say no, Miss – '

'Gwen.'

'Gwen. If I were a kid just starting out I'd be happy to donate some hours, but I have a family to take care of, so you see – '

'No, Greg, I guess I haven't made myself clear. Money is not something we have to worry about. Whatever we need will be provided.'

'Right. What's the catch?'

'Wellington.' She laughed. 'You'd have to live in Wellington. But before that scares you off, let me give you some more information.'

They talked for nearly two hours. By the end of the phone call, Greg could only keep saying, 'Thanks. You don't know how much I needed this. Thanks.'

Over the first weekend in April, Greg moved his daughters to Wellington. He depleted the family savings to buy the modest cottage Gwen had suggested, one that had belonged to a member of the Wellington family. The cottage was situated back from the road in the center of a garden now overgrown with wild morning glories, quick grass, and plantain weeds. Greg's plan was to rehabilitate the cottage and grounds, to make ready a place for Leslie's return. He worked past one every morning and all day on Saturdays and Sundays. He had Molly painting shutters and Emma polishing drawer pulls. Carpets came up, and old wood floors were scrubbed. He bought five-gallon buckets of egg shell latex and painted all the interior surfaces the same shade of white, rolling over spiders, flies, and dust. They ate pizza every night, doughnuts every morning. They washed every window with vinegar and newspaper until the entire cottage gleamed like a box meant for holding light.

On the fifth morning in May, just as the sun had crested and was settling into its afternoon descent, Leslie stood on the frost-heaved walkway outside her new home, a suitcase in each hand. Emma darted about the garden like a dragonfly, shouting, 'Look, Mommy! This is where my swing is going! Look, Mommy! There's a nest in this tree!' Molly, standing apart, bounced a plastic bag full of her mother's possessions off one knee, then the other, and stared at the house. 'I painted the shutters,' she said to the lengthening shadows. 'If you don't like that green color, you can change it.' Greg waited by the front door, watching Leslie for signs he feared he wouldn't recognize.

'So, what do you think?' he asked.

'It's beautiful.'

'Come in then. See the rest.' Greg opened the door. She hesitated and then walked forward. When she reached the door, Greg took her bags and moved aside.

Leslie stepped over the threshold. In doing so, her story became one with mine.

Three

THAT EVENING, GREG TOOK them to Dandy's Big Burger drive-in. They ate Big Burgers and french fries from window trays in the car. Emma and Molly took turns listing the life necessities Wellington did not offer; there were no malls, no movie theaters, no McDonald's.

'It's awful,' said Molly.

'It's not so bad.' Greg straightened the rearview mirror to see his older daughter. 'All those things are just up the road in Rutherford.'

'Rutherford is like an hour away.'

'I've ruined her life.' He looked at Leslie, who was poking at her half-eaten hamburger. 'Feel like taking a tour?'

She smiled at him, relieved by the idea of motion. 'Yeah. Sure. I'd better start getting my bearings.'

Greg drove the long way home. The girls entertained themselves with Rock-Paper-Scissors as he steered up and down the small crumbled streets of Wellington, pointing out local conveniences to Leslie. She saw the post office/city hall, the tiny grocery store, both bars, the diner, the nice restaurant, and the catalog outlet. There was one dentist, one pediatrician, one family doctor –

'No shrinks?'

– one chiropractor, three churches. Wellington boasted a combination bowling alley and billiard room. It was a minor hub for bus traffic. There were a couple of antiques stores that Greg believed to be old-timers trying to sell off the contents of their homes. Many of the houses stood empty on untended lots. Most were big Victorians with rounded turrets and generous verandahs, every eave, every upper nook holding filigreed woodwork. At the lower levels, however, much of the gingerbread was missing.

'Actually, it gets stolen. Dealers drive up from the city and help themselves. No one's here to argue.'

Leslie pressed her palm against the car window. She imagined Hansel and Gretel, on making their escape, turning back for one last bite. The image gave her a chill. 'So, where'd everybody go?'

'Wellington was never anything but a resort place. A lot of these were summer homes.'

'It is good to be rich.'

'Well, it was until the Depression. The money went away. The people followed. Wellington got forgotten.'

'But it's still here. What do the locals do?'

'There's a big concrete recycling plant outside of town; other than that, it's just tourist biz. Tourists, that's what I think the Five Mile fix-up is about.' He ignored the stop sign at an intersection and made a left on to the cross street.

'It's just another big old house like these, right?'

Greg glanced again at the rearview mirror. 'Later, Les. There's the Garretts' place.' He pointed to a house, a trim little Cape Cod painted in blues and white, set back a distance from the curb. At the curb was a sign carefully lettered in a flowing Art Nouveau style: SPIRITUAL CONSULTATION. DIVINATION. HERBAL REMEDIES. AUTOMATIC WRITING. INQUIRE WITHIN.

'That's your Garrett person. That's Gwen?'

'Yep. She practices – what do you call it? Wicca?'

'You mean she's a witch?' Leslie couldn't help herself; she covered her mouth to hide her laughter, but without much success. 'Did she tell you this before or after you took the job?'

'She didn't tell me. Her husband did. Had us out to dinner one of our first nights here, and Joe offered me their services – at a discount, mind you – because Gwen and I are colleagues.'

'Their services? Her husband is into it, too?'

'Joe runs the business end of it, I think. Mostly, he sighs a lot. Drinks, too.'

'I bet he does.'

Again he looked in the rearview and then gestured for Leslie to lower her voice. 'We have to be nice, Leslie. Gwen's pregnant.'

'Oh, baby witches.' Laughing had given her the hiccups.

Greg wagged his finger at her. 'Just because you're not Nature Girl doesn't mean there's anything to make fun of. I mean, she's just doing the kinda thing that's been done all over the world for centuries.'

'Yeah, at medicine shows.'

'Stop being mean and hold your breath. Count to ten. Slowly.' He steered the car through a wide right turn, as he pointed out a long gravel road running straight into the woods. 'That's how you get to the lake. There's a park and the girls seem to enjoy the beach.'

'What there is of it,' said Molly, confirming her parents' sense that she had been eavesdropping.

Greg cleared his throat. 'Oh, and the founders' original home is down there. Town's kept it up best they could. It's open to the public as a museum and library.'

'What hours are they open?'

'Why?'

'I don't know. Just looking for something to do. Is that a problem?' She looked over Greg and saw the tendons in his jaw working to keep his mouth shut.

'No problems, Les. Let's talk about this later.'

They drove the rest of the distance to their house without speaking. Greg pulled into the driveway, and Leslie saw a small yellow lump tucked against the front door. 'What's that?'

Molly and Emma leaned over the front seat to see what Leslie was seeing. A second later, they were shouting, 'It's Sam! It's Sam! Sam came back!' They were out of the car before it had completely stopped. The yellow lump became a stumpy-legged missile covered with short yellow hair, thumping tail at one end, panting tongue at the other. The puppy raced to greet them. Molly swooped down and picked the puppy up like a piece of firewood. She ran toward her parents, with Emma squealing in pursuit.

'Uh-oh,' said Greg. He opened the door of the car to 'It's Sam! Dad, you said if Sam came back we could keep him! You said so.'

In anticipation of what was coming next, Greg and Leslie locked eyes through the windshield. Leslie raised her hands in resignation. Greg relayed the news, and the joy began in earnest. Molly and Emma jumping, shrieking, while the puppy itself bounced in

Molly's embrace, helpless in the wake of little-girl love. Molly skipped to Leslie's side of the car with Emma close behind. Bright-faced, breathless, she held out their prize. Leslie rolled down her window.

'I love him. It's a boy. I checked. He came out of the woods on the day we moved here and Dad said he probably belonged to someone but he didn't have a collar and then Dad said we could keep him until someone came looking for him but then he ran away and now's he's back so we can keep him and his name is Sam.'

'His name is Sam,' echoed Emma. 'You want to pet him, Mommy?'

Molly extended the puppy halfway through the window. Leslie reached up to stroke the floppy yellow ears, at which point Sam clamped his jaws shut on the tender flesh between Leslie's thumb and finger.

'Hey!' Leslie smacked the puppy's nose. 'Bad dog!'

The puppy yelped and let go. Molly clutched the dog to her chest and glared at her mother before running off toward the back of the house.

'Those three are out cold,' Greg said as he came downstairs.

'Finally.' Leslie sat on the floor of the empty front room, running her fingers along the curving grain of the wood planks as if following a map. 'So, what did you do with all our stuff?'

'Our priceless antiques?' He carried a wooden chair with a broken armrest from the kitchen to where Leslie was sitting. 'I thought you hated our stuff.'

'Yeah, I do. You didn't throw it away, did you?'

'No. Of course not. It's in storage. I thought – well, it's a new house, and I thought you might like to sort through it, and you know, decide what you want to keep.'

'I want to keep it all.'

'Then I'll call tomorrow and have it all sent over.'

She said nothing.

'Les? Did I do something wrong?'

'No. Don't worry about it.'

'I just thought, you know, the past. I thought maybe you'd like a change.'

'I've had a change. I was kinda hoping to change back. It's okay, Greg.'

He inched his chair a bit closer to her. 'You must be very tired.'

'That's one word for what I am.'

'Let's get you to bed, then.' He stood and offered her his hand. She took it and pulled him down to the floor beside her.

'I am not a piece of your mother's good china. Try to remember that, okay?'

'What does that mean?'

'Never mind. I'm going to bed.' She squeezed his fingers. 'You coming?'

'Not now. I can't. I've got to take a look at next week's work.'

'You're kidding. I thought you were going to tell me all about Five Mile House.'

'That is no bedtime story. I'm sorry, Les, but I really do need to work. We'll talk tomorrow.' The muscles in his hand flexed against her grip. She let him go. He stood, picked up the chair, and carried it back to the kitchen.

Their bedroom was as small and plain as the rest of the house. The air smelled of lemon oil and turpentine. The lack of furnishings gave it a hollow quality that made an echo of any sound. Greg had managed to get the bed there, the frames and the mattress at least. He'd put folding tray tables on either side with a small lamp in the center of each. The clock radio was on his side, on hers a battalion of amber prescription bottles. It was after ten. Time for an Ambien and its dead drop into sleep. Leslie selected the appropriate bottle and sat at the foot of their bed. Greg had overmade it with white flannel sheets and white thermal blankets tucked up tight against a bank of white pillows. White curtains shifted at the open window. She snapped off the plastic bottle cap. The soft light of the lamps made the surrounding white softly luminous, and Leslie, in dark jeans and dark sweater, thought of herself suddenly as that tiny speck of irritant that necessitates pearls. She dry swallowed a little white pill.

The bedroom walls were bare except for a framed family portrait, Leslie's favorite picture of them together. They'd had it done at a local department store for Emma's first Christmas;

it had been their gift to each other that very lean year. Greg looked stiff and stoic in his too-small suit, the only one he owned. Molly, front tooth missing, had insisted on pigtails, and Leslie could still remember trying to even out the red bows on her daughter's pitch-colored braids. Emma's long-bald baby head was just beginning to show dark brown fuzz. She'd been teething and miserable. The photographer had to snap each shot as Emma inhaled between screams. Leslie was in a borrowed red velvet jumper and white blouse, her own black hair piled in loose curls atop her head. The photographer had said she looked like 'Snow White's sexy sister,' for which she blushed, even though she knew it had been an order-more-prints sales ploy.

Now, Leslie sat on the end of the bed and studied the picture with the same determination she'd seen in parents as they pored through mug shots of underage hookers and junkies. The four souls in the photograph stared in blue-eyed unity back at Leslie. They looked alternately stunned, tired, amazed. They floated in their eight-by-ten-inch walnut frame on the blank sea of freshly painted whiteness, survivors in a lifeboat drifting mercifully away from the wreckage.

Leslie went to the wall, removed the frame from its hook, and returned to the bed. She lay down with the portrait cradled to her chest, and fell asleep.

When she awoke, it was still night. For a second her throat closed in panic; her heartbeat accelerated hard; she didn't know where she was. Wellington, she remembered. I'm in Wellington. Her heart slowed. Leslie propped herself up on one elbow. The bedroom lights were still on. She was alone in bed. The portrait was back on the wall. She raked back her hair and checked the clock. Nearly three-thirty. The window had been lowered to a crack, the roller blind drawn so that the edge scraped the sill with each breath of breeze. It sounded like someone trying to get in. Leslie cursed her imagination and got out of bed.

She went out into the hallway that ran in an L-shape around the top of the stair. Her and Greg's room was at the short end of the hall, the girls' at the long. In between was the bathroom in which a fluorescent fixture above the mirror was glowing with a faint, agitated flicker. Leslie walked carefully to her daughters' room, each step greeted with floorboard creaks and sighs.

Except for overflowing suitcases at the foot of each twin bed and the puppy stretched out on the floor between them, Molly and Emma's room was bare. Emma had kicked off her covers, and in an effort to preserve body heat, had tucked herself into a ball, sleeping rump up. She was breathing through her mouth, long, deep whistling ins and outs. Leslie pulled the blankets up to Emma's chin making her look like a curly-headed snail.

Molly, on the other hand, burrowed into bed each night as though it were the start of hibernation. Some mornings, Leslie had to strip the linens to find her. At this moment, the only visible part of her child was fingertips peeking above the edge of the comforter. Leslie folded back the perspiration-damp bed clothes. Molly mumbled a generic 'Leave me alone' and wriggled her sweaty body until the covers had covered her again. Leslie blew them each a kiss and then went downstairs to find her husband.

Greg had fallen asleep where he sat. She found him, snoring, head on forearms, slumped on to the laminate pillow of the kitchen table. The tabletop was cluttered with drawings and books marked with yellow slips of paper, each scrawled with Greg's impossible handwriting. One of the books was open to a black-and-white photograph, full page, of a stern old house. The caption read PLATE 27: FIVE MILE HOUSE CIRCA 1892.

So, this was the big deal? Leslie sat down and carefully pulled the book away from Greg. She angled herself out of the glare of the overhead light. The photograph was a bit fuzzy, as if the house had moved just as the shutter closed. Then again, thought Leslie, the uncertain focus may have been deliberate, a photographic veil over an unsightly reality. She'd learned enough from Greg to recognize the architecture as Victorian, but its austerity, its complete lack of ornament, made it look more like a condemnation of an age famous for its excess. The structure itself was massive, its lines unbroken verticals bridged by stunted horizontals, like a fortress. And it was symmetrical, absolutely symmetrical as though a mirror had bisected the thing so perfectly that the reflection was indistinguishable from the solid. The main part of the house, which looked to be about three stories in height, rose in equal sections on either side of a broad tower-like element built out from the front. The tower cleared the roof line and continued upward for a couple more floors at least. Dark rows of slate shingles crowned the tower and were repeated on the lower roofing. The exterior was finished with wood clapboard painted white. Shutters hung at each side of the squat, mullioned windows. The paint on the clapboards and shutters was peeling. A small verandah sheltered the front door, casting the space beneath it into shadow. Leslie could just barely make out the figure of a man standing next to the door. She brought her face closer to the page, but was not rewarded with any greater detail. The area around the house, what the photograph included, appeared to be an overgrown tangle of bramble bushes and vines.

Greg yawned. 'Lovely place, don't you think?'

Leslie looked up to see him studying her with sleep-heavy eyes. 'Let me guess. They called it Five Mile because that's as close as anyone wanted to get?'

'It's called Five Mile House because it was built on – wait for it – Five Mile Hill. And that was taken on one of its better days. Wait till you see what's become of it.'

'I'm not sure I want to. Who did you say you're doing this for?'

He stretched, and then scratched at the stubble on his cheek. 'I didn't really say, because I don't really know.'

'Who's signing the checks?'

'Well, I told you how Gwen Garrett put me on to this, right?' Greg rolled his head to the left and then back. He winced at the popping sounds. 'Yeah. From there it gets complicated. Gwen and her husband moved here to Wellington about four years ago. She travels quite a bit for Mansfield Custom but they live out here because Gwen says she had this addicted-to-country-living-thing.'

'It's hard to be a witch in the city.'

'Be nice. Anyway, the Wellington family – '

'Wellington? Like the town?'

'Right. They still own most of the land around here. I figure they also own Five Mile because it was the Wellingtons who started inquiries into the restoration options. Somebody representing the family called Mansfield Custom and was told that Mansfield doesn't do the kind of work the Wellingtons were looking for, but they did have a representative living in town who might be able to line up some local expertise.'

Leslie frowned at him. 'You're hardly local, Greg.'

'No, but Gwen had heard of my interest in country properties and she knew something about our situation, so – '

'She thought we might want to get the fuck out of Dodge?'

Greg shrugged. 'Yeah, but she had to okay it with her client. A couple weeks later I got a call from one of the Wellingtons' attorneys, a guy named Hogarth. He said the Wellingtons wanted me to do it but there was one stipulation: I had to put my crew together from Mansfield Custom's roster.'

'So it's a Mansfield project, after all. Why are they so insistent about having Mansfield Custom on site?'

'Nobody's obliged to explain me nuttin', sweetheart. A guess? Perhaps because Mansfield retains independent craftsmen and that keeps the unions out of it. I think it's also because Mansfield requires all their guys to be bonded. They work in a lot of security-sensitive environments, you know, art museums and CEO offices and government buildings.'

'Are we talking carpenters or secret agents?'

'Very funny.'

Leslie looked at the photograph again. 'And they consider this dump a security-sensitive environment?'

'It's probably just a lot of public relations crap. If that's what the Wellingtons want, who am I to argue with their money?'

'I don't get it.' She peered at the figure caught forever in the darkness by the front door. 'What's so special about this house?'

'Its past,' said Greg.

'So, they're fixing it up for the historical register?'

'I think it's more like they're trying to fix history.'

'Now we're getting somewhere.' Leslie leaned forward. 'Do I smell gossip?'

He grinned. 'Like stink on a pig farm.'

'Spill.'

His playful expression dulled. 'I don't know, Les.'

'You don't know what?'

'Whether this is a story you should be hearing.'

'Oh.' She sat up straighter. 'Will I find large blocks of print missing from the morning papers? Maybe you should listen in on my phone calls, too?'

'Leslie. Christ. I'm only trying to help.'

'You are trying to protect me. Stop.'

He dropped his head. 'There's a terrible world out there.'

'No? Really?'

'What do you want from me?'

'What I want? What I want?' She caught herself, eased back on the accelerating fury. Unclenched her fists. Breathed. 'Greg, there is nothing out there more terrible than what I'm carrying in here.' She raised a trembling finger to her temple.

He reached across the table and lowered her accusing hand, held it. 'Everything's going to be all right. Everything's going to be okay.'

'No,' Leslie said, pulling her hand free, 'everything's going to be exactly what it is.'

Four

M ONDAY MORNING CRAWLED IN on the misery of a long night of puppy howls. Molly and Emma, in their efforts to comfort the creature, nearly missed the school bus. They went running out into the glaring brightness without kisses, hugs, or hopes for a good day. Greg was stomping about the upper floors, mumbling vague, sleepy complaints. Leslie, in nightshirt and dirty socks, slumped in a kitchen chair and watched bleary-eyed as Sam, the newest family member, urinated on the linoleum.

'Man's best friend,' she said to the dog as it sniffed its work.

Greg, still stomping, came down the stairs and into the kitchen. Barefoot.

'Watch where you're walking . . .' Leslie tried to warn him.

The puddle splashed halfway to his knee. Sam tried to make amends by licking Greg's shin clean. He sighed and stroked the dog's head. 'Aw, hell. What's a little puppy pee?'

'Another mess for me to clean,' said Leslie, as she got up and grabbed the paper towels.

He took the roll from her. 'You okay?'

'Yes, Greg. I'm okay. I mean – I didn't sleep, that's all.'

'I'm going to take old Sam here up to Five Mile with me, teach him the fine art of being the official site dog,' he said, petting the dog's snout. 'The house will be quiet. Maybe you can nap.'

She leaned into the counter and squinted at him. 'Yeah, I'll lie down, take a little snooze, and the movers will silently pile furniture around me.'

'I'm just trying to help, Les. Besides, Mitch said he wouldn't be able to get the truck here till late this morning. I'll be back by then.' His hands full of urine-soaked paper toweling, he motioned for the plastic wastebasket behind her. She tried to slide it in his direction, but it toppled over, spilling cereal boxes and orange peels at his feet. 'Nice,' he said.

'It was an accident.' She righted the basket and tried to help him refill it. He brushed her hands away.

'Leslie, go get some sleep.'

Whether it was an effect of the medication or a symptom of the depression, Leslie didn't dream anymore, and for that she was grateful. Sleep always came quick. It was thin, but darkly vast, a sort of fluid stillness that would not allow her to submerge. She floated on it, skimming the boundary line of consciousness, always on the verge of waking. It no longer surprised her to be, as she was now, suddenly awake. It did, however, take her a few moments to realize that the doorbell was ringing.

The clock next to the bed said ten after nine. The movers were early. 'I'll be right there,' she shouted as she jumped out of bed. She yanked off her nightshirt and threw on a pair of shorts and a tank top. She shoved her feet into canvas sneakers and ran her fingers through her curls as she trotted down stairs.

'Yeah,' she said as she opened the door, yawning. It wasn't the movers. It wasn't anyone. An obnoxiously red sports car idled in the drive, but its owner was nowhere to be seen. She took a step out the door, shielding her eyes from the sudden flood of sunlight. 'Yeah? Is anyone there?'

A figure, just beyond the corner of the house, moved. The motion glanced against the edge of Leslie's peripheral vision. She was being watched. In a city-bred response, Leslie turned her entire body toward the watcher, meeting his assessment with her own she-wolf stare that demanded he look away or suffer the consequences.

But that did not break his gaze, if anything it intensified as though he did not trust his eyes. His eyes, heavy lidded and deepset, seemed too large for his skull. Everything about him was ever so slightly out of proportion. His torso was a bit too long for his legs. He stood with an uneven, slope-shouldered ease, casual in his manner, yet the artlessness seemed artfully achieved. His collar-length hair fell in gray-flecked chestnut layers about the broad bones of his thin face. He wore a pressed white shirt and khakis and a tweed sports coat. It was the shoes, suede loafers, that gave him away.

Lawyer, thought Leslie and smiled.

He smiled back, wide-mouthed, showing his teeth. All the better to eat you with, my dear. 'I didn't think anyone was home – ' the lawyer walked toward her – 'You must be Leslie.' He offered his hand. 'Phillip Hogarth.'

'Oh, yeah. Hogarth. You're the one who got us into this mess?' She laughed as she shook his hand and surprised herself with an immediate awareness of how completely his grip encompassed hers. Heat blossomed in her cheeks. She silently cursed her schoolgirl fluster and pulled her hand from his. 'What can I do for you, Mister Hogarth?'

'First, you will call me Phillip,' he said, his voice low, conspiratorial. Leslie wanted to look away from his face but could not. His eyes held her with their frank interest. How long had it been since she had seen anything in another face but the false kindness that served as a feint for fear?

'I can do that,' she said, her own tone imitating his. 'Phillip.'

'Second, you can tell me how I might get in touch with, ah, your husband . . .'

'Greg?'

'Greg. Right. I have to let him know Harry and Diana, the Wellingtons, are in town. I tried the number up at Five Mile, but no answer.'

'Can't help you there,' she said. 'There's only one number. He's due back here in an hour or so. You're welcome to wait. Or, if it's urgent, you can try to find him up at the site.'

'I cannot recall a single moment in this project that wasn't a matter of utmost urgency.' He winked at her as though they already shared a private joke. 'As much as I appreciate your invitation, I'm afraid I'll have to trek up hill. But before I forget . . .' He loped over to the car, removed an oblong basket from the front seat, and hurried back, holding it out to Leslie. She looked at the package, its contents wrapped in a white cloth and tied with a heavy twine. She looked at him.

'This should have crossed the threshold with you. My Ukrainian grandmother would never forgive me,' he said, indicating she should take it. She did. He pulled the free end of the twine and the cloth fell open. The basket held a small loaf of dark bread, a slender vial of shimmering crystals, and a bottle of dark wine with a label in a language Leslie didn't recognize.

'Old country house warming. The salt is to protect you from doubt, the bread is to protect you from want, and the wine is to protect you from unhappiness.' He laughed. 'That's the old country for you – good luck measured by the absence of bad.'

'Sounds like good luck to me.'

His dark eyes grew even darker as his expression clouded with a vague sadness. 'I need to be getting along, I guess.'

'Thanks for the gift, Phillip.' Leslie clutched the basket to her middle. 'I – I mean, we appreciate the thought.'

He nodded and turned back toward his car. Leslie didn't wait for him to drive away but went back into the house, closed the door by falling against it with her full weight. She looked down at the basket and pulled it closer to her. The bread, still warm, wafted a rich yeasty perfume. She lifted the loaf and tore off a piece with her teeth. Her mouth filled with the caraway and cocoa of pumpernickel.

Chewing, she carried the basket to the kitchen, where the table was covered with Greg's file folders, clippings, blueprints, and photographs. She tore off another chunk of bread and then surveyed the materials laid out around her. She coveted the pleasures of meaningful work – although what exactly Greg was working on was still unclear to her.

Whatever it was he obviously felt it a threat to her. Why he felt so was a question to which she could only intuit answers because Greg had so far avoided giving them directly. Leslie hated this haze of intuitive impulses. She wanted a clear path of logic and fact. And there she was with all this information, Greg gone to work and the girls off to school. How much of this could she get through before he came back? The anticipation fell away as quickly as it had risen. If Greg left this lying around it was only because he didn't care what she saw of it. The important information would be elsewhere. Her husband knew her better than that.

Leslie looked again at the basket and wondered about the wine, realizing the brown glass of the bottle was the same shade as Phillip Hogarth's eyes. She shook her head at her silliness. She set the basket down on the table as a centerpiece for Greg's Five Mile work. She pulled off another piece of the bread and then went outside.

The day was broad-skied and brilliant. Irises the color of oxblood bobbed their yellow beards in the front beds. The newly leafed trees swayed in the now gusting, now calm breeze. Leslie settled on the front steps to soak up some sun. It was too cold for the shorts and tank top she was wearing, but the hospital stay had left her looking grub-pale and depleted; she was eager to get a little color in her skin. The May sun had an accumulative effect, and as the warmth saturated her body, her eyes grew heavy. She leaned back, letting herself drowse.

She was startled back to wakefulness by a repetitive beeping. A panel truck with the words WARD BROTHERS MOVING AND STORAGE painted on the side was backing – or attempting to back – into the driveway. It shunted forward and then reverse, forward, reverse, trying to find the correct angle of entry. She stood and went to the edge of the drive where the rear of the truck finally halted. The cab doors opened in unison and out came two big men with well-rounded bellies and large, straight teeth that shone from behind their dark beards. Each wore a khaki shirt with his name embroidered on it. One was Mitch, the other Dan. Leslie couldn't be certain if they were twins by birth or by habit.

'The Ward brothers, I presume,' she said to the one labeled Mitch.

'Yep,' Dan answered as he fastened a thick black support belt around his middle. He then wrenched open the latch on the cargo door and shoved it upward. A wave of heat rolled out of the truck's interior darkness, bringing with it a mixture of odors at once familiar and repellent, like the scent of a victim's perfume lingering at a crime scene.

'Missus Stone?' Mitch had her elbow. 'Hey, Missus Stone, are you okay?'

'What?' She pulled away. 'Yeah, I'm fine.'

Mitch snorted in good humor. 'Pardon me, Missus Stone, but I know what fine is and you look a few feet short of close.'

Leslie stared at the man who was studying her with the earnest sort of sympathy one offers zoo exhibits. Oh God, she realized, I'm Wellington's newest tourist attraction. 'Look guys, do you need me to do this?'

Mitch glanced at his brother, who hunched his shoulders in a quick shrug. 'No, ma'am, we don't need you here, but we ain't, you know, interior designers.' He grinned.

'Me neither,' said Leslie. 'Wing it.'

Dan came over with a clipboard. 'We'll be right careful with your things, Missus Stone, but our insurance company needs – '

She took the clipboard from him and signed her name without reading any of it. 'I'm going to take a walk. A long one I think. If my husband gets back before I do, tell him Leslie said not to worry.'

'But he's going to worry anyway, right?' said Mitch.

'Why don't you just unload the truck?' She handed the clipboard back to Dan. 'If I wanted to get to the lake, which direction . . .'

Mitch pointed to the left.

Five

WELLINGTON PARK ANNOUNCED ITSELF only on a brown metal sign the state highway department had put up. The sign's white reflective arrow assured that, contrary to appearances, the slight parting of trees in the woods was the park's entrance. Leslie stood at the edge of the gravel road and stared into the uncertain light of the forest. How far could it be, really?

'Stop being ridiculous,' she said aloud. 'It's just a bunch of trees.' She headed off into the shadow. She made herself walk slowly, securing each step on the shifting surface of chunky gravel. Bird-sound reeled over her head. Black flies tried to fly into her nose and eyes, her ears and neck. The blanket of last autumn's leaves was composting, perfuming the air with a fragrance both vital and foul; she recognized the top note as that of skunk. A chipmunk darted into her path, sat up on its haunches, and glared at her.

'What's your problem?' Leslie glared back. It chattered a series of chipmunk curses and continued on its way. 'Right back at you, I'm sure.' Christ, how much further?

It wasn't far at all. Just a few hundred feet of slender birch and sugar maples and then she could see the silver line of the lake sparkling in the distance. The road emptied out onto a parking lot, vacant but for one bottle green Volkswagen Beetle. From there, it was a choice between a steep descent down a stone staircase to the water or a paved walkway marked with a plaque that read WELLINGTON HOUSE MUSEUM.

She crossed the parking lot and stood on the top step. The lake, deep blue and cold looking, stretched wide at the shoreline below her and narrowed toward the horizon, hemmed in by hills. Greg had told her about the lake already. Beyond those hills, the expanse of water broadened again and more fully. The Indian name for it was Katata, which was Lakota for *blunt*. The shape of the entire lake was that of a blunted ax. Geographical maps still labeled the area by its original name. When the Wellingtons had moved in, however, the lake, like everything around it, was assumed as de facto virginity. It was Lake Wellington, now, and to those who lived here it was simply The Lake.

At the foot of the staircase was a concession stand, boarded up until the start of summer. A slender white sand beach clung to the water's edge like a rim of ice. Lifeguard towers marked each end of the swimming area, and although it wasn't there to be seen, Leslie knew that by Memorial Day there'd be a big platform on floats in the middle of the water. The safe swimming area would be cordoned off by nylon ropes and orange plastic buoys. The concession stand would be selling soft ice cream cones, and the air would be dense with the smell of coconut oil and barbecue. She knew this not because of what Greg had told her but because she had grown up in a summer lake place and all these summer lake places were exactly alike. It was as if each had been deliberately intended to duplicate the exact same postcard-perfect fantasy: *Having a great time! Wish you were here!!*

The fact that she had ended up in a place so much like the one from which she started carried unavoidable premonitions with it. The idea of this doubling back to begin again produced a momentum, a sort of slow rolling blast field Leslie knew would flatten the walls between her and all she had fortressed herself against. She closed her eyes and concentrated, a sort of reversed meditation where the purpose was not to calm herself but to actively quash those parts of her that refused to remain buried. Success depended upon finding the image that held more power than her fear. This time she succeeded with an aggressive imagining, a picture profound in both its clarity and surprise, that of her body wrapped tight and writhing around the lean irregularities of Phillip Hogarth.

Her eyes snapped open. There was no denying the heat arcing through her pelvis. She was suddenly unsure of what posed more threat, the past or the future. She turned away from the lake and started down the path toward the Wellington House Museum.

The walkway curved into the woods a good quarter mile from

the parking lot. Wellington House was less grand than she'd expected, more an ambitious bungalow than a family estate. A rough stone foundation supported the five-gabled structure. Gingerbread scrolls braced the eaves; other than that, the house was plain, sensible in its gray clapboards and white trim. The windows had been opened to take the breeze, which stiffened suddenly and sent a shower of maple seeds pirouetting to the earth. Leslie held out her hand to catch a winged pod, but let it fall away at the sound of a voice coming from the other side of the building. A woman was part humming, part singing a Brahms lullaby.

'Hello?' Leslie left the paved walk and made her way toward the song. She rounded the corner but found the side yard empty. 'Hello?' The song continued from behind the house. She followed it. What she found made her forget, for a moment, the reason she was here.

Behind a fence of tall and pointed iron bars lay a small cemetery. The headstones were few; Leslie counted seven marble crosses of identical size. These were centered about a stone angel, maybe five feet in height. The angel's arms were thrown over her eyes, her head hung in grief. The base of the angel was engraved with the name Bly. Leslie ventured closer to the fence, to the gate from where she could make out the names carved into the crosses: Bartholomew, Abigail, Marie, Simon, James, Matthew, Justine. Beneath each name was the date of birth and the date of demise, which was the same on each one, September 23, 1891. With quick arithmetic, Leslie figured that all had been children, the eldest but sixteen. Another fall of maple seeds danced down from above, scattering, disappearing in the long grasses covering the graves. Leslie attempted to open the gate. It was locked. The singing began again. Behind her.

Leslie spun around to look behind her. 'Hello!'

The song stopped. 'Oh, hi,' the voice called back. 'I'm up here.'

Leslie shielded her eyes and looked up to see a woman resting her elbows on the sill of a second-story window. The end of the woman's long, white-blond braid dipped and bobbed, Rapunzel-like, in mid air.

'You're Leslie Stone.'

'And you know this how?'

'I've seen your picture. On Greg's desk? We work together. I'm Gwen. Gwen Garrett?'

'Oh, yeah. Hi. I guess I should say thanks for giving him the opportunity. You're a historian, right?'

'Among other things.' Gwen smiled.

Leslie remembered the sign in the Garretts' front yard and for a second indulged the image of pointed hats and broom sticks. She willed the picture away. 'What happened here?' Leslie pointed to the graveyard.

'Those are Eleanor's children.'

'What was it? A fire or something?'

'The "or something." But let's not spend the morning yelling at each other. Come on in. I'll make tea and we'll chat.' Gwen pulled her head back inside. The tip of her braid slithered in behind her.

'Yeah,' Leslie said to herself as she looked over her shoulder at the weeping angel. 'Let's go have tea with the witch.'

'Pick your poison.' Gwen fanned an arc of colorful tea bags on the counter in the museum office. Leslie thought immediately of some of the better-stocked drug dealers she knew back in the city. She reminded herself of the difference between good friends and useful friends and then nudged a ginseng-peppermint concoction out of line.

'Good choice. Very restorative. The body knows what it needs,' Gwen said as she went to quiet the whistling kettle. She was a graceful woman, fine-boned, long-limbed. The rope of braid hanging down her spine brushed the small of her back. She wore a purple jumper that fell to her ankles, the skirt of which swelled slightly over her pregnant belly. Gwen caught Leslie's inspection and laughed.

'Four and a half months, since you asked. I'm due end of August.' She dunked the tea bag up and down in a cobalt-blue mug, blinking her eyes against the rising steam. Leslie thought she'd never before seen eyes that color, a mist shade, like lavender fog. The Garrett woman wore no makeup, still her pale, pale complexion was highlighted by an interior light of vigorous health. The beaklike line of her nose gave Gwen an appearance more regal than attractive.

She smiled – thin lips revealing slightly crooked teeth shining in her wide mouth.

'This should steep a few minutes. Want a quick tour?' Gwen was out the door before the offer could be accepted or declined.

She waited for Leslie in the tiny foyer inside the front entrance. 'The Wellington Historical Society has two presentations.' She gestured toward the staircase like a trained hostess. 'The first is the saga of Daniel Wellington, town father, how he came to this country, a poor boy with no skills and no education but still went on to establish a dynasty, yada-yada-yada, classic American Dream stuff.' She yawned with exaggerated boredom. 'Or we can do the infinitely more popular Eleanor Bly, Killer Mommy, Tour of Terror.'

'Eleanor killed her kids?'

Gwen frowned. 'You didn't know? I thought Greg would have already filled you in on the old Five Mile story.'

'Greg isn't much of a storyteller.'

'Oh. Well, maybe he's saving it for a special occasion. I wouldn't want to ruin his fun.'

Leslie felt the small space with its dark woodwork and filtered light grow much smaller. 'Did Greg tell you not to tell me?'

'No.' Gwen sat down on the stairs. 'But if he hasn't told you by now – I wouldn't want to jeopardize our working relationship.'

'This is ridiculous. Just tell me.'

Gwen played with the end of her braid. 'I know. How 'bout we leave it to the Wellington Historical Society?' She reached in her pocket, pulled out a brochure, and opened it. 'We give these out to visitors. Something to remember us by.'

Leslie took the brochure and tilted it into the light.

TRAGEDY AT FIVE MILE HOUSE: In September 1889, Joshua Bly laid the cornerstone of the house he intended as a peaceful shelter for his scandal-besieged family. The land that is known locally as Five Mile Hill was given to Joshua by his sister, Isabel, herself the new bride of William Wellington, a grandson of Daniel and Maeve. The house took nearly two years to complete. But what was to have been the Bly clan's bright new start fell quickly to darkness. Joshua and his wife

Eleanor and their eight children had spent less than a week in their new home when Eleanor, still gravely depressed from the trials of the previous years, killed her children, all but the eldest son, who managed to escape. Before dawn that terrible day – September 23, 1891 – Eleanor had thrown herself from the tower window of the house.

Leslie tapped at the passage with her forefinger. 'That must have been some scandal.'

Gwen nodded. 'Joshua was the prime suspect in a mass poisoning at a bordello run by a woman with a reputation as a sorceress – the bad kind of sorceress.'

'Criminy. That's all? He was acquitted?'

'Never tried. There wasn't enough evidence. Or what evidence there was up and disappeared.'

'Oh,' said Leslie. 'Good chance he did it?'

'Good chance he did something. Part of the disappearing evidence was the testimony of two witnesses who saw him running from the house. He was the only one seen going in who was alive to walk out. What do you think of that, Detective?'

Leslie smiled. 'I think that was a long time ago. When you take their daddy's little adventures into account, however, anyone with common sense would think to ask about the autopsies on Eleanor's kids.'

'There was no record of any autopsies performed. The killings were accomplished very, ah, gently. Not a mark on any of them.'

'Pillows,' said Leslie. 'Probably did them with pillows. Back then no one would have seen the fiber evidence. What did Joshua have to say for himself that morning?'

'It's a Gothic horror tale to the end.' Gwen smirked slyly. 'Joshua is said to have gone instantly and irrevocably insane. That very morning he started building.'

'Building what?'

'The additions. On Five Mile? Wow, Greg really hasn't told you anything.'

'Apparently not.'

Gwen patted her belly. 'Well, it's understandable, I guess.'

'Why?'

'All right, I'll show you, but your husband is going to be very pissed with me.' Gwen stood and started up the stairs. Leslie followed her. Once they reached the top, Gwen led Leslie down a hallway that smelled of mothballs and mold. They came to the dark wood door at the end of the hall. Gwen reached in the pocket of her dress and pulled out a skeleton key. 'Normally, we don't open this room to the public.'

The latch slid back with a dull metallic thud. Gwen opened the door, held it for Leslie. The room was bright with sun. The low, angled ceiling danced with rippling shadows, and Leslie felt as though she were underwater. From the window, she could see the little cemetery. The room was furnished with a small bed and a rocking chair. It had been a nursery, maybe. Or a nurse's quarters. The walls were papered with a trellising vine pattern that looked hand-painted. Over the head of the bed was a framed photograph, a black-and-white miniature that Leslie had to move closer to see. It was a wedding portrait. The dark-haired woman in the photograph stood straight with unsmiling Victorian propriety in her high-collared, corseted gown of heavy white lace. Leslie looked again.

'Oh, my God.' She started laughing.

'You have to understand, Leslie. It's just about the only picture of Eleanor anyone's found. The family destroyed almost everything connected with her at the time of her death.'

'So, that's why everyone is staring at me?'

'You have to understand that Greg wasn't aware of any of this, not until a day or two before you arrived. He didn't know.'

Leslie looked back over her shoulder. 'Yeah, but you must have.' She sat down on the bed and began to twist the brochure back and forth in her hands. 'If you had any idea how many times I've seen people mistakenly recognize – and I mean absolutely recognize – family members in photographs . . . there's a reason we use fingerprints and DNA for positive IDs.'

Gwen settled in the rocker. 'You must admit the resemblance is amazing.'

'It's one photograph. It means nothing.'

'Do you understand Greg's concern?'

'What I understand is that my husband has probably figured out that his lucky break is based on a coincidence you spotted in the metro section of the newspaper.'

'Greg and I have already had this discussion.' Gwen sighed and glanced out the window. 'I'll point out to you what I pointed out to him: yeah, his wife bears a twin-like resemblance to Eleanor, but what are the chances Eleanor's twin would have married the man who could rebuild that house. Huh?'

'That's the best you can do?'

'Are you going to argue with a gift because you don't care for the color of the bow on the box? Good fortune deserves a little gratitude, honey. It was this marvelous bit of coincidence that convinced Harry Wellington that your hubby – who has no previous experience in this sort of work, mind you – was the guy for the job.'

Leslie turned to the window. 'You know what I did, back in the city?'

Gwen began to rock. 'Yes.'

'Maybe Eleanor and I have more in common than our faces.'

'I don't think so, Leslie. If you want my opinion, Eleanor Bly was a full-scale lunatic. What you did was as sane as anything I've ever heard. As a mother, a mother-to-be, I'd like to think I'd do the exact same thing.'

Leslie twisted the brochure harder. 'There are laws.'

'Yes, there are. Gravity – now there's a law. Just ask Eleanor.'

Leslie looked down at the twisted wad of the brochure. 'You know, Eleanor may have been acting to protect her kids from their wacked-out father.' She shoved the crumpled brochure in her pocket.

'That Eleanor was protecting her children is a favored theory, and it only supports the sanity of your actions; you went after the threat. You made certain he was stopped.'

A chill scuttled across Leslie's shoulders. 'I'd better be going. Greg's going to be – '

'Wait, I'll drive you home,' said Gwen as she stopped the rocker.

'No. Really. I need to walk. Exercise, you know.' Leslie stood.

'Well, it is a lovely day. Nice meeting you, Leslie.'

'You too.' Leslie walked out of the little room, down the mothball-fumed hallway, down the stairs, and out the front door. At some twenty steps beyond the house, she started to run.

44

Six

S HE REACHED THE MAIN road. Her lungs clutched for air, her thigh muscles were doughy, and her skin was clammy damp with a cold sweat. She could not, however, stop. Running – the slamming impact of bone against earth – running felt real. She fell into a pain-pointed rhythm, a syncopated persistence of footfall and breath, one act necessitating the other.

She ran. Every so often a car or truck would whisk past, and Leslie, sinking further into her trance, paid no attention. She fixed her eyes downward, unseeing. Her path drifted from the packed dirt of the shoulder onto the pavement. The sudden bleating of a car horn shocked her into awareness, shocked her to a stop in the middle of the road. The oncoming vehicle swerved around her. The driver, in the moment their eyes met, stared at her with disbelief. He honked the horn again, long and loud for emphasis, then was gone.

Leslie gestured with her middle finger and then, sucking down gulps of air, hobbled back to the roadside. She bent forward, supporting herself on her trembling thighs, and blinked against the pinfire stars swirling before her. Her heart wouldn't slow; she sat, hoping she wouldn't faint. Dust and dead grass clung to her drenched skin. She was polka-dotted with itchy swellings and bloody bite marks. 'Dumb,' she said on some exhalations. 'Stupid,' she said on others. She had no idea where she was.

Her right calf muscle cramped, a hard, living knot of hurt. Leslie hauled herself upright, and against the protestations of the rest of her body, started walking. The knot in her leg loosened; the fire in her chest began to subside. She continued forward, thinking she'd flag down the next passing car and ask for directions.

No cars came along. The woods to her right seemed denser the

45

further she went. The closely huddled trees were blanketed in vines. Looking more carefully, she saw the points of iron fence work breaking regularly through the greenery. She rounded a broad bend in the road and came upon a widening in the shoulder.

Leslie didn't fully recognize her location until she saw the big iron gates flung wide. Great, toothed tracks of bulldozers and dump trucks scarred the soft earth by the road. The tracks led through the gates and up the hill in crisscrossing trails of flattened plant life. This was the entrance to Five Mile House.

The truncated shadows along the roadside told her it was nearing the noon hour. Greg would be home. The thought of him drumming his fingers and waiting for her return to his sense of safety brought a certain satisfaction. Leslie started up the hill.

The steep, rutted drive was deeply shaded by the overhanging tree branches. It was muddy and the ground gave off a rank odor. Humming about her, close to her ears, were busy insect noises; with the exception of this insect sound, the woods were silent. She could smell the freshly bled sap of branches broken by the careless advance of big machines. *Dozers and graders and backhoes, oh my.* She hiked past bright green fiddleheads of new ferns unfurling amidst the skeletal remains of last summer's growth. The oaks and maples gave over to scraggly pines and bramble. Then the pines thinned and fell away.

She reached a second gate. It leaned, broken outward, against a toppled wall of granite boulders. These served as little more than catches for stagnating rainwater, death-still nurseries soon to erupt as flights of mosquitoes. On the other side of the wall, the drive split in two, each side arcing around a center yard, now the resting place for the earth movers and trucks that had made it up the hill. The yellow heads of dandelions filled the empty places between the machines and dotted the treads of the huge tires. Piles of gravel and sand lay at the edge of the yard, partially blocking the drive; no matter which direction she took, Leslie would only end up at the front steps of Five Mile.

Leslie had stopped walking. She was shielding her eyes to take in a full view of the house. Save for the broken windows and missing shingles – understandable effects of neglect and time – the house looked as it did in Greg's book, except there was more of it. Much, much more of it. Additions trailed away like tentacles from every exterior wall of the main structure. Each addition branched and bent about the others in what looked to be a deliberate attempt to reconstruct the Gordian knot in wood and stone.

She crossed the yard through its center, threading the maze of machines, the last being a dump truck with the words WELLINGTON CONCRETE RECYCLING painted on its door. Beyond that, only a few feet of dry, dusty yard lay between Leslie and the house. Greg, or some Mansfield Custom workers, had posted numerous signs about the property. NO TRESPASSING. DANGER! HARD HAT AREA. CONSTRUCTION ZONE. Leslie looked up at the house and thought the warnings more vanity than necessity. The house, with its many additions, was more like a many-tailed reptile that had puffed itself up as an illusion of threat.

She spotted the engraved numerals on a cornerstone. It was almost completely hidden by the wild grasses growing along the foundation line. She was about to head over to clear them away when there was a definite gust to the breeze. Five Mile's front door inched open. Leslie's heart shifted into higher gear. She had to laugh at herself. 'It's the wind, idiot. It's just the wind, and you' – she said to the house – 'are nothing but a big old cliché.'

She climbed the sagging front steps. The weathered oak of the front door had been draped over with a curtain of heavy-grade plastic. She pushed the plastic aside and entered Five Mile.

Disappointment was her first reaction. The interior of Five Mile was hardly equal to the great houses of infamy she'd seen in films. The foyer was barren of fancy woodwork and ornament. The plaster walls were cracked, broken through to the lathe in many places, lending the impression of a scabrous pox. A stairway ran razor straight to the second floor. It had been blocked off with yellow tape with the word CAUTION printed again and again. To her right and to her left were archways that opened on to the front rooms. Another passage ran past the stairs and led presumably to the rear of the house. Over her head a lantern on a long chain swayed in the crosscurrent of drafts.

She chose the room to her right. It had been a parlor she guessed. She also guessed that Mr Bly and the missus hadn't planned on entertaining much. Like the entry, this room was angular and austere. It had the same single lantern hanging from the same central spot. The floorboards were stained in rippling patterns

47

that mirrored the watermarks on the ceiling. Exposed lathe lent the room a certain character, a humanity Leslie sensed it had originally lacked. Two windows, which faced the front yard, allowed the room the full sun, although this brightness was muted by the plastic now covering the frames.

Leslie went to the middle of the room and paced off a measure of steps, on the diagonal, to one corner. Then its opposite. The room, as she had sensed, was perfectly square. It was the same precision symmetry she'd seen in Greg's book. And no fireplace. A public room with no fireplace?

On the exterior wall was another archway, curtained with milky plastic, beyond which lay darkness. This, like the stairs, had been taped off to prevent use. She figured it must be an entrance to the additions. She had no intention of taking these on, but still, since she was here, she wanted to see. Leslie pulled the plastic aside and stuck her head into the corridor. The light from the front room revealed the first few yards of a passage quickly overtaken by shadow. Her nose wrinkled at the smell of rot and the rancid stink of mouse. There was another smell, though. She leaned in further, trying to distinguish it. Something almost Christmasy, a spicy scent, very faint, but there. Probably one of the Mansfield guys' aftershave, she told herself, as she stepped away from the passage and let the plastic fall back into place.

'What did Bly think he was building?' Leslie asked aloud. Then she remembered the Historical Society brochure. She pulled it from her pocket and smoothed it out as best she could. The print was smudged. She turned pages, scanning until she found reference to the continued building on the house. The short paragraph offered no explanations for Joshua's obsessive construction other than to compare it to a better known example of such 'arguably paranoid and delusional' behavior in the Winchester Mystery House in California. The section closed with a warning that the current state of Five Mile House was hazardous and all trespassers would be prosecuted.

Leslie tucked the brochure back in her pocket and reconsidered the front room. It wasn't only the additions that were curious. Something else was wrong here, but she couldn't place what was troubling her. She left this room behind and crossed the foyer to find an identical room on the opposite side. Same squared off proportions, same placement of an access to the additions, same windows.

It wasn't in keeping with the architecture of the day. Houses of Five Mile's era had been built like railroad cars, one room opening directly on to another. It was not uncommon to find the only route to the kitchen was through the parlor, then the dining room and the pantry. Things became even more awkward in the private chambers because there was no privacy. Of course, there had been pocket doors partitioning one room from the next, but Five Mile's completely enclosed spaces were unique. And why no fireplaces? Why keep these rooms unheated in winter? Or – she went to the window to make certain her assumption: although the glass was gone, it was certain the frames had been designed not to open. These rooms would be suffocating in summer. Why build a house so that it's impossible to live in?

She left the front rooms and wandered down the passage behind the stairs. The light was dimmer back here, and she noticed a narrow opening to another set of stairs. Those were too dark to try, so she continued forward until, startled, she found herself in a space exactly like that of the entry, complete with stairway and main door and square rooms to the left and right. For a moment she thought she'd lost her way, been turned about somehow, but realized it was the house that turned back upon itself. Or rather turned its back on no one. Doubly vigilant, Five Mile watched what came before and behind it.

She headed back the way she came, but paused at the opening to the darkened stairs. Leslie went in and looked up. The staircase climbed, in herky-jerky angles, up into shadows. She realized these stairs must lead to the tower but they too had been blocked by yards of yellow plastic warning tape. Leslie placed her right foot on the first riser; it felt steady enough. Greg was going to be furious with her. And yet, and yet – She ran her finger along the edge of the tape. She needed to see. Leslie tugged at the tape with increasing force until it broke. In the upward pull of a backward gravity, she started to climb, testing each riser before trusting it with her weight. She steadied herself against the wall, dragging her fingers along the cool broken plaster, cutting trails through the thick dust.

She took another step upward. In fact, she thought, except for the shape of it, the emptiness that Five Mile House defined, there was nothing remarkable about the place. No glorious examples of woodcraft or stained glass. No precious metals or rare materials or genius in design. It was only a sad, sick old house. Why fix it up at all? Why not merely pull it down and let the earth heal this hillside?

Up again. It might have value as a curiosity, a circus freak of architecture, but wouldn't that appeal be more tangible in its current condition? Right now, Five Mile House could be called truly haunted, if only by the discernible passage of time, the affects of loss. Erase those changes, and wouldn't that erase the power of the past? It would be like the crews that go in and clean up after a murder. They wash and wipe and polish until what was real, absolutely undeniable, has disappeared, leaving behind only its ephemeral tracings in words: a statement, a report, an argument and the opposition to it. Stories, thought Leslie, stories are the ghosts. If the Wellingtons undo the Five Mile's present, they undo its past as well, and then there's no way to separate fact from hope, fear from wish.

She stepped up one, two more. So, what in the Wellingtons' history would justify the expense of these restorations? Whose ghost were they trying to bury? Eleanor's? That couldn't be. It was Eleanor's story, her ghost they wanted to hide behind. What could be so heinous that the death of seven children and their mother seemed palatable by comparison?

She glanced at her hand on the wall. The trail of dust had gone red. She looked at her fingers. The tips were bleeding, the skin abraded away by the plaster. Blood on the wall. Leslie's breath hooked tight in her throat. The floor beneath her feet listed, and she felt herself fighting to remain level. Not successful, she fell, tumbling a short distance down the stairs until, reflexively, she reached out and caught herself. Her hand found the newel post. She sank to her knees, bent over in the middle, certain she was about to be ill, when from above came a sound so precise as to be unmistakable: a child running toward her. Leslie shut her eyes. Still she could see. The little black patent party shoes in descent on the stair. The little white socks. A scabbed knee. She heard the voice.

'Is he here?'

Leslie covered her ears. 'No.'

She squeezed her eyes tighter. She waited.

When the silence assured her that she was alone, Leslie straightened. She forced her eyes open. 'Move,' she whispered to herself. 'Goddamn it, move.' She was still urging herself forward as she broke free of Five Mile.

Seven

THE WELLINGTON HISTORICAL SOCIETY'S telling of Five Mile's history amuses me, but I am uncertain as to why. Is it because the words reveal so much or so little? What was their phrase? *Joshua's scandal-besieged family*? Is that an attempt to distill the essence of the facts or merely an attempt to avoid them?

The sorceress had a name. She was Della Rosa Benevista, and she reigned unquestioned in a brownstone house of infamous address. Had anyone referred to her establishment as a 'bordello,' she would have seen to it that was the last word to fall from the offending tongue. She was Spanish of birth and rearing, a small woman, waspish in size and demeanor, reputably a gifted dancer, a mistress of the flamenco. If asked the nature of her business, Della would snap, stiletto sharp, her ever-present painted fan and demur that she was not conducting business but was merely the privileged hostess of a nightly salon. That her salon comprised married men of great wealth and half-clad girls of great beauty was a detail that seemed beneath her concern.

I, of course, had never set foot within the rooms, but I could imagine them. I did spend much time imagining them on those evenings when Joshua was away cocooning himself in strange perfumes he claimed to be my invention. I imagined walls covered in velvets the color of a bull's blood and hide. Chaise longues draped in embroidered shawls and languid flesh. Gaslight tripping off polished brass doorknobs and crystal decanters of port. Scents of spiced oils and lavender. Laughter. Music. Whispers. This is how I imagined it. I never asked Joshua if my imaginings of Della Rosa's came close to reality. After that last night, when all but Joshua lay dead, I never asked Joshua anything again.

Had it been an ordinary evening, they might have been found earlier, some in time to save. But it was late September, the autumnal equinox and Persephone's return to the underworld. These pagan dates were important to Della Rosa for reasons I, at that time, could only guess. She marked them with lavish Bacchanalia, days and nights of feasting and debauchery that left mothers to concoct fairy tales explaining mysteriously detained fathers. Accustomed as we were to such doings, three or four days passed before anyone thought something amiss behind Della Rosa's shuttered windows. When the constables came knocking, came to inquire on the behalf of angry wives, they found – oh dear Lord, what they found.

As reported by the newspapers, the doors had to be broken in with battering rams. This was because the building had been barricaded, not by mere hasps and locks, but by boards purposefully nailed over the exits, as well as the windows. Those inside had apparently walled themselves in, although, at the end, it appeared some tried to escape; the investigating constables nearly tripped over the bodies of a trio of young whores, their small fingers torn to bloodied rags from tearing at the rough wood planks. Bodies of loved ones and their lovers lay everywhere, contorted in the last ravages of searing agony. Many were naked and embraced about each other, male and female, in orgy. Open wounds on some had sped the engines of decay, and the house effused a liquefied stench. Della Rosa was found drowned in her bath, bound with ropes and rock weights in poisoned water tinted pink by her blood. A witch's death.

There was rat poison in the cistern. There was nightshade in the caviar and belladonna in the port. There was black hellebore in the figs and a suckling pig basted in savin oil; pears poached in oleander honey; quail fed on hemlock seeds; custards flavored with Barbados nut; flasks meant for body oils and perfumes filled with flesh-eating acids. And as though this were not sufficient, the gas lamps had been extinguished and left to sough vapors meant to suffocate those foolish enough to fight for survival.

What no one dared speak was the obvious: this was not murder but some horrific dark ritual, an appeal to powers that no saved soul could imagine. The complicity implied by the self-inflicted carnage proved more than the moral mind could contain, and as such, it was decided that these were victims of an elaborate plot of extortion and murder as designed by my husband, the sole patron to enter Della Rosa's that September who still remained among the living. He was arrested based on the accounts of the two street whores who placed him at the cistern. As the news of Joshua's arrest spread, a different feasting began.

I understood the outrage. There was not a heart in the city, not one, more disturbed than mine. For each question the authorities asked of Joshua, I had ten. All this, all this, Joshua, and yet you live? Not a mark upon you nor a single moment of physical distress? I knew my husband. I had long before fathomed his vast shallows and sudden depths. Whereas his run past the cistern was seen by the public as incrimination or cowardice, I sensed an implication more dire. The reason Joshua continued to live was that he had left Della Rosa's in order to be somewhere else, somewhere far worse, I reckoned. If not, why not make an account of his actions and silence his accusers? Instead, he spoke nothing except to his coterie of stiff-faced attorneys. Not one word of excuse or explanation did he offer, even to me. During my visits to his cell, he might ask after the children or pat my hand and whisper that all was well, not to worry. *Not to worry* – I wanted to shout his words back at him. I wanted to claw that implacable expression from his features, put my hands about his throat, and choke the truth from him. Where were you, Joshua? Where were you and what in God's name were you doing?

The attorneys did their work, making calls upon the grief- and horror-stricken families. I don't know if they carried money or threats or both; all I can report is that one by one the charges fell away like so much rotting fruit. Finally, the two whores who had sworn it was Joshua at the cistern found their memories failing them. They could no longer even be generally certain if it was Joshua or some man resembling him they had seen. In fact, they might have seen nothing but a shadow or perhaps a large dog. Having lost credibility as witnesses, both women set sail for France having come, incredibly, into simultaneous inheritances.

Without evidence or witnesses there were no remaining grounds for the charges. So certain were the authorities of public outcry that they brought Joshua word of his freedom in the dark of midnight. When Joshua arrived on the threshold of our home there was nothing in his face, no joy, no relief, nothing but a certainty of purpose. It had been advised that we leave the city immediately, he said, for the populace at large did not function with the same cool logic of the law. So there we were rushing, rushing about in the middle of the night, rushing to the train, rushing out of the city, rushing to sanctuary at his sister's home in Wellington. During our haste, our rush to collect our things, I caught a glimpse of what I was not supposed to see: Joshua dislodging a large satchel from one of the children's wardrobes. The satchel opened and Joshua was pelted in the face by a thick shower of bank notes. As he hurried to gather them up, he saw me watching him. He smiled as a thief might smile when he is certain not only of his loot but his safety, his skill.

Had I known, had I guessed, I might have saved the children and myself sooner.

I can, however, guess what you are thinking. Given my own actions, who am I to accuse anyone? But what you have before you, the tale as it is told by the Wellington Historical Society is only that, a tale, not truth. I cannot say, even now, precisely what truth took place in this damnable house, only that my dying occurred upon the very brink of larger events. I remember the advent of terror in the realization of what I had done. I remember the blue-gray of dawn and the pale glimmer of late-setting stars. I remember the soles of my shoes upon the sill. The sweep of cool air before my descent.

I do not crave the truth; I dread it. Logic assumes the necessity of reasons for why I have been denied my eternal rest. Yet, without the opportunity to tell my story, all that is left me is the ephemeral, disjointed speculations of others. It is for this reason I protect Five Mile House, to hold my story safe. I protect it from the living who climb the hill to see the relic of a mad woman and pay no heed to the implications of madness in the house itself. They throw rocks at windows and drink beer and fornicate among discarded bottles in the yard. They tell one another obscene parodies that only add to the confusion of tales I sift through. They call my name, summon me forward to ask inane questions about their futures. Their futures? I have yet to find an audience for an accurate report of my own past.

It was her past and not my presence from which Leslie ran.

I watched her flee, watched her scramble and slide down the slope toward level ground, and I came to understand that she was haunted by a thing more perverse than mere regret. Nothing would be gained from telling her my story. Leslie had fought her way to the center of the whirlwind to hide in an illusion of order. I might as well stand by her ear and scream; she would not hear me. I understood this in Leslie as I understood it in myself. I could not, at that point, put a name to her terror, but I recognized it.

Imagine yourself falling from a great height. It does not matter from where, a cliff, a bridge, a tower. Nor does it matter why you are falling. Did you slip? Were you careless? Do you blame gravity? Your own desperation? Another's? The answers, true or otherwise, are of little concern. What matters is how to make it stop. You clutch at anything: the sharp, broken rock of ledges; flesh-severing suspension cables; the air itself. Impossibility, injury, pain are of no relevance, for what matters is stopping. All else will wait. You must, if you can, stop the fall.

Eight

LESLIE LIMPED DOWN THE road to her home with her mind fixed absolutely on a single question, the point of reason that had snagged and held her, held her fast, if still suspended and swinging over the abyss. She reached her driveway to find it full of automobiles: Greg's pickup, Gwen's VW, Phillip's Jaguar. The yard was stacked with boxes both empty and unopened around which Mitch and Dan scurried in the antlike activity of moving. Leslie braced her weight on Greg's pickup and rested. Then she went on, steadying herself against the VW and finally the Jaguar. Okay, that's it, she thought, closing her eyes. That's as far as I go.

But then Mitch Ward was patting her cheek and saying softly, 'Missus Stone? Hey, Missus Stone?' and Greg and Gwen were there fretting over the scrapes, the bruises she couldn't feel. She squinted at her husband as he instructed Gwen, who was already hurrying back to the house, as to the location of the first aid supplies.

'You didn't do your homework, did you, Greg?' Leslie said.

'Come in the house. You need to get off your feet.' He took her arm.

She resisted his gentle tug forward. 'You signed onto Five Mile without looking into any of it.'

'Tell me you didn't go up there.'

'Oh yes, I did.' She pulled away. 'And maybe you should start calling me Eleanor.'

'Christ. How'd you find out?'

'Not from you, obviously.'

'I was going to tell you. I never got the chance. I swear I was – '

She ignored his attempt at explanation. 'That house. It's so . . . so naked. It's just a big box painted to look like a house. It's not meant for people, Greg. Why the hell did he build it?'

'Leslie, please come inside. You're bleeding – '

'It took a lot of money to put that thing up on that hill. Why spend that much money on nothing?'

'Les – '

She scratched furiously at a bug bite on her collarbone. 'The Blys certainly weren't into creature comforts; I've seen prisons that looked more like a home. There's something seriously wrong with that place.'

'I don't know what to tell you, Les.'

'You should have done your homework before – forget it.' She flung her hand at him and limped off toward the backyard, only to hear Phillip Hogarth call after her. She turned back.

'And what do you want?' she said.

'I brought you something to drink.' He was watching her again, that same authentic curiosity. She was not about to ask which past life sparked his interest. She avoided his eyes. Instead she looked at the wineglass he carried, the dark contents threatening to spill with each step he took toward her.

'Have some of this,' he said. 'You'll feel better.' He held the glass for her as she took a sip. The wine tasted like warm blackberries and sage. She pressed the glass back toward him, and thought, so much for magic potions to ward off unhappiness.

'Thanks.'

'My pleasure. You were asking about the money?' Phillip cupped his palm beneath Leslie's elbow, coaxing her into motion, back toward Greg. 'Five Mile House was built as financial insurance for the Bly family business, and the "Bly family business" is Wellington-speak for a scheme to funnel Wellington funds into Joshua's shit pit full of gambling debts and sixty-percent-interest notes.' He released Leslie a few feet shy of her husband.

'So why use up even more money building that horrible house?'

'Okay, Detective, that's enough.' Greg went to her and put his arm around her shoulder. 'You need to rest.'

'To bring in more money.' Phillip raised the wineglass to her in a semisalute.

'Ah-ha.' Leslie's posture shifted in understanding. 'His sister –

what's her name? Isabel, right. Isabel got the Wellingtons to pay to have the house built and – '

' – and Joshua padded the expense sheets – ' Phillip continued.

' – and that's why there are no fireplaces or working windows – '

' – so he could pocket the monies he claimed he spent on them.'

'Okay,' said Leslie, 'now things are starting to make a little sense.'

Phillip laughed. 'Sense. Now there's a word not often associated with the Bly clan. But I'm happy to make sense of anything. I'm here to help.'

She became aware of her husband's tightening grip on her shoulder. 'Just what sort of help do you think we need?'

Greg pulled her closer, and spoke in her ear. 'Phil said he was by earlier and told you that Harry and Diana – that the Wellingtons are in town. They want to meet us for dinner to discuss – well, apparently there's been a change of plans about Five Mile.'

'Oh good.' Leslie steadied her eyes on Hogarth. 'More changes.'

'Only your husband and Gwen Garrett have been summoned to the dreaded business end of the evening. I hope you will join us for the dinner.' He laid his hand, for a moment, on her forearm. 'Please, Leslie?' Their eye contact did not falter, and Leslie felt a vague shift of alignment in her pelvis.

'I won't be there,' said Gwen, striding back with an open cardboard shoebox full of cotton gauze, bandages, and various tubes and bottles of medicines.

'Ah, Gwen, don't be shy. It's not a party without you,' said Phillip.

'I'll send Joe to take notes for me. Joe and Harry can talk bottom lines. My husband loves that shit.' Gwen poked through the box. 'I know you, Phillip. You just want me along so you won't have to be the sole member of the Diana Wellington entertainment committee.'

'Guilty,' he said.

Leslie took the box away from Gwen. 'This sounds better and better. I think I'll pass, too.'

Greg said, 'Les, they're already expecting you. It would be rude . . .'

'Rude? I'm nothing but a sideshow exhibit to these people. Go without me, Greg. I've got a lot of work to do and besides, I don't want to leave the girls alone.'

The silence that followed only amplified the anger in Leslie's words. Finally, Gwen said, 'You know, Leslie, if you want to go, I'll be happy to watch your kids. As long as you're home at a reasonable hour. I still get tired pretty early.' She brushed a smudge of dust off her belly.

'You're very generous, but I couldn't impose like that,' said Leslie, sensing she was being cornered by an unrefusable kindness.

'It's hardly an imposition. Besides, this is your big chance to sample the nightlife of Wellington.' Gwen nodded slightly, encouraging acceptance.

'Come on, Les,' said Greg with a laugh, 'don't embarrass me in front of my boss by telling her she can't baby-sit for us.'

'You are sure you don't mind, Gwen?' Leslie said, resigned.

'Not at all.'

'Count me in,' said Leslie. She said it to Phillip Hogarth.

Before the very end when the days darkened irreversibly and I no longer believed in reason, I paced the corridors of our city house, sleepless, searching myself for some indication of exactly what manner of spiritual illness had drawn me to Joshua Bly. By then, even though worse was to come, I no longer comforted my conscience with the luxury of delusions; my innocence had not been seduced by his deceitful charms nor had my trust been ensnared by his cunning disguise. Before the end, well before, I recognized the weakness as mine, always mine.

I loved Joshua before we met. More than that, I craved him. I brought him into existence out of my own emptiness. We were introduced at a wedding reception. It was late summer and one of the first social events my family had attended since the death of my brother, Samuel. The bride's family, clients of my father's law firm, had been acquainted with the Blys for ages. Joshua, all dark intensity and honest appetite, took my arm, and in front of my own father, bent to whisper in my ear: Would I not care to escape this dreary company?

He escorted me out to the garden where the last of summer's roses dripped withered petals. We walked together. It was Joshua who spoke, his low tones implying a shared vision as he expressed wicked opinions about our hosts, the bride, the groom, the choice of music, the menu, the ragged-winged butterflies that had the misfortune of fluttering through his line of sight. Not one word of kindness nor good regard did he utter, and yet the sound of his voice filled me with longings so far removed from propriety that I feared myself possessed. In the days that followed our meeting, I gave myself fevers with scandalous imaginings of secret encounters in the cook's pantry or Father's study, of the different means by which I might improve his view of the world.

Our next meeting sent me into a dead faint in the middle of Sunday services, or rather, into the horrid pretense of fainting. It was early autumn and we had been stung by a week of unseasonably cold air. Killing frosts had taken what remained of summer's pastels, and we walked to the church, my parents and myself, under a canopy of oaks with curling leaves the shade of old rust.

The coal stove at the back of the sanctuary was stoked to full blast, making the air hot and thin. The organist, a dear man with more devotion than skill, was pounding at his keys, surely impressing Our Lord, if not us, with his sincerity. My father ushered us to our usual pew. A moment later Joshua Bly, whom I had never before seen among our congregation, slid into the pew in front of us. Mr Bly? My father tapped his shoulder and after exchanging the expected pleasantries, Joshua seated himself directly in front of me.

I was wearing my green wool dress. The wool itched my skin like horse hair. The bones in my corseting caged my breath. Reverend Fallsworth entered and we stood and sang. My lips were dry. We prayed. The first scripture reading, announced the reverend, was from the book of Romans. It was then I noticed the perspiration rolling ever so slowly down the back of Joshua's neck. Tiny, glistening beads emerging from the fine strands of dark hair, they slipped down his skin to collect and be absorbed on the edge of his collar. Reverend Fallsworth, with his high-pitched bee-buzz drone, was explaining how Paul's letter to the Romans bridged the centuries to instruct us in how best to keep our Christian faith. Yet, I knew, at that moment, I could keep faith only in Joshua. I knew he would taste of seawater. The knowledge was fascinating and the fascination demanded resolution, as though by discovering water I had, by necessity, discovered thirst. As Reverend Fallsworth read from Romans of Paul's admonition to help the sinful without falling into sin ourselves, I found that against my reasoned will, I was leaning forward, the tip of my tongue sneaking out from between my heat-tightened lips, reaching for a drop of the mortal moisture that would both quench and petrify me.

At that moment, I heard a small hiccup and glanced sideways to see my mother's horrified expression. Without other recourse, I was compelled to rescue mine and my family's dignity by rolling my eyes upward and pitching forward in full faint. How much better it would have been for so many if the Lord had not waited, but had chosen that moment to strike me down.

Therefore, it is with resignation that I report Leslie's acceptance of Phillip Hogarth's dinner invitation. Perhaps it was but a directional marker on the parallel path of our stories, hers and mine, a sign by which I might recognize my chance of redemption. Then again, it may have been nothing more than another testament to the inevitability of human nature: those of us who desire destruction tend to draw or be drawn, as if by magnetic forces, to the steel-hearted ones most willing to indulge us.

And so drawn, Leslie climbs the stairs toward her bedroom, to bathe, to rest, to make ready for her first social outing in months. She is very much aware of the aura of warmth on her arm. The place where Hogarth touched her. From below, behind her, comes Gwen's quiet concern.

'Are you all right? You want some help cleaning up those scratches?'

Leslie turns back, exasperated. 'I'm fine. Why is everyone so hot to trot to help me?'

'Ah, because we're nice people who help each other when we can?'

Leslie exhales, drops her chin. 'I had that one coming. Sorry.'

Gwen dismisses the remorse. 'At the risk of offending you even further, thanks for letting me sit tonight. I'm not up for a trip to Diana-land. Oh, but don't let me discourage you; everyone should visit there once. It's an interesting experience.'

'You're not helping me feel better about this, Gwen.'

Gwen laughs, says goodbye, and Leslie continues up the stairs. Once in the bedroom, she closes the door and begins to undress, trying to distinguish which marks on her body are injuries and which are mere dirt. She tosses her dirty clothes on the floor amid the cardboard boxes the Ward brothers have stacked against the wall. There is not much room to move about. What space is not filled with boxes is taken over with Greg and Leslie's furniture. He was right; she should sort through it. The old things are overwhelming.

There is no point in dressing the scratches and scrapes until after she washes. She is sorting through suitcases, looking for clean towels, when a soft knock comes at the door.

'Greg?' she says absentmindedly.

'No. Missus Stone. It's me. Mitch Ward.'

'Mitch . . . I'm kinda in the middle of something.'

'Please, Missus Stone. It's important.'

Leslie curses under her breath. She pulls the sheet off the unmade bed and wraps it around herself. 'Yes,' she says even before she's cracked the door, just enough to see him, the worry in his heavy face. 'Yes,' she says again.

'Look, Missus Stone. I know this is none of my business, but I couldn't help hearing you talking with Gwen Garrett.'

'And?'

'And I wouldn't be a decent man if I didn't warn you.'

'Warn me about what?'

'Don't leave your girls tonight, Missus Stone. Whatever you do, keep that woman away from your kids.'

Forgetting her state of undress, Leslie pushes the door further ajar. 'Excuse me?'

Mitch looks away. 'She's not right, Missus Stone.'

'Gwen thinks she's a witch. Yes, I know.'

'It's not that. And they like it better these days if you call 'em Wiccan.'

'They?'

'Oh, yeah, there's a big – what do you call it? – coven in Wellington. They went and made a whole dang religion out of what the old ladies round here used to call housekeeping. Every full moon or so, you see 'em dancing in one of the fields. Long white dresses and flowers in their hair. Bunch of gawky, middle-aged hippies. They're harmless enough, not that you'd have caught my grandma out there among 'em. But Gwen's what they'd call a solitary. Word is the coven wouldn't have her.'

'Why not?'

He shakes his head. 'Wouldn't know for sure. But there are stories.'

'About Gwen?'

Mitch stretched his mouth taut, thinking, but before he can speak, Gwen's voice calls up the stairs.

'Leslie? You there? Everything okay?'

'Yeah. What do you need?'

'Greg says I should be here by seven but to check with you, so I'm checking with you.'

'Seven's fine, Gwen.' Leslie looks at Mitch for a moment. 'There are stories about me, too.'

Mitch's shoulders hunch. He sighs. 'All right.' He looks failed. 'Please remember, Missus Stone, I tried to warn you.' He walks away, and Leslie closes the door.

Nine

A T A QUARTER PAST seven, the principals – all but one – begin to gather about the large round table in the center of Tate's, a once elegant dining establishment now as frayed about the edges as the linens on its tables. Greg, in chinos and a sports shirt, sits next to Leslie, who is playing with the salt shaker trying not to feel frumpy in her navy-and-white polka-dot sundress. To Greg's left is Joe Garrett, wearing a suit and tie. Gwen is conspicuous in her absence, on which Joe makes no comment, even after Greg says, for a third time, how kind it was of Gwen to look after the girls. Joe just grunts an acknowledgment and goes on sorting through a folder stamped with the Mansfield Custom logo. Phillip Hogarth is introducing Harry and Diana Wellington and their six-year-old son, Jack. Harry looks to be in his midfifties and Diana quite a bit younger. He is wearing jeans and a white polo shirt – a sport he plays. Gray and balding, Harry Wellington moves with vigor, a sort of physical enthusiasm that speaks of weight lifting and treadmills. Diana is petite, dainty, to use the old-fashioned term. She talks very fast, gestures broadly, and laughs at her own remarks. Her hair is short and artificially colored with many shades of gold. She wears a short blue dress that shows off her tanned legs. Jack is small, like his mother, towheaded with a dimpled chin. Dressed identically to his father, he doesn't smile or speak, but hangs by his mother's hand, leaning into her hip.

Harry seats himself next to Joe so that they might discuss the papers in Joe's folder. Diana takes the chair next to her husband and Jack is given the one beside her. Phillip sits between Jack and Leslie. The circle is complete.

A waiter, or perhaps it is the owner, lights the votive candle in the center of the table. Harry jokes with the man and then orders Champagne. They toast new friendships, productive endeavors. Leslie sips at the bubbles and watches how first Diana's, then Harry's eyes dart to glance at her. She knows they know. She knows also that they will not speak of it. That would be far too impolite, too forward, even if they were only adults at the table. But they know, and she has to wonder how much of Diana's fidgety perkiness and Harry's back-slapping zeal and Joe's distraction and Gwen's reticence to be here are, like Greg's protectiveness, based on the realization that a madwoman, a murderess, sits among them, toasting their futures.

The predinner conversation follows approved social paths: Harry Wellington's other children; the Stones' two; the Garretts' expected arrival; prospects for favored sports teams; books read, movies viewed. Jack sits quietly, his chair pulled up close to his mother's, and draws stick figures on paper napkins with a pencil. Leslie tries to engage him, telling him about Emma and Molly, but it is Diana who answers her questions about his likes and dislikes. Leslie gives up, returning to the adult conversation. When she speaks, she garners the full attention of the table. They study her with expressions both curious and afraid, like a group of eager young scientists at the discovery of a new, possibly poisonous species.

Finally, mercifully, dinner arrives. Leslie picks at her salmon in its congealing hollandaise. What little she eats is tasteless to her. She pushes a fork full of the pink flesh around her plate and wishes she were elsewhere. Harry Wellington clinks his spoon against his water glass as though he were fighting the din in a large, crowded hall. He stands. Leslie cringes internally; this can't be good, she thinks.

Harry begins by lying, kindly, and thanks Tate's for a great meal. He remembers, he tells them, coming to Tate's when he was about Jack's age on another sort of family errand. Leslie steals a peek at Jack, who is yawning and still drawing. She doubts Jack will remember this evening when he wakes tomorrow. Harry is now on the subject of history, of the Wellingtons' history and how this town is a part of that history and he feels a certain, he doesn't quite know the word he wants, *responsibility* to that past and hence to its future.

Then he sighs and looks around the restaurant, shakes his head. 'I have a vision,' he says, and next to her, Leslie hears Phillip Hogarth suppress a laugh.

'I have a vision,' Harry continues, his eyes focused in middle distance above their heads, 'of a Wellington rebuilt, a Wellington with a thriving economy, yes but more, a Wellington that is a symbol of a place and time in this country, a place and time that unless we actively set about preserving it will be lost to us forever.'

'Cut the crap, Harry,' Diana says as she strokes her son's hair. 'Stop selling it and just deliver the vision thing. Jack's tired.'

Harry takes this instruction with a grin. 'I do get going sometimes. Anyway, I don't know why I didn't see this earlier, but instead of limiting ourselves to the old Five Mile place, why not restore the whole fucking town? Don't scold me, Diana, the boy's heard the f-word sixteen times already today.'

Joe Garrett sits suddenly upright, like a sprung catapult. 'What do you mean, the whole town?'

'I mean the whole town. Wellington buys up the old houses and Mansfield renovates them and we're in business.'

'As what?'

'A planned resort community, but with more of an entertainment element.'

Diana emits a low growl of frustration. 'Harry.'

'All right, Diana. I'm talking about Wellington's history of witchcraft. The only town on this continent that can compete with us for witches is Salem, Massachusetts, and hell, all they have to offer is witches.'

'Whereas we' – Phillip is rubbing his eyes with fingers – 'have the added bonus of mass poisonings, child murder, suicide, and insanity.' He drops his hands and looks at Leslie. She smiles slightly to indicate that no offense has been taken.

Harry, rapt within his own belief, continues his plea for converts. 'Phil, if we're going to turn Five Mile into a tourist attraction, why not use the whole historical potential of the place? Wellington's lousy with witches.'

Greg, his eyes starting to shine with the glaze of a new faith, cocks his head. 'You're talking about cultivating a specialized tourist industry?'

'I am talking,' says Harry, 'about turning Wellington into a fucking theme park.'

'Hotels,' says Joe. 'Hotels and a convention center.'

'No, son. You don't understand. We use what's already here. Take old Elm Street, for instance. Mansfield Custom renovates the hell out of those houses, fills them with antiques, and presto! We have an open-air mall of upscale bed-and-breakfasts. We also develop all the in-town business, so it supports us thematically. Our staff wears period costuming – '

'Like year-round Mardi Gras,' says Greg.

'Like those Renaissance fairs Gwen's always dragging me off to,' says Joe.

'Hell,' says Harry. 'Like fucking Disney World.' He downs a large gulp of wine. 'The one thing we don't do is make Salem's mistake. We don't try to be anything else.'

Phil leans back and says quietly, 'That shouldn't be a problem. It's not like Wellington has a Nathaniel Hawthorne to account for.'

'Our goal then' – Harry, finger raised, is preaching to his newly collected flock – 'is to get up and running as soon as possible. I want Five Mile ready for the public no later than Hallowe'en of this year. That's Salem's big date, and I'm giving the world notice up front that Wellington's witches are no mere wannabes. I want to open Five Mile with a party, a Hallowe'en party – invitation only, of course – and a midnight candlelight tour of the place. Can it be done?'

Greg and Joe exchange a look and nod in unison.

'Great. That's just great. Oh, and here's the topper – Diana's idea. During the party, in secret, we have Leslie here, in costume, wander around the additions, so our guests can report back that they saw the ghost of Eleanor Bly. What d'ya think?'

The table falls silent. Leslie grabs the table edge and holds on to it as though without it she might float away. She can feel Greg beside her, feel him begging her, begging, begging not to lose herself. Not now.

Harry prods. 'You do know how much you look like her?'

Leslie looks down at her hands, the blue-green tracery of veins, the rough knuckles. She inhales and smiles up at Harry. A bright, beaming smile. She feels the muscles of her face stretching far beyond their normal range. She says nothing.

Harry accepts this as consent and is now talking about calendars, about deadlines. Joe is asking Greg questions about time frames and costs. Diana is tapping the table with a butter knife, insisting that she is to be deferred to in certain matters; the party is hers. Leslie, still smiling, still clutching the edge of the table, has stopped listening. A hand is on her thigh, a gentle squeeze.

'You all right?' Phillip Hogarth's voice in her ear.

She shrugs.

Without further encouragement, Hogarth stands and says that he is driving Mrs Stone home. Greg squints up at him.

'Must you go so soon?' Diana says.

Leslie speaks to Greg. 'I promised Gwen she'd be off duty by nine. Remember?'

Phillip jangles his car keys. 'And I'm not needed here until you four finalize something, which doesn't appear likely any time soon.'

Leslie says her good-nights and thank-yous in a voice that sounds, to her, prerecorded. She pats Greg on the shoulder, and then follows Phillip Hogarth to the parking lot. The sky has clouded over, and the night air is thick with drizzle.

Phillip stops. 'Look, you need to know that Harry may be an idiot, but he's not a deliberately malicious idiot. He's just hyped up about this new – what shall we call it? – project. I apologize for him. And if you like, I'll make certain the topic is never raised again.'

'I'm fine. I was ready to go home.' She strides off ahead of him toward the red sports car glimmering wet in the parking lot lights.

'Nice car,' she says when he catches up with her. It's Leslie's way of announcing the subject officially changed.

Hogarth considers her a moment and then grins. 'Want to drive?'

'Man, oh man, I haven't driven anything in a very long time.'

He tosses the keys in a gentle arc in her direction. She catches them.

The interior is soft, pale leather. Leslie finds the switch for the headlamps, and the dashboard lights up. Phillip Hogarth leans in closer, pointing out controls. After a few moments of basic instruction and the staccato uncertainty of finding the rhythm of the gears, they are speeding down the streets of Wellington, Leslie behind the steering wheel.

The rain picks up. Hogarth reaches across her to adjust the wipers; his arm brushes hers. He, apparently, is no more familiar with the town than Leslie and makes several directional suggestions that serve of no use but to get them lost. Before long, they are far beyond Wellington, laughing at their mutual ineptitude. The headlamps catch a widening in the road's shoulder. Leslie slows and pulls off. She is still laughing. The halogen beams glare off chain-link fencing, and beyond that, wet slabs of broken concrete heaped in jagged mounds. A sign on the fence reads WELLINGTON CONCRETE RECYCLING. Leslie shifts into reverse, but does not release the brake. Instead, she stops laughing. She shifts into park, turns off the headlamps and the windshield wipers. She turns off the key in the ignition, removes it. The engine is silent. The rain beats at the roof, the windows, the road. Leslie closes her eyes and turns her mouth toward Phillip. He is already there, waiting for her.

They kiss with a kind of desperate abandon, as those who are drowning might inhale water if only to end the struggle. Then they part, trying to see each other in the darkness, through the rain-drenched night. Leslie is breathing hard. Phillip finds her face with his hand, touches her cheek.

'Do you want to talk about what just happened here?' he says.

Leslie shakes her head, knowing he can feel her answer.

'I understand,' he says, his fingers lifting the hair away from her face. 'I imagine it gets exhausting, having to talk about every little thing you've ever done.'

They sit like that, in the dark, in the quiet, until Leslie believes there will be no more questions from Phillip. Then she slips her hands about his neck and pulls herself on top of him, legs straddling his hips, her mouth sealed to his mouth, her sex sealed to his. Leslie takes Phillip Hogarth as the rain closes over them in torrents.

She drives them back to her house, a little box of yellow light. They clutch hands momentarily in farewell. He gets out of the car to stand in the rain and watch her run to the door. After the door has closed, she hears him drive away.

Gwen is on the couch, feet curled beneath her. She is knitting what looks to be a blanket in baby shades of yellow, blue, and green. Gwen is humming. She smiles at Leslie, who thanks her again for looking after Molly and Emma. 'They were great,' says Gwen. 'Are you okay?'

When Gwen has gone, Leslie climbs the stairs to her daughters' room. She uncovers Molly and recovers Emma. Then she sits on the floor between their beds. The puppy crawls into her lap. She stays there a long time listening to her children breathe.

Leslie lies sleepless in the dark of their bedroom. Greg is downstairs working. She hears the calculator's endless ratcheting of numbers. The meeting with the Wellingtons ended late. He apologized when he came in, but to Leslie he sounded more relieved than sorry. He shook the rain off his clothing. He said he was happy to see that she and Gwen seemed to be hitting it off. He doesn't want Leslie to feel alone.

'Alone?' Leslie laughs in a throaty whisper. She's certain of what she should feel, ashamed, appalled at herself, her lack of loyalty and gratitude. Leslie, however, feels none of those things, and that saddens her. She is solidifying inside herself, molding or being molded into an instrument of what she can only qualify as some grand purpose. Leslie lies in the dark, mesmerized by the echoes of chaotic sensation coursing through her flesh: her beard-burned face, the virgin ache between her legs. It takes her a while to recognize it, to recognize herself.

Alive, it finally occurs to her. I'm still alive.

Ten

THE WOMAN AT THE Wellington Historical Society told Leslie over the phone that the volunteer positions at the Wellington House Museum were not among the most exciting duties they had to offer. If Leslie wanted to help out with the newsletter, she'd be busier and there'd be the company of other Historical Society members.

'The museum is dead this time of year,' said the woman. 'The area schools have finished with their field trips for the year and the tourists don't really come round till later in the summer. Really, it's just a dusting job.'

'That's all right,' said Leslie. 'I'm looking for something quiet.'

If Leslie was sure about it, they were looking to fill the Monday –Wednesday–Friday morning slot as their regular volunteer had medical concerns that had forced her to resign.

'I'll take it,' said Leslie.

The woman instructed Leslie to be at the museum the next morning. Leslie would be able to get the keys and the materials the Society used for guiding tours. She also said that if Leslie found it too lonely or boring, to give them a call and they'd find more for her to do.

'I'll keep myself occupied.' Leslie hung up the phone and opened the bright red bound composition book she'd pilfered from Molly's school supplies. At the top of the first page she wrote: *M/W/F AM. Meet Wed.* She realized she'd forgotten to ask the woman on the phone whom she was to be meeting. So she added a big question mark at the end of her notes.

Leslie was not surprised, however, to discover Gwen's green VW in the parking lot that Wednesday morning. Gwen was sitting on the front steps of the Wellington house, the calico print of her dress pooled over the risers. Her hair was unbraided and blowing about in her face. She was swinging a set of keys on a cord. She saw Leslie on the path and waved.

'I hear they tried to talk you out of this,' Gwen said before Leslie even reached the house. 'You probably should have listened to them.'

'Probably.' Leslie sat on the step below Gwen and used the red notebook she'd brought with her to scrape a cluster of dandelion fluff off her jeans. 'I guess the whole town knows about the resurrection of Eleanor by now.'

Gwen nodded. 'The big debate at the Society yesterday was whether you would attract visitors or scare them off.'

'What do you think?'

Gwen smiled down at Leslie. 'I think you're looking for something that isn't here.'

'Yeah?'

'Yeah. This is the family's version of itself, Leslie. It's cool and sensible and clear.'

Leslie raised an eyebrow. 'In other words, completely false.'

'No, just incomplete. You can't see the storm if you're standing at the center of it. You'll need to head up to the university at Rutherford. Check out the info in the library up there. That's where I've done most of my research.'

'Or you could answer my questions,' said Leslie.

Gwen wagged her head and chuckled. 'I'd be wasting my breath. You, Leslie Stone, don't trust anything you don't see for yourself.'

'And you say that why?'

'We're a lot alike, you and me.'

Leslie waited a moment, thinking Gwen would elaborate. When she didn't Leslie decided to change the subject. 'They said you had medical concerns. Is everything okay?'

'We're not sure. I was bleeding a couple days ago. That's how it started last time.'

'Last time? Oh, Gwen, I'm sorry. I didn't know.'

'No reason you should.' She looked out into the woods. 'I conceive; I just can't seem to hold on to them. The last one made it to five months. That was a year ago. Anyway, this time they stitched up my cervix. The bleeding's stopped but the doctor wants me off my feet as much as possible.'

'Is there anything I can do?'

Gwen dropped the keys into Leslie's lap. 'Take care of Eleanor for me.'

'Really. I mean it, Gwen. If you need anything, will you call?'

Gwen patted Leslie on the shoulder. 'You're sweet.' She stood up, braced her hands at the small of her back, and stretched. 'I'll be fine,' she said, but Leslie couldn't tell if it was confidence or hope. 'Come on, then. I'll show you around.'

They went in the house, and Gwen showed Leslie where the brochures were kept and the closet with the cleaning supplies. She instructed her on how to book tours. In the museum office, she gave Leslie a copy of the Historical Society directory with numbers to call if she needed help. She presented Leslie with the skeleton key that would open or lock all the interior doors, and then pointed to a door tucked beneath the staircase.

'The library's in here,' said Gwen as she pushed open the door with a plaque that labeled this the reading room. It was a small but bright corner room lined with glass-paneled barristers' bookcases. A single, square table and four chairs furnished the center of the room. 'We're not a lending library. Nothing leaves here, understand?' She stretched her back again. 'I think I should be heading home now. I've got to call up to Five Mile and check on how Greg's doing with our new marching orders. I'll tell him you're well situated here.'

'Please don't. I'm not sure he's going to like this – you know, my bonding with Eleanor.'

'Gotcha.' Gwen winked at her.

'Thanks. And please, let me know if I can help out in any way.'

'Sure thing, love.' Gwen glanced around the reading room. 'Have fun now.'

Leslie walked Gwen to the front door and watched as she made her way to the parking lot. When Leslie heard the chug of the VW fade, she went back to the reading room. She opened the glass door on the first bookcase and went to work.

When the next volunteer arrived at one, Leslie was still in the reading room. Her head hurt from trying to decipher intricate handwritten journal entries and ledgers; it hurt more with the frustration of not finding any real information. Her notebook had few entries; most of those were questions the Wellington House library refused to answer. She did learn that Eleanor's maiden name was Bitterford and that Isabel and Joshua Bly had been sent to America from England as young children. The relatives charged with meeting the children never arrived at the docks. A young woman they'd met on board ship invited them into her home, where they stayed until other family could be located. They remained in her care for nearly a month until arrangements had been made. Where they'd ended up was not mentioned. Neither was there reference to how Isabel had met and married William Wellington.

Leslie reviewed the notes as her replacement scurried about the reading room, pretending to wipe down the glass doors while studying Leslie. Unnerved by the scrutiny, Leslie closed the notebook, and said, 'Weird, huh?'

The woman with the dust cloth nodded.

From the museum, Leslie drove the van into town. She stopped at the little diner facing the fountain in the town square. Inside, trying to ignore the outright stares of staff and customers, Leslie ordered two bowls of vegetable soup and tuna salad sandwiches to go. She then took the cardboard soup cartons and wax paperwrapped sandwiches back to the car and drove – getting only a little lost – to the Garretts' house.

Leslie stood on the front porch considering the Spiritual Consultant signboard for a second before ringing the door bell. When Gwen answered, she giggled. 'You are such a mommy,' she said as she motioned Leslie inside. She led Leslie back to the kitchen, which was bright and stark and antiseptic looking. The air was dense with a fragrance both smoky and green.

'Not what you were expecting?' Gwen asked.

'I don't know.'

'Sure you do. You were expecting an alchemy lab and not a chemistry class. Everybody who comes in here the first time gets that same disappointed expression. You wanted eye of newt. Everybody does.'

'Yeah, well – ' Leslie put the food down on the marble-topped worktable – 'I've never met a – well, someone who was in your line of work.'

'You've never met a historian before?' Gwen winked and took two white pottery soup bowls from a cupboard.

'You know what I mean. Oh, the soup's for you. I've got to be getting home to Molly and Em.'

'This is very nice. Maybe next time you can stay and we'll do something witchy. We can read your cards and find out if there actually is something between you and Eleanor.'

'Hmmm,' said Leslie. 'Maybe. What is that smell?'

Gwen smiled. 'Sage. You bundle it up and heat it until it smokes. Then you take the smoke from room to room. It chases away evil spirits.' She rubbed her belly. 'Just in case.'

Leslie drove home. Molly and Emma, just home from school, were planted before the television watching the music video channel. She turned off the set and sent them outside to play while she made a snack for them. In her kitchen, which was small, dim, and messy, Leslie laid out four slices of white bread. She took the peanut butter and potato chips from one cupboard and the grape jelly from the fridge. She grabbed a knife from the dish drainer. She put it all on the counter and then went and sat down at the kitchen table. The telephone was in the middle of the table. Leslie stared at the telephone for what seemed a very long time. She was waiting for a reason to change her mind. None arrived. Leslie picked up the receiver and dialed the number she had memorized. Phillip answered.

She didn't say hello. 'What do you know about Rutherford?'

They agreed to meet the next afternoon. The second Thursday of May.

Eleven

BY THE LAST THURSDAY of June, life for the Stones had taken on the numbing comfort of routine. School was out, and Molly had agreed – for a sum slightly higher than her usual allowance – to serve mornings as her sister's keeper. Greg rose at daylight, packed his lunch, and drove off to Five Mile with Sam, the site dog, in the back of the pickup. He left notes for Leslie on sticky squares of yellow paper. She'd find them in the morning, neat yellow rows on the breakfast table, reminders of bills to be paid and calls to make. He promised with routine sincerity not to be late, a promise he routinely broke. He ended his notes with X's and O's and LOVE-YOU's. She'd peel them free, crumple, and dispose of them. When she headed up to bed each evening, Leslie left sticky yellow notes in return: which bill had been paid already and which calls were successful or not. She wrote that she understood how hard he was working. She wrote that she missed him. She ended with LOVE-YOU, TOO's. In the morning those notes, like Greg, would be gone.

Monday, Wednesday, and Friday mornings were framed by her commitment to the Wellington Historical Society. With the summer crowds at the lake, her job had taken on the new dimension of directing wet, sandy visitors to the public restrooms at the end of the beach, cleaning up ice cream spills, and the like. These afternoons were spent either in the yard, where she was trying to coax a vegetable garden from the rocky soil, or at Gwen's house, where Gwen good-naturedly attempted to coax Leslie into experiments in the arcane. Neither effort could be termed a success.

Tuesdays were for grocery shopping and general errands, an

exercise in public appearance. Her hope was that the more Wellington saw of her, the less remarkable she would seem. As such, Leslie walked the aisles of Wellington business, chatting with clerks, complimenting shopkeepers on their selections, sympathizing with how hard it was to compete with Rutherford. Mostly, she listened to the locals' increasingly acrimonious debate over the shape of their town's impending reinvention as the haven for a subculture of the strange. Leslie took no sides in the matter, only nodded and empathized, doing her best to seem harmless. No matter her efforts, the buzz of gossip followed her like a halo of diseased mosquitoes. Justified, homicide, resemblance, curse: these were the sorts of words that trailed after her. There were exceptions: Mitch Ward, when she saw him, would ask after Emma and Molly, the family, as though they had more to worry about in the world than Wellington's rumors. Leslie dreaded these Tuesday excursions, but knew if she didn't show up, smiling, alert, talkative, on a regular basis, those mosquitoes would multiply and swarm, bypassing Leslie for the tender ears of her children. The girls were hearing enough already from their classmates and friends.

If Tuesdays were the chore, Thursdays were the reward. Thursdays had meaning, purpose. On Thursday, Leslie drove forty miles to the state university in Rutherford and settled herself at a table in the quiet, quiet library to pore over materials associated with Five Mile House and the Bly family. Gwen had been right; so rich was the trove of information here that Leslie, at first, thought that she might easily spend years trying to organize an approach to understanding it. But that was in the beginning when she mistook the sheer number of documents as a sign of usefulness.

In moments of self-analysis, Leslie sensed her fascination with the house was indeed connected to something else, and if she stared at Five Mile House long enough the image before her would rearrange itself into the form of what she really sought. Then again, she'd argue, perhaps it had nothing to do with the house. Perhaps it was a simple matter of pride. Leslie wanted to solve the riddle before she was given the answer. More specifically she wanted to find the answer before having to defer, at long last, and ask for help. 'Okay,' Leslie heard herself saying, 'Okay, Gwen, you win. What am I missing? What am I not seeing here?' The thought of having to admit to such incompetence put a foul taste on her tongue. Leslie resolved to narrow the gauge of her filters and sift again. She had been, after all, a good detective. Once upon a time.

Whatever her motivation, Leslie was finding sanctuary in the process of the search. There was a tactile satisfaction in effective methodology, solace in the rules of evidence. At the library table, surrounded by texts, or in the cool glow of the microfiche screen, Leslie remembered what she had liked most about policework: the abeyance of speculation before that which can and must be proved. *Your honor, if it so please the court, in the case of the People versus Bly, I would submit the following list of tangibles: one complete set of blueprints of the structure known as Five Mile House, both original and those commissioned to document Joshua Bly's additions. I would submit also copies from newspaper articles dated eighteen-eighty-nine. These articles relate the sequence of incidents involving an extraordinarily elaborate mass poisoning at one Madame Della Rosa Benevista's and the subsequent arrest of Joshua Bly, who was the only visitor of Madame Benevista's that weekend to survive. These articles note that in spite of eyewitness accounts placing him in the vicinity of the poisoned cistern, there were insufficient grounds on which to convict him. All charges were dropped. In addition, I offer clippings from a Rutherford daily that notes the Bly family's move to Wellington. We have official records of the hill, known as Wellington South No. 11, being deeded over to Joshua by his sister Isabel. The land was to be held by Joshua's heirs until that time when there were no heirs to lay claim and the land would revert to the Wellington family. There are photographs of the house in various stages of construction. And of course, this series of obituaries detailing the deaths of Eleanor and her children.*

In what she knew to be a clear case of obstruction, Leslie willfully withheld other matters of evidence from consideration, in particular the city tabloids' reporting of the Bly family tragedy. Leslie had spent hours studying these pages with their lurid pen-and-ink depictions of a madwoman, her hair tangled like a nest of serpents and her face contorted in fury, as she dashed her babies to the ground. One paper featured a large portrait of poor Eleanor herself. It was a head-and-shoulders photograph and Leslie had to abandon her arguments of faulty perception; she might as well be looking in a mirror. *On this point, it troubles the*

People that supposedly reliable sources have deliberately misled investigators –

'Gwen? This is Leslie. I'm up here in Rutherford. Why did you tell me that picture of Eleanor in the museum was the only one left? Yes, I found the old newspapers; you knew I would. You didn't want to upset me. Yeah, I know: nobody wants to upset me. Well, how do I sound right now?'

Leslie never made such calls. The luxury of unmonitored anger was too costly. Still she constantly imagined slipping free from her straitjacket of appearances. How she longed for the simple pleasure of raising her voice or slamming a door. These imaginings, these fantasies of old angers indulged, had become a low hum in her head, a steady drone that kept her jaw tight and her shoulders knotted. She knew only brief moments of respite, an ebbing of the inner noise as it was forced against the boundary of an outward act. Thursdays, at around three o'clock, after leaving the university, she'd drive down Marshall Boulevard past the gaudy familiarity of fast-food restaurants and inexpensive motels, until she reached the appointed place.

The red Jaguar was parked around the back. He was always there first, and Leslie, who felt herself beyond loving anyone, would say she loved him for that. She'd park and lock her car doors, then walk to the room he'd taken on long-term lease. Rarely would she have even to knock, because Phillip would open the door before her, open it onto a cool and quiet darkness.

It was like diving into her own shadow. They didn't speak much. Words would only complicate the vortex of fingers and tongues and perspiring flesh. Sound, such as it was, came from the television, or from Leslie as she muffled her screams against the back of her hand.

When it was over, they'd shower, dress, and perhaps share a beer while watching the early headlines. He'd leave first, kissing her on the forehead. He knew she liked to have the room to herself for a while.

In these times alone, Leslie might consider the disheveled bed and think that maybe she could ask Phillip about the house, maybe he had privileged information that he'd share, whispering in her ear, a lover's secret. She resisted such an impulse because it would mean allowing him into her Five Mile House, the one she was building out of her time, her study, her needs; such entrance was something she had no intention of permitting. Besides – she reasoned as the drone in her head commenced once again – she didn't come here, to this room, to further her understanding of Five Mile. Leslie knew why she showed up here week after week. She had not asked Phillip to name the appeal she held for him. She had no need to. His interest was of little interest to her. Leslie came here to listen, because after Phillip had pulled her back into herself she was, for an hour or so, able to hear clearly.

On occasion the voice would come from behind one of the hotel room walls. Sometimes it came from the bathroom, as soft as the steam fogging the mirrors. Lately, it was closer, as though its owner were sitting on the bed. A child's voice, earnest in its curiosity.

Is he here?

It wasn't that voice she came to discern, for that voice, the child's question, Amy's question, ran in loops and eddies and echoes through her every cell. It was her own voice she needed to be sure of, if only for a few minutes, so that when Amy asked, Leslie could be certain of having answered.

Is he here?

Alone in the motel room, attuned to herself by a lover she didn't love, Leslie Stone nodded in response and heard herself say what she should have said, what she would have said, if she had known.

'Yes. Yes, Amy, he is here. Run.'

The last Thursday evening in June, Leslie arrived back in Wellington to find her home unlit and empty. A yellow sticky note on the table informed her that Greg had been summoned to a meeting with Harry and Diana. Unable to reach Leslie, he had taken the girls over to the Garretts'. Leslie flattened the note, pressing the glued edge hard against the tabletop. Greg was annoyed with her; she could see it in the slant of his letters. She also knew his displeasure had more to do with trying to arrange last-minute care for his daughters than finding Leslie not at home. She caught, as well, the fact he was not only calling his employers by their first names, he had underlined those names. Important people.

Leslie drove to the Garretts' under a gathering fatigue. It was nearly eight o'clock, and the sky was fading into half light. The Garretts' windows shone, the interior lights muted by sheer white curtains. Leslie could see Gwen's belly-swollen figure moving from room to room, followed by another, slighter form. At first she thought it might be Molly, but just then Molly, Emma, and the dog came tearing around the corner of the house. They were soaking wet, the three of them. Leslie raised her hand, but they didn't see her. They just kept running round to the back again. As she approached Gwen's front door, she heard the scolding *tusk, tusk, tusk* of a rainbird sprinkler, above that the squeak of Emma's giggles and Sam's play-with-me-damn-it bark. They were having fun. The fatigue was suddenly crushing.

Leslie rang the doorbell and rubbed the back of her neck while she waited. It wasn't Gwen who opened the door.

Diana Wellington in shorts and a tee-shirt went up on her barefoot tiptoes with apparent delight. 'Leslie! Great! You're just in time.'

'Oh, well, hello, I, hmmm . . . my kids are here.'

'Come in. Come in – no, you must. We were just about to start. Do you want a glass of wine?' She had Leslie by the wrist, pulling her through the house. 'Hey, Gwennie! Leslie's here.'

Diana dragged Leslie back to Gwen's study, a comfortable sort of parlor filled with tightly packed overstuffed bookshelves and chairs upholstered in deep green chintz. Gwen, in a long, pale blue shift, was busy lighting candles with a taper. The low chimes of the grandfather clock in the hall toned a heavy eight counts. Gwen turned her head to throw a wry smile at Leslie. 'The more souls at the table the better our chances.'

'For what?' said Leslie as Diana handed her a goblet of red wine she had not requested.

'We're going to have a séance.' Diana giggled and then bit her lip. Her face was flushed with wine. She danced lightly to the place where she had left her own glass, settled cross-legged in a chair, and laughed again.

'We are not having a séance.' Gwen blew out the taper and shook her head, the tip of her candlelight color braid swinging perilously close to the real thing. 'Séances are for scam artists and slumber parties. We were, Leslie, going to try a little automatic writing.'

'Yeah. Hmmm. Well, I'll collect the girls and get out of your way.'

'No, no. Stay. Please.' Diana pleaded. 'I'll chicken out if I'm here by myself.'

'I thought you were supposed to be at a meeting with Greg – '

'Oh, that. I blew it off. It's just Harry touching base with the Mansfield Custom guys. His excuse to make another round through the area, shake a bunch of hands. Harry's a people person.' Diana pointed at the chair next to hers. 'Leslie, would you please sit down? Besides, Jack is having a much better time out there in the yard. He adores your girls.'

Leslie glanced out the window to see Jack's thin white arms straining to drag Sam into range of the sprinkler. 'They seem to be getting along.'

Gwen had settled on the floor, big pink pillows supporting her back. On the coffee table before her there was a large tablet of paper, a rough sort of newsprint, and a palm-sized platform of dark, varnished wood. The center of the platform held a fine-pointed pen. 'It's called a planchette,' explained Gwen, adjusting the pillows, grimacing. 'Automatic writing works just like the old Ouija board, but I prefer plain paper because sometimes the energy chooses to express itself as a picture.'

'Gwennie's a witch,' Diana announced as though it were news.

'Hmmm.' Leslie gulped at the wine, grateful for its heat and sting.

'This has nothing to do with the craft, Diana. There are those confirmed antispiritualists who still employ automatic writing as a portal to the subconscious. It's useful with schizophrenics and certain kinds of psychoses. Anyway, divination is more about interpretation than method. We see what we want to see. What we need to see, well . . .' Gwen grinned hard at Leslie. 'It's talk like that gets a girl kicked out of her coven.'

Perhaps it was the wine or the flickering candles or the fatigue or all or none of it, but Leslie's interior sentinel dulled. 'I heard about that. What did you do to piss off the witches?'

'What didn't I do? Mostly it was this.' Gwen pulled a large photo album from beneath the table. She opened it and passed it to Leslie. There among the family photos and prints of medicinal herbs was a certificate from the state university at Rutherford bestowing upon one Gwendolyn Louise Van Der Walles a doctorate in psychology.

'You're a shrink?'

Gwen took a pinched breath. 'No. The paranormal is my field, so technically I'm a weird sister even to the scientific community. The girls here in Wellington felt, or rather Delores Jacobi felt, they couldn't trust me anymore, thought I might turn them into a research project. There was also some conflict about money, diversifying ourselves beyond the concrete plant.'

'Wait, wait, wait –' Leslie finally sank into a chair – 'The witches invest in the concrete recycling place out on – '

'Not invest,' Gwen said, 'own, operate.'

'The Rubble Witches,' Diana announced. 'That's what they call themselves. Rubble witches. Harry's right; Wellington's lousy with them.' She drained her glass. 'WCR: Wellington Concrete Recycling. RWC: Rubble Witches Coven. CRW: Certifiably Ridiculous Women. Old Wellington joke.'

Gwen gave Diana a tight little smile. 'It's a long story, Leslie, and frankly I'm not all that interested in retelling it tonight. Let's just say a coven works like a board of directors. Challenge their decision-making capacity and they'll simply decide to get rid of the challenge. I wasn't exactly devastated. Joe and I were getting serious, so we left the coven together.'

Leslie felt her jaw drop. 'You met Joe Garrett, Mister Don't Touch My Hair, at a witches' coven?'

'Hey, he's a good guy. A lot of men are drawn to Wicca because, well – '

'Because,' said Diana, 'they hear the word *witch* and they instantly think "easy pussy." Are we going to do this thing or what?'

'Yes. Let's.' Gwen shifted her weight, her face skewed by discomfort. 'This kid's been giving me grief all day. So, who are we going to talk to?'

Diana leaned forward, candlelight glinting in her wine-brightened eyes. 'Call Eleanor Bly and ask her why she did it.'

'Oh please, no,' said Leslie as she shoved the photo album back under the table.

'We couldn't even if I wanted to.' Gwen frowned. 'Christ, Diana. It's like this, Leslie. I'll give you the official speech I make every time a tourist shows up on my doorstep with the same request. The energies left behind by suicides are not able to displace themselves. In other words, the delightfully ironic punishment for taking your own life is never being able to leave it. If you want to talk to Eleanor, Diana, you'll have to trek up to the tower at Five Mile, a move I don't recommend. With the state that place is in, such a trip might be its own form of suicide. Besides, even if you managed to get up there without breaking your neck, Eleanor has to decide she wants to talk to you.'

'Yeah, but Gwen, that excuse won't work anymore. I was up there today,' Diana said. 'You can come and go as you want. You know that. It's not pretty or anything, but it's all reinforced. Absolutely safe. Greg took Harry and me on a tour. So, let's grab the kids and go.'

Leslie stood. 'No way am I traipsing up there tonight. Gwen, if I could borrow a couple towels, I'm going to wrap up Molly and Em – '

'Please.' Diana pleaded with a full-body sort of pout, and Leslie knew exactly how this woman got to be Mrs Harry Wellington.

'Not tonight, Diana.' Leslie made no attempt to keep the disapproving maternal overtones from her voice. 'Anyway, has anyone ever considered that Eleanor was not a suicide? She might have been helped out that window.'

'What makes you say that?' Gwen asked as she heaved herself to standing.

Leslie shrugged. 'I don't know. Nothing really. It's just the sort of question we, I mean, I was trained to ask.'

'You really do look like her,' Diana said softly, and sipped at her wine.

'Hmmm.' Leslie stared down into the red of her glass; everything was suddenly so very red. And then she saw it, the great spreading sea of it on Gwen's pale blue dress. 'Gwen, you're bleeding.'

Gwen looked down and then back to Leslie. A faint sob broke in her throat. 'Oh no,' she said, her hand reaching out. 'Oh, please no. Not again.'

Leslie caught her. 'Come on, we're going to lie you back down right here, okay Gwen –'

'Diana, call an ambulance and then get hold of Joe – '

'It's okay, Gwen – it's okay – are you having contractions? – '

'I'll take that as a yes – hold my hand –

'Yes, it's early, you're right, it's early – breathe – just breathe – don't worry about that –

'I'm going to raise your legs a little bit – you're shivering, are you cold? Let's get this blanket on you – '

'Any sign of that ambulance, Diana?

'Diana!'

In the end when everything that could be done had been done, it was still not enough. The doctors would determine that the baby had died in the womb, probably a day or two before, and Gwen's body had simply sought to expel it. This is how nature works, they assured Joe. Gwen would be fine, physically, in a week or two. The rest of her recovery would take longer.

After the call came from the hospital, Leslie told Greg that she wanted to stay behind and clean the carpet, as best she could, before Joe returned. Molly and Emma, except for the sirens and shouting, had not been aware of the greater part of the evening's tragedy. Confused, tired, they asked to see their mother before they went home. Leslie met them out in the hallway, the door closed on the bloodied room behind her. She yanked off the rubber gloves, dropped to her knees, and pulled them to her body. Leslie kissed and hugged them until Greg crept forward and prised them away from her.

'Come home soon,' he said.

Leslie, still on her knees, nodded. As he led them down the hall, away from her, Leslie heard Emma say, 'Daddy? Did Mommy get mad again?'

Twelve

'LESLIE, YOU LOOK SO sad.' Gwen closed her robe and pushed herself up against the thin hospital pillows. She patted the blanket, gesturing for Leslie to come sit on the bed. 'There's nothing to be sad about.'

Leslie sat on the edge of the bed. 'Nothing?'

'Not a thing. Every life fulfills itself, even the short ones.'

'I envy your faith.'

'I'm not sure that's what I'd call it.' Gwen picked up a brush from the bedside table, leaned forward, and started to brush her hair. 'I do feel more at peace with this one than the two before. Maybe that's because I don't have to try again. I had them, well, I can't try anymore.'

'Joe told us.' Leslie took the brush from Gwen. 'Let me.' She guided the bristles through the thick, almost-white strands. 'To lose one child is brutal. I think it took a hell of a lot of courage to try as many times as you did.'

Gwen laughed. 'Courage is for choices.'

'You had choices.'

'Not as many as I first thought. Do you think you had a choice?'

Leslie stopped brushing. 'If you're talking about what I think you're talking about, then yeah, of course I had a choice. I didn't have to pull the trigger. I chose to.'

'I don't agree. The idea that somehow it could have all gone differently is just an artifact of aftermath. The definition of the effect always comes before we start naming the causes.'

'Yes, Professor Garrett.'

'All I'm saying is that I don't think you had a choice. I don't

86

think you ever did. It only looks that way because that's the way you look at it.'

Leslie put the brush back on the nightstand. 'You need your rest.'

Gwen sighed. 'I didn't mean to upset you. It's just that over the past few days I've begun to see the inevitability in the way events play out. Choice, all that free will crap, that is the myth. Each of us, at any moment, is at the conjunction of countless random events. We do what we do because it's the only thing we can do at that moment. We take the path of least resistance not because it's easy, but because it's the only one open to us.'

Leslie stood and looked at her watch. 'Visitors' hours were over fifteen minutes ago. I do have to get going.' She turned to leave.

'Would it be easier,' Gwen asked, 'if you knew for sure? If you knew absolutely that you got the right guy, would it make you feel better?'

Leslie stopped. She looked back and shook her head.

'Didn't think so, you aren't that pragmatic. And I bet you'd feel even worse if it turned out to be the wrong guy because the bastard who killed that little girl had gotten away with it, correct? Either way, Leslie loses, right? So, why then did you do this thing so contrary to your true nature, so guaranteed to cause you nothing but pain?'

'I don't know.' Leslie pushed open the door and went out into the corridor. As the door swung shut, she heard Gwen call out behind her.

'Because you had no choice, Leslie. You never did.'

Gwen called Saturday morning to thank Leslie for her kindness. 'Kindness' was Gwen's word. Gwen then informed Leslie that she and Joe were going away for a while to her sister's home in the eastern mountains. It was a good place to work at recovering her strength. Leslie said she understood. Gwen asked if Leslie might look after her garden, turn the water on now and then if the weather got too dry. Leslie said she'd be happy to.

And so, Leslie added a daily visit to Gwen's garden to her lockstep routine. She did little more than run the hose, arcing misty rainbows over the burgeoning greenery. She worried that it wasn't enough. Perhaps she should be weeding the neat little rows or pruning one plant back to prevent its overgrowing another, but she dreaded doing harm. Leslie had never seen such intricately planted beds. Gwen's garden was centered on beds of herbs labeled with medicinal-sounding names like ERUCA SATIVA and TANECETUM VULGARE. These were flanked by beds of strange conical flowers with fleshy peach petals. Roses the size of a child's thimble nestled against the sinuous trunks of the massive clematis Gwen had trained over a lattice arbor. Beyond the arbor lay patchwork beds of vegetables, each section outlined in the yellow marigolds that kept the insects away. Gwen's garden was lovely, thought Leslie, but also deliberate in a way that made her uneasy, almost fearful of disrupting Gwen's sense of order. Should an errant pink open among the frothy sea of white roses, Leslie knew she'd feel compelled to cut it away – that or correct its coloring with paint. She could see Gwen, long finger pointed in accusation as she bellowed, 'Off with her head!'

Leslie was more than a little relieved when, in the third week of July, Gwen called to say she was back in Wellington. Leslie asked if she might come by for a visit that afternoon, and Gwen said that no, play time was over; her days were going to be spent up on the hill. She was feeling much better and was eager to get back to work on Five Mile House; so many decisions had been postponed in her absence. Besides, work would be a comfort. Leslie could not argue with that.

'Come up to the house with me,' said Gwen. 'I'll show you around.'

'No thanks,' said Leslie, who felt her first visit to Five Mile had been more than adequate. 'I'd just be in the way.'

'Come by tomorrow morning then,' said Gwen. Leslie accepted the breakfast invitation.

She sat in Gwen's kitchen feeling awkward and helpless as Gwen bustled about preparing the meal. Gwen chopped herbs for the omelet she was making and chatted happily about how well the garden was coming on, thanks to Leslie. Gwen was wearing her purple maternity dress and every so often, she'd absentmindedly pat herself where the baby had been. At one point, Gwen caught herself doing it.

'Old habits, huh?' she said with a laugh. Leslie didn't join in.

Within days Leslie had reinvented her daily caring for Gwen's garden to simply caring for Gwen. She brought casseroles or muffins or an exotic tea she thought Gwen might enjoy. As Leslie had studied the careful management of the garden, she now studied the woman who, although given to an occasional distant glance or shallow sigh, appeared to be handling her loss with an equally careful management of self. This appearance of peace troubled Leslie; in contrast to the profound and unquestioning acceptance, Gwen was still wearing her maternity clothes.

Leslie did not ask questions, however. In part, she wished not to breach the privacy barrier, a breakthrough of which would grant Gwen equal rights to inquire after Leslie's state of mind. There was another reason, as well. It was something different in Gwen, not new, but more intensified. Gwen in her garden pulling up the tender sprouting dandelions; Gwen in the kitchen making soup; Gwen in the study reading. It was the expression on Gwen's face when she saw Leslie in approach, the mist-gray eyes slitting in concentration, the quick, thin smile, and then the set in her posture of an unswayable resolve. It was more than an expression, it was a gesture. It unnerved Leslie each time she saw it; it was as though Leslie had suddenly realized that she had wandered off the path in a notoriously dangerous wood. Nevertheless, Leslie could not fathom what the danger might be. It was still and only Gwen.

Leslie, alternating between feeling threatened and ridiculous, responded to Gwen's unsettling cheeriness by fostering a distance between them. Leslie made sure her daily visits were pleasant but empty, framed by the small talk people use to define the silences that forbid real words. It was cowardice on her part, Leslie would condemn herself, fear that Gwen's strange, soulless grieving was but a front for emotions Leslie herself would not dare name, let alone indulge. They talked of the heat, the humidity, the price of tomatoes, progress on the Five Mile project which Gwen had taken to calling 'her baby.' They talked of these things not because that was easier for Gwen, but because it was easier for Leslie.

The small talk continued through the end of July and most of August, until one hazy morning, when Leslie was helping Gwen to thin a row of ornamental chives. Having exhausted conversation, they worked along without speaking, troweling up the fine white bulbs, brushing off the dark soil, separating the large clusters into smaller groups and replanting them. Bees bounced about in the onion-scented heat. It was pleasant work that lulled Leslie into a mindless automation. She was uncertain of how much time had passed in that state, but she became aware of eyes upon her. Gwen, at the far end of the next row, was watching her from under the edge of her broad-brimmed sun hat.

'What? Am I doing something wrong?' Leslie scanned the row she'd been working.

Gwen rubbed at the back of her neck. 'Do you truly believe Eleanor might *not* have been a suicide?'

Leslie stuck her trowel in the soil and prised up another set of bulbs. 'Where did that come from?'

'I remember you saying something that night, but we never got a chance to talk about it.'

'Gwen, Eleanor died over a hundred years ago. Whatever I do or do not believe isn't important.'

'It's important to you, important enough that you've spent time considering the alternative possibilities. Are you still playing detective, Detective?'

'I'm poking around a little. It's something to do. I'm going to start on those carrots.'

'There is no need to get defensive, Leslie. You might like to know that you aren't the only one.'

Leslie sat back on her heels and looked at Gwen. 'The only one?'

'You aren't the only person to question certain assumptions made by the so-called authorities. I, like you, see inconsistencies.'

Leslie laughed. She shook her head and plunged the trowel deeper into the earth. 'I'm really not up for any more of the horror stories of Wellington.'

'If you don't want to talk about Eleanor, tell me what you think about Joshua. Did he poison all those people?'

Leslie put down the trowel. 'Why do you want my opinion?'

'Just curious.'

'Okay. From what I've seen of the story, I'd say yeah, he was involved, but that was some pretty fancy poisoning. Obviously, he wasn't working alone, and since poison is more a woman's weapon, my case theory would be that the Benevista chick was his partner. It was Joshua who did her, the tub and rope and whatever. The old double-cross.' She picked up the trowel again.

'Why?'

'May we talk about something else now?'

Gwen stood, walked to where Leslie had begun digging, and sat beside her. 'Look, I know you don't want – well my *case theory* is you don't want anyone's help with anything. You need to listen to me, Leslie, because there's more going on up on that hill, in this town, more than a restoration project.'

Leslie didn't stop working. 'They're looking for something, aren't they?'

'Something extraordinary.'

'Which is why Mansfield Custom, the CIA of remodeling firms, is doing the work, right?' Leslie tossed aside the bulbs she had just dug free. 'Joshua hid something up there, something he stole from Benevista? Money? Jewels, paintings? What?'

Gwen leaned in close. 'A book. At least, they think it's a book. It might be part of a book. It might be only a fragment, a sheaf of parchment, say, or a palimpsest, or a scroll, or a tablet or something else. No one is sure what it is, only that it's somewhere in Wellington. The restoration of the town is an excuse to dismantle every building in it. That's why Harry Wellington keeps coming through here. He's checking in on what they may have turned up.'

'I thought he was building a roadside attraction.'

'That part is true; the project needed a credible cover story and this also insures local cooperation. It's not all a rigged façade. If done right, everyone in town is going to benefit.'

Leslie dipped her chin. 'So tell me about this book.'

'I can't.' Gwen took up the trowel and began to twist the point into the earth.

'You can't? You're the one who brought it up.'

'And you're the one who doesn't want stories. That's all I have.'

'You mean they're looking for something that doesn't exist?'

Gwen freed the trowel and used its edge to scrape smooth the soil in front of her. With her finger she drew a circle in the dirt. 'This is nature.' She then drew a line bisecting the circle vertically. 'One side is order; the other is chaos.' Again she drew a line through the horizontal axis. 'The creative is one side; the destructive is the other. Therefore, we have four primary forces at work: creative order, creative chaos, destructive order, and destructive chaos.

The circle comprises everything, including nothingness. Follow me so far?'

'Hmmm.' Leslie couldn't see Gwen's face beneath the hat.

'High school geometry: an infinite number of lines can be drawn through the center, right? It gives us an infinite set of possibilities within a bounded universe centered on the point where all possibilities converge. Or radiate outward. In other words, the godhead.'

'Please don't go mystic on me.'

Gwen ignored the comment. 'Suppose there existed a collection of equations that allowed the plotting of all possible outcomes in all dimensions, a kind of calculus of metaphysics. You could hypothetically locate the ultimate center, the secret of the circle. When worked to completion, this set of equations would result in the spontaneous generation of an artificial godhead, the ability to create and destroy absolutely. Suppose such a collection of equations had been split up and scattered through wars or theft or just plain common sense. Over the centuries certain fragments may have surfaced, passing through such hands as those of Pythagoras and Nostradamus and perhaps even Albert Einstein. Now, suppose a syndicate of powerful individuals were trying to put the book back together because with the advent of computers it might be possible to actually work the book to its solution, thereby gaining unimaginable powers. And just suppose one of the final missing pieces had been traced to Joshua Bly.' Gwen pushed the hat up and the pupils in her strange gray eyes constricted to nothing.

'You're telling me they believe the key to all creation – '

' – and destruction – '

' – is hidden up on that hill?'

'Yes and no,' said Gwen. She wiped out her diagram with a single sweep of her hand. 'Every word of what I just told you is pure invention. I made it up as I went along.'

'I don't understand, Gwen. You're lying to me?'

'I told you a story, that's all.'

'Which is it? Is there a book or isn't there?'

'That book is my field of expertise, Leslie. That book is what I've spent my life on, and let me tell you it doesn't matter whether the book is real or not. What does matter is that there are those among us who believe the book is real. They believe it is up at Five

Mile. Their beliefs may or may not be delusions, but their appetites are authentic. The more pervasive their belief, that is the more they can anchor it to empirical reality, then the more those appetites will grow and the more dangerous those believers become. Make no mistake, they will have taken your resemblance to Eleanor as a sign.'

'So, they're a bunch of loony-tunes.' Leslie sat forward, resting her chin in her palm. 'I'm the last one to hold that against them – as long as their checks don't bounce.'

'Be careful, Leslie. No matter what you think you understand about Five Mile House, you must remember that everything about the past is story and legend. It's easy to get lost there.'

'Are you talking about the house or its history?'

Gwen smiled her thin, sad smile. 'If you're looking for the truth, stay in the here and now.' She pressed her dirty hands against her flat, empty belly. 'Only now is real.'

Leslie waited up for Greg that night. Work on Five Mile had accelerated to a level of near twenty-four-hour effort. It was not uncommon for Greg to be out until midnight or later. When he came in this night, it was close to two. He smelled of old sweat and sawdust. He had a torn blue bandana wrapped as a makeshift bandage on his right hand. Tired beyond explaining, he simply looked at it and sighed. 'It's nothing.'

Leslie fetched the shoebox containing their first aid supplies. When she returned, he was sitting on the bed in his shorts. She kneeled on the floor in front of him. Carefully, she unwrapped the bandana, then winced when she saw his palm.

'You should have gotten stitches for this.'

Greg inhaled through his teeth as the air hit the wound. 'No time.'

'It's pretty deep. What did you do to yourself?'

'Grabbed hold of a saw blade that wasn't quite done sawing.'

'Criminy.' She moistened a gauze pad with hydrogen peroxide and gently dabbed the surface of the wound. The peroxide foamed, sending flumes of white up and down the valleys created by the calluses on his skin. She folded another oblong of gauze and laid it against the severed skin. She then slowly wrapped his hand in a clean white bandage, weaving figure eights between the thumb and forefinger, around the back of his hand, down around his wrist and back up to the place she started. She finished with a length of tape to secure the ends. 'There,' she said, looking up to see he had fallen asleep, his head dropped to the side. Leslie placed her hand on his scruffy, sun-darkened cheek and ran her fingers up along the distinct tan line left by the hard hat he wore. Suddenly, he seemed a stranger to her, not her husband, not any one she'd ever known. She leaned forward and brushed her lips against his, leaned in further and whispered in his ear, attempting to wake him.

'Greg, go take a shower. You'll feel better. I'll wait for you.'

'Too tired. I'd drown standing up.' For emphasis he fell back on the bed.

'Okay. You sleep.' She helped him haul his legs onto the mattress.

He yawned. 'Everything's all right, right? You and the girls?'

'We're great. I just wanted to talk to you about Five Mile, you know, find out how things are going. Anything interesting happen?'

'Other than nearly slicing my hand in two?' He was still yawning. 'Can we do this tomorrow, Les? I have to be up there again in four hours.'

'Sure. We'll do it tomorrow. But I won't be home till late, remember.' She turned off the light beside him. 'It's Thursday.'

Thirteen

L ESLIE BYPASSED HER USUAL place in the reference section of the university library, going instead to the main desk to inquire about the doctoral thesis of one Gwendolyn Van Der Walles Garrett. In a few minutes, the librarian – a very tall and constricted-looking young man, who gazed down on her with the same bland interest one might show any innocuous pest – returned with a thick volume bound in blue vellum. The title of the work looked to be at least twenty-six words in length. Less than half of those were familiar to Leslie, but at least Gwen's name appeared beneath the academic hocus-pocus. This was enough to satisfy Leslie. She signed out *Deus ex Machina: Codes of Ritual and Sacrifice as Technologies in the Actualization of the Godhead in Sacred Texts with Particular Emphasis on the Mythos of 'The Analecta Seriatus'* and settled with it in a vacant carrel.

She ran her hand over the cool blue cover and remembered Gwen's admonishments to caution. Was the warning meant to direct her toward or away from Five Mile's true nature? She had to admit that her research so far had only led her down the thoroughly trodden paths of history. The lack of tangential byways that might have led to new insight left Leslie feeling no recourse but to tramp again and again a course she already sensed would take her nowhere. Perhaps it was that frustration which forgave this lapse into the speculative and arcane. Gwen had already instructed her not to believe any of the legends, but until Leslie had learned what the legends were, the disbelief would be frail, unsteady. 'Okay, Dr Garrett,' Leslie said as she opened the blue cover. 'Tell me a story.'

In spite of its intimidating title, the work proved more readable than Leslie first hoped. The *Analecta Seriatus* turned out to be the true name for what Gwen had shrugged off the day before as 'a book.' The title came from a Latin pronouncement on the source of the document: *Analecta* was Greek for a collection of fragmented writings; *Seriatus* was Latin for sequence or series. This title, the mating of terms from differing languages to form a larger whole, was of such self-referential symbolism that scholars were uncertain if the title was original to the work or purely descriptive of its content. Some held the *Analecta* to be as old as time itself, believing it to be the metaphorical 'Tree of Knowledge' due to the branching nature of the formulae contained within its pages. The scattering of those pages had been, essentially, the shattering of Eden; the work of mankind being solely that of restoring the *Analecta* to its proper *Seriatus,* thereby restoring the Deity.

Taking notes as she went, Leslie read about the historical search for what some took as the scientific equivalent of the Grail. Theories abounded: the *Analecta* was the mystery at the heart of the ancient Mystery Cults; the Pythagorean Monad from which all numbers were created; the holy treasure both sought and guarded by the Knights Templar. Alchemists, Kabalists, numerologists, code-crackers of all sorts had spent years, wealth, blood in pursuit of a thing no one had seen but believed real all the same. Gwen had found stories of Arabian concubines with *Analecta* equations tattooed on their inner thighs in hopes of secreting them from the armies of the Crusades. Mere segments of *Analecta* code woven into the ornate patterns of oriental rugs supposedly permitted levitation, hence the mythic flying carpet. Experts were trying to untangle an *Analecta*-based language believed hidden in the intricacy of the Celtic knots gracing the Book of Kells. Leonardo Da Vinci had reportedly disguised one of the code keys on a canvas over which he painted the *Mona Lisa*; it was for this knowledge she smiled. Modern seekers postulated that the recordings sent into the farthest reaches of the solar system on the Voyager II space probe were in actuality a set of *Analecta* proofs; if there were a universal language, this would be it. And yet, not one of these efforts was founded on anything more substantial than hearsay.

Others evaded the arguments for tangible evidence by holding the *Analecta* as an article of pure faith. When the fragments were reunited in proper sequence, the portals to paradise would be thrown wide, and we would all be gods. The *Analecta*'s powers, therefore, were not to be located in the physical realm but to be invoked through demonstrations of unquestioning spiritual obedience as framed by ritual acts of immense sacrifice. The definition of what such sacrifice might entail was vague, but references to the *Analecta* had been reportedly found in the records attributed to the Inquisition, Hitler's Germany, Jonestown.

Leslie closed her eyes, and saw the little graveyard behind the Wellington museum with its weeping angel standing watch over the seven small crosses. All of Eleanor's children gone. Sacrificed? All of them? No, not all. Leslie blinked. She turned to the first pages of her notebook, where she had scribbled details of the Bly family history. All the children had been killed, it told her, except, except, except . . .

'The one who was old enough,' she read aloud, 'to take off on his own.' She turned a few pages forward, cursing her lack of organization, until she found the list of names copied from the headstones: Bartholomew, Abigail, Marie, Simon, James, Matthew, Justine. Old enough must mean first born. To take off on his – *his* – own. Male child.

Leslie closed her notebook and leaned, rocking her weight back, throwing the chair onto a precarious two-leg balance. She chewed at the end of her pen and tried to concentrate, to will forward the question taking shape in the shadowed corners of her mind. When it did at last emerge, a simple query of ghastly logic, the implications of asking it overwhelmed her chances of immediately seeking the answer: if one sets out to kill all of one's children, wouldn't sense dictate starting with the eldest and working back toward those of greater vulnerability? If there were a Joshua Bly Junior and he survived the tragedy at Five Mile, was it because he was intentionally allowed to escape? If so, why?

'It's the house.' Realization caused her to fall forward. The chair thudded firm, all four legs on the floor. 'Again with that damn house. Five Mile stays in the Bly family only as long as there is a Bly family. They sent him out there to breed.'

She felt both elation and despair at the prospect of having a plausible, if outlandish, explanation for her likeness to Eleanor. The thought of putting together a genealogy of her own huge and scattered family was daunting, and Leslie slumped in the carrel, exhausted by the mere contemplation of the work. There had to be a more direct route. She glanced up at the clock. It was almost three.

Leslie pitches her body forward over Phillip, holding him inside her and heaving her thighs, her hips, her breath in the great rolling waves of a sea at storm. She arches her neck and swings her head, sweeping, beating his chest and neck with her hair. He holds her wrists, a measure of self-protection. When, at last, she breaks, her body exorcised or reunited with its nameless, private demons, she collapses against him, quiets. He releases her hands. Phillip smooths her hair, pulling it back in a loose grip as he tightens his arms about her in embrace.

'Is it me?' she whispers.

'I'm sorry? Is what you?'

She rolls off him and stares at the ceiling. 'You've been looking for the heirs to Five Mile, and here I am with my ever-so-freakin'- remarkable resemblance to Old Lady Bly. Am I a member of the family?'

'Would you like to be?'

'I'm serious, Phillip.'

'Why would I keep that from you? I mean, if you were, and Five Mile House were your responsibility, don't you think I'd have you take it off our hands?'

'Likely chance I would.'

'Then I'd be seeing you in court, darling.'

Leslie shifts onto her side to face him. 'Who got out? I mean, which of the Bly kids survived?'

'None of them.'

'No. The brochure says that one of the kids – the oldest boy?'

He shakes his head. 'None of them lived. I know, I know, but small-town historical societies are about perpetuating small-town propaganda. The oldest kid, Samuel, was said to have figured out he was in danger and ran away. In reality he died of tuberculosis in a sanitarium months before the others were killed. It was the same way Eleanor lost her brother. I've always thought that might have been what drove her over the edge, you know. TB is a terrible way to die. Eleanor might have believed she was saving them from the same fate. After the murders, the story

98

developed that he'd taken off in the middle of the night to save himself.'

'If they're all gone, why are you bothering to look for heirs?'

'Why are you asking me all these questions, Detective? This is more than we've talked in weeks.'

'Just trying to figure out what's what.'

He traces his finger down the length of her sternum, following a bead of perspiration as it curves and disappears under her breast. 'Joshua, as you've probably heard, was a rather randy gentleman. Randy gentlemen sometimes leave behind awkward souvenirs.'

'And the Wellingtons want to be certain their big investment in fixing up Five Mile doesn't go to some long lost oops on the family tree.'

'Basically, that's it.'

'And there's nothing else? No buried treasures or priceless artifacts?'

'Am I supposed to know something else, Detective?'

She closes her eyes. 'Would you tell me if you did?'

'Leslie, you know the drill. I'm bound by certain ethical – '

'Yeah, yeah. I shouldn't have brought it up.' She opens her eyes and sits up. 'Did you bring any beer?'

'A whole six-pack.' Phillip pushes himself up against the headboard and points to a brown paper bag next to the TV. 'I brought you something else, too.'

'I've been smelling it since I got here.' Leslie pads over to the table, opens the bag, and grins back at him. 'Pastrami.'

'On rye with mustard.'

'How did you guess?'

'I've tasted it on you.'

'Food of the damned.' She brings the bag back to the bed. 'Want some?' They share the sandwich and drink most of the beer and then couple again. Leslie dozes while Phillip showers. He wakes her and points at his watch.

'Shit!' She jumps out of bed, grabbing her clothes.

He crumples the sandwich bag and lobs it toward the wastebasket. He misses. 'I've got to meet Harry in about fifteen – '

'Yeah, go,' she says, waving him away.

Leslie stopped at the grocery store on her way out of Rutherford.

She found the pay phone and called Greg to apologize for getting caught up, for being late, for inconveniencing him again. He sounded tired, perhaps too tired to even express his exasperation. He asked only what he should do with the girls; he had to get back to work. Leslie suggested Gwen, and Greg said he'd thought of that, but there'd been no answer when he phoned.

'I'll take them up to Five Mile with me.'

'Greg, I'm not sure that's a good idea.'

'It's not like I have much choice. I have to get back up there.'

'Look, Molly will be okay keeping an eye on things until I get back. Just put them in front of the television and tell them I'm on my way.' She heard him responding to voices in the other room.

'I think Molly has hit her limit on Emma-watching for today. I'll take them up to the house. You can pick them up whenever you get here.'

'I said I was sorry.'

'You say that a lot, Les.' He hung up the phone.

She stared at the silent receiver before returning it to its cradle. The rage-driven drone in her head sped up a notch, still blurred but getting clearer as the beery haze lifted. Leslie took a red plastic basket from a stack of red plastic baskets and wandered the grocery aisles. She thought about Five Mile and her daughters and her husband and Five Mile and then Phillip and then Gwen and her stories and then Five Mile, going round and round in mental circles, inciting a dizziness that no amount of alcohol could emulate.

She had been wandering in such a distracted state for a while when a white-haired man in a red apron asked if there was anything he might help her find. Leslie said no, no thank you, and handed him the empty basket. She went out to her van and drove home.

When she pulled into the driveway, she was mildly surprised to see Greg's truck there. Perhaps he had finished earlier than expected. Or the girls had been too much to handle. If that was the case, she was certain to find him even more ill-tempered than when they had spoken on the phone.

The lights were on in the front room but the house was quiet. She hung her keys on the hook by the door. All right, where were they?

Greg's voice responded to her unasked question.

'I'm in here, Les. The girls are up the street at the Widmarks'. They're fine.'

She went to where he was waiting. At a glance, she knew something was wrong. 'What happened?'

'Come here, sweetheart. Sit down.'

Leslie didn't move. 'What happened?'

Greg folded his hands and looked down at them. 'Right after I talked to you, Joe Garrett called. Gwen . . .'

He lifted his face to meet hers and although Leslie could read it in his expression, she wanted the words. 'Gwen what?'

'Apparently the miscarriage was harder on her than any of us realized.'

'How?'

'They're not sure yet. It looks like something she mixed herself, something herbal, from her garden.'

'I don't believe it. Not for one goddamn second.'

'Leslie, she left a note.'

'I don't care if she left a videotape and a half dozen eye witnesses. I don't believe it. Not Gwen.'

Greg stood and walked toward Leslie, who backed away with each approaching step he took. 'I understand how upsetting this is for you. That's why I wanted you to hear it from me.'

'Suicide?'

'I'm sorry, Leslie.'

'I don't believe you.'

Greg drew his hands over his face. 'Leslie' – his voice was choppy with fear – 'I don't know how to help you with this.'

She was backed up against the door, her arms locked over her chest. 'I want to see her.'

'Sweetheart.'

'I want to see the body. Right now.'

'Sweetheart.' He spoke so very softly, she felt the words drift up and beyond her reach. 'Gwen was hurting, hurting more than any of us could have guessed. She found a way to make the pain stop. People do that sometimes. You know that.'

'What I know?' she said, yanking her car keys off the hook. 'What I know is nothing.' She stared at him hard for a second and then left, slamming the door behind her.

Fourteen

MY BROTHER SURRENDERED TO death the spring I turned
sixteen, a mere season before I met Joshua and my own
peculiar illness took hold. My brother's name was Samuel, and
yes, I named my first boy for him, apparently dooming the child
by doing so. My brother contracted consumption when he was
just ten. I was eight. We were, by doctor's edict, separated from
that point forward, and I lost my truest friend. He lived the next
eight years as a recluse, poor little boy, quarantined to the sunny
side of the house with only nurses as companions. On Christmas
mornings and Easter, occasionally a birthday, he might be wheeled
down in his chair to join us for a short time until his cough and its
attendant unpleasantness overwhelmed him.

By the time of his death he was too weak for even his chair. In
mid-March, a week after his eighteenth birthday, my mother woke
me in the early light of day to tell me that Samuel's struggle was
ending. She wondered if I might like to come say my goodbyes. I
pulled on my dressing gown and followed her to a part of the house
from which I'd been for nearly a decade forbidden. In Samuel's
room, where the golden hues of the rising sun drowned the candles
on his nightstand, I knelt by his bed and studied the stranger who
had devoured my brother. Consumption is the correct name for this
monstrosity. He, whom my parents called Samuel, was nothing but
a translucent sack of rattles and pain. And I remember, as I feigned
my farewells and prayers for his salvation, that I knew only one
true emotion. I hated him. I hated his frailty, hated his pathetic
incapacity to accept the inevitable. For what have you fought? I
asked him silently. What good has such stubbornness done you?
Why torture yourself, torture us with the continual reminders of

your absence? If a memory of love led me to his bedside that dawn, it was contempt for his weakness which drove me out, running from the room retching with great, unstoppable sobs.

It was a similar contempt for weakness that drove Leslie Stone to knock at the Garretts' front door. Joe answered, his usually perfected person skewed by shock, sleeplessness, and the alcohol Leslie detected on his breath.

'Leslie? What the . . . it's . . . I don't know what time it is.'

'It's nearly four, Joe. I couldn't sleep, so I came over to see how you're doing.'

'I've done better.' He motioned her into the house.

'Joe, I'm just so – I don't know what to say.'

'Thanks. Can I get you something?'

Leslie took his arm and steered him into the kitchen. 'Why don't I make us both some coffee, huh?'

'Nope,' he said, sitting down at the table where he'd apparently been spending the night. He picked up a shot glass and filled it from an almost-empty bottle of scotch. 'I think I'll stick with this. You sure you don't want some?'

'No thanks.' She took the coffee canister from the cupboard. In the past few weeks she'd come to know Gwen's kitchen as well as she knew her own. The woman had been a fastidious housekeeper, and Leslie hoped, as she moved about the room, to see something amiss: one of the spice jars out of its alphabetical order, a canister of tea out of place. A hint, a clue, but there was nothing. She took a mug from the under-shelf hook and went to sit at the table, where Joe was wavering, eyes closed, a man in a fugue.

'Gwen was a good friend,' said Leslie. 'I'll miss her.'

He didn't respond. Leslie poured him another shot. 'Joe? Can I ask you a couple questions?'

His eyelids fluttered as he came back to wakefulness. He saw the drink and downed it. 'Yeah? I answered a bunch of questions already. She was in bed when I got home. I thought she was taking a nap. She was still sleeping when I went back to work. I tried phoning, but she didn't – so, I kinda got worried and came back to check on her. She wasn't sleeping.' He swallowed and then began to weep. 'I'm sorry, Leslie. I'm sorry.' He bent forward, covering his face with his hands.

Leslie stroked the back of his head. 'Greg said she left a note.'

He straightened, wiping his eyes and nose against his arm. 'Yeah, there was a note. The police took it even after I told them I was sure it was her handwriting.'

'That's what they do, Joe. They'll give it back to you soon.' She filled the shot glass again. 'I know this is really painful, but what did the note say?'

'Not much. Just that she couldn't go on after losing another baby and it wasn't anybody's fault' – he started to laugh – 'just your basic suicide note.'

'Joe, you need to get some rest.' Leslie stood and offered her hand. 'Let's go.'

He shook his head. 'I can't sleep in the bedroom.'

'I know. I want you to lie down on the couch for a while. You don't have to sleep, just rest.'

'You won't leave?'

'No. Not if you want me to stay. You mind if I look around a little?'

''Kay. You look around. Don't leave.' He let her pull him upward. Halfway to the living room, Joe fell dead asleep, and Leslie had to drag him to the nearest chair. She eased him down and draped Gwen's old afghan over him, tucking it up around his shoulders. 'Almost as good as a warrant.' She went back to the kitchen and took the yellow rubber gloves from under the sink. She put them on, and then she headed upstairs.

The bedroom gave her nothing except the forlorn evidence of Gwen's physical impression left behind in the bed linen. Leslie laid her gloved palm lightly on the dent in the pillow. 'I don't believe it, Gwen,' she whispered. The rest of the bedroom was spotless, the furniture gleamed – dust free – in the overhead light. She opened closets and dresser drawers but found nothing to indicate Gwen or any one else's intent. She wished she could see the note, see the photographs of the body – if there were photographs, that is. Small towns, sensitive to their citizens as individuals, tended to fortress the grief-stricken in sympathy. For suicides, or perceived suicides, the rules became amorphous; things were accepted as they appeared. Leslie, however, knew how easily sympathy can make one thing look like another thing, displacing truth in the transformation.

She went back downstairs, to the back of the house, to Gwen's study. She switched on the lamps and scanned the bookshelves. Other than the arcane nature of the titles, nothing struck Leslie as odd, everything still in Gwen's library-perfect alphabetization. The prints on the walls were level and smudge-free; the photographs were of no one Leslie recognized. Gwen's desk was orderly; her appointment book was opened, but nothing was written in it for that day, nothing for the previous week or the one after. The coffee table in the middle of the room held the big pad of paper Gwen used for her automatic writing experiments. Its cover was closed. The planchette sat on top of the pad.

Leslie vaguely heard herself say 'Hmmm' as she crouched to look more closely at the planchette. She lifted the cover of the pad. The current page was blank, but it was obvious the preceding pages had been torn out recklessly, in haste, leaving behind a goodly portion of paper. Not like Gwen at all. She let the cover fall back into place, replaced the planchette, and then went into the living room.

'Joe. Wake up. I need to talk to you.' She shook him. 'Joe!'

'Uh-uh. Hi, Leslie. Oh, God. Leslie, Gwennie is dead.'

'Yes. Joe – stay with me – where exactly did you find the note?'

'Next to the bed.' He rubbed at his eyes with his fists.

'The same bed where you thought Gwen had been sleeping?'

'Yeah.'

'What kind of paper was it on?'

'I don't know. Paper.'

'Was it the kind she used for automatic writing? Did it look like it might have been torn from that big pad in her study?'

'Might have been. The paper wasn't real important to me.'

Leslie looked at her hands and pulled off the yellow gloves. 'Was she meeting with anyone this morning? A client? Was there anyone else in the house today?'

After a few seconds, the implication of her statement sparked a sudden alertness in his face. 'What are you talking about?'

'I am talking about what you need to do. You need to make sure there is an autopsy for Gwen. You have to get on the phone and insist on it. Right now.'

The spark faded. 'Well, they're doing one already to find out, you know, what she took.'

'I'm sure they're going to find something, Joe, but we need to know how it was administered. You have to get on the phone and tell them you've had second thoughts. Tell them you suspect – '

'I suspect what?'

She sank next to Joe's chair. 'Do you really believe Gwen was the type to do this?' She watched the words hit, watched him deflate, become small, something beyond hope.

'Leslie, go home. Go now. Leave us both alone.'

'Okay.' Leslie nodded. 'We'll talk later.'

'No, we won't,' he said. 'Not about this.'

'Joe, I can't believe –'

'Go away, Leslie. Leave us alone.'

'All right, but we will talk later.' And Leslie left him sitting staring straight ahead into nothing.

Fifteen

JOE'S PREDICTION PROVED CORRECT; they did not speak of it again. Later in the day, Greg called Leslie to say that Phillip Hogarth had been up at Five Mile House to let everyone know that Joe was taking Gwen back to her hometown, where her family would lay her to rest. The autopsy reports, according to Hogarth, had been inconclusive. Whatever Gwen had taken, a still unidentified organic compound, had caused her heart to stop. It was, in the words of the coroner, a quiet death. When Leslie asked about further investigation, Greg paused. She heard him sigh, and then he said no, there'd be no further investigation. Gwen's body was to be cremated, as she had requested in her farewell note. Joe apparently felt he had all the answers he required.

Leslie thanked Greg for the information. She hung up the phone and went into the kitchen. She filled a tumbler with cold water from the tap. She gulped it down, and filled it again, and drank. Then she hurled the glass against the porcelain sink. It exploded upward, sending shards within a nerve's width of her eyes, head, throat. She did not flinch.

Molly came running downstairs. 'What was that?'

Leslie became aware of her hands gripped on the edge of the counter. She willed her fingers to flex free. 'It's okay, Molly. Just a little accident.' She turned to face her daughter and forced a smile.

Molly stood in the door to the kitchen, her eyes large with comprehension. She had heard these explosions before, seen the shattered aftermath glittering about her mother's presence. 'Mom?' she said, and Leslie heard all the fear and fury.

'You're right. It wasn't an accident.' She sighed and bent over to gather the larger pieces of debris. 'I'm upset about Gwen. Sometimes it helps to break things.'

Molly dropped her shoulders in obvious relief that they weren't going to pretend. 'You want some help cleaning it up?'

'No. My mess, my responsibility.' She dropped what she had collected in the under-sink trash can.

'I don't mind, Mom.'

'I do.' Leslie stepped over the remaining fragments. She looked down at Molly, who was looking down at the floor. Leslie put a finger under her daughter's chin and gently lifted her face. Molly's sullen expression didn't alter, nor could she seem to bring herself to meet her mother's gaze. Leslie, having nothing left to offer, simply took Molly in her arms and rocked her. The embrace was not returned.

At long last, Leslie kissed Molly on the crown of her head, inhaling deep the warmth of her child. Then she let Molly go.

'Really, Mol. I'm all right.'

'Well, I heard and so . . . okay, I'm going back to my room now.' Molly turned and made good her escape.

That evening, for the first time in weeks, they sat down to dinner as a family. Leslie had made baked ziti, garlic bread, and a salad with vegetables from their garden. They talked quietly about their day's work, remembering to say 'please' and 'thank you' for each portion requested and received. Emma spilled her apple juice and they – Greg, Leslie, and Molly – assured her it was no great loss as the dog busied himself licking the floor. After dinner the girls took Sam outside. They wanted to play on the tire swing their father had put up earlier that afternoon. Leslie was on her hands and knees, wiping up the last bit of juice from beneath the table, when the doorbell rang.

Greg got up and went to answer it. Leslie recognized the voice of their visitor at once. She pushed herself back to her feet.

Greg had ushered him into the kitchen. 'Hey, Les, you remember Phil Hogarth?'

'Of course.' Leslie dried her apple-sticky palms on her jeans, and she and Phillip shook hands. 'How are you?'

'Things have been better, wouldn't you agree?' He offered her a weak smile and then turned back to Greg. 'I met with Harry. Five Mile is all yours now.'

Greg leaned against the doorjamb, his face full of uncertainty. 'I'm going to be needing some help, Phil. I can't manage the site and the historical shit and get it all in by October.'

'It's already taken care of. I'm going to look after the money end.'

'And why do I hear a "but" coming?'

'Yes, but, there is another supervisory concern coming on board, and I'm not certain how you're going to feel about it. Diana has decided she wants to spend the rest of the summer up here overseeing the more, ah, cosmetic aspects of the restoration, the interior decoration.'

'Right.' Leslie went to the sink to rinse out the wash cloth. 'Wouldn't there have to be some original decoration to restore?'

Phillip laughed. Greg said, 'Les has a point. What's to decorate? I thought the goal was to get it up and running as a tourist attraction by Hallowe'en.'

'Yes, but that was before Diana fell in love with Five Mile and the idea it might be haunted. She has' – he hooked the fingers of both hands into quotation marks – ' "this thing about ghosts." '

Leslie dropped the cloth on the table. 'You mean they're going to live up there?'

'It's what Diana wants, and what Diana wants is what Harry wants. Her reasoning is there are a lot of family estates that are both private homes and open to the public.'

'Five Mile ain't no fucking White House.' Greg pulled up a chair and sat. 'I don't know if that can be done, not by October. You're talking eight weeks? It would mean . . . crap, I can't even begin to think of what it would mean.' He took a pencil from his shirt pocket and began to sketch on a paper napkin.

'They have kids.' Leslie spoke directly to Phillip. 'She wants to move kids into that house?'

He shrugged. 'The older three, from Harry's first marriage, are either in college or off on their own; they wouldn't be living here. The little guy, Jack, will be seven soon, and Harry has already started shopping for boarding schools – although he's yet to break that one to his wife. Diana can be a ditz but she's one hell of a devoted mother. It's all very Oedipal.'

'Where is devoted Mommy going to stash little Jack while she's playing interior designer?'

'Well, she'll keep Jack with her during the day and they'll live at the Garretts'. Diana's made arrangements to rent it from Joe – Leslie, you don't even have to say it. It's not what I would have chosen for them either. But I think Diana wants to play with Gwen's toys.'

'Hmmm.' The tone in her voice caused Greg to glance up from his drawing. Leslie, realizing both men were staring at her, raised an eyebrow and said, 'Maybe I'm being obnoxious, but that Wellington woman is warped.'

'Keep your obnoxiousness to yourself, please,' Greg said, and went back to his sketching.

Phillip cleared his throat. 'Diana is young and easily bored. Although we might question her motivations, in terms of placating local opposition to the Wellington project, nothing could be more useful than a gesture demonstrating that the Wellingtons hold their personal investment in the town's future of equal importance to their financial ambitions. I can't think of anything that would smooth the way more effectively than Diana's very public efforts to make a home for her family here.'

'Extremely well spun, doctor,' Leslie said, clapping her hands in exaggerated applause.

He bowed his head in acknowledgment of her compliment. 'So, Greg, what do you need from me in the meanwhile?'

Greg kept drawing. 'Only your soul and twenty-seven hours a day of your time.'

'You realize I have other commitments.' He glanced at Leslie.

'Not anymore you don't.'

Leslie turned to the window to watch her daughters. Emma, in the center of the tire, was holding tight to the rim as Molly pushed her in a circle, twisting the rope until it buckled back on itself. Then Molly let go and Emma went spinning, fast. The dog barked and tried to give chase. Emma threw her head back. Her arms slid down the black rim and her legs extended, trusting herself to forces she couldn't name or control. Leslie looked at Phillip. 'I'll let you guys get to work, then.'

'Not tonight. I have to get going; there's paperwork and logistics to be seen to. But Greg, I'll be up at Five Mile first thing in the morning.'

'We generally get started before what you suit-and-tie types call morning.'

'I'll be there.'

'Fine,' answered Greg.

After a long, silent minute, Leslie said to Phillip, 'Well, I was going to take the kids out for ice cream. I think you'll have to move your car.'

'Yes. Right.'

'Bring you something, Greg?'

'I'm fine.'

Phillip and Leslie walked out together into the darkening day. 'And what part of that could you not have done on the phone?'

'I was worried about you. I had to see for myself that you were all right.'

'Because of Gwen?' She folded her arms over her middle.

'Yes. This is tough, huh?'

She didn't answer. She searched his face, trying to see beyond the flesh and bone, the muscle and sinuous tissues, trying to see beyond what she could touch. She could take him into every part of herself, every part but one: she would not allow him to see her surrender.

'Leslie?'

'Tough? Why should this be tough? My friend killed herself. No big deal.'

'I only wanted you to know that I am concerned. If you want to talk, if you need to talk – '

'I have doctors for that.'

'I meant, well, talk about matters that are best kept between friends.' He opened his car door and slipped inside.

'Thanks. I'll keep that in mind.' She made to shut the door and then stopped. 'You up for a lawyer-type favor?'

Phillip turned over the ignition and the engine engaged. 'That depends.'

'I want to see Gwen's note. The one she left.'

'Why would you want to see that?'

'I'll settle for a photocopy. Not just a transcription of the words, though. I want to see her handwriting.'

'What the hell for?'

'My peace of mind.'

'You, my lady, have a strange sense of peace.' He revved the engine. 'But if that would help, I'll see what I can do.'

'I'd appreciate it,' said Leslie. She shut the car door, and watched him back down the drive. He waved at her, then drove away, his tires raising a thin cloud of dust that swirled red and gold in the last light of the sun.

Sixteen

'YOU MUST THINK I am so weird,' Diana said as she snuggled deeper into one of the chairs in Gwen's study. 'But I have this thing about death, well, really about what comes after death.' She lit her second marijuana cigarette of the afternoon. Leslie sat on the other side of the coffee table, sketch pad and planchette between them.

'I suppose we all wonder about certain things,' said Leslie, who was still wondering why she and her daughters had been summoned to this audience.

'Exactly! I wonder about it. Harry says I obsess, but really, I just wonder. Do you think it's weird that I want to live in this house?'

'Why should it matter what I think?'

'I guess everyone thinks it's weird to want to sleep in the same bed where someone died. Maybe I think so, too. But remember what Gwen said about the punishment thing for taking your own life?'

Until that moment, Leslie had not recalled the conversation. 'Not quite. It was something about leaving – '

'Exactly. If you commit suicide your spirit can't depart. You're stuck in your life forever.'

'So, you want to be here because you think Gwen will talk to you?'

'Through the automatic writing thing, yeah. Exactly. Gwen showed me how to do it.'

'She did?'

'Before, obviously. I used to come here in the evening, and she'd go into a trance thing. Well, I'm not sure if that's what it was, but that's what I'd call it. Then her hand would move. Sometimes we got words, sometimes pictures. I didn't understand most of it, which was frustrating because Gwen said that she was receiving on my behalf and it was my job to interpret the writing things, the symbols that showed up. Oh well.' Diana grew quiet, took a deep inhale of the sweet smoke, and held it. 'You sure you don't want a hit?'

'It's a little early for me.'

'Well, if you change your mind . . .' She exhaled slowly and then turned in the chair to peer out the window. 'Oh, look, the kids are waving at us. Hi, Jack! Hi, honey!' Diana turned back. 'Your girls are adorable.'

'Thanks.' Leslie waved at her daughters and the slight, yellow-haired boy who looked exactly like his mother. 'Diana, what did Gwen do with the readings, I mean the writing itself?'

'She tore them out of the pad there and gave them to me so I could meditate on them, try to see if I could figure out what they meant. I'll show them to you if you want. They're upstairs in one of my suitcases.'

'You kept them all?'

'Yep. All except the ones from the last session. The last time I saw Gwen, we did this reading that went on and on. She went through a ton of paper. When she came out of the trance or whatever, she looked over all she'd written and said something like "garbage" or "crap" or something like that. She apologized for wasting my time.'

'Did you see any of those pages?'

'No. What was the point? I wasn't able to do anything with the ones she said were "static free."'

Leslie leaned forward and drummed her fingers on the cover of the pad. 'When was this, Diana?'

'Two days before she – do you want to see the readings? It'll only take me a minute to find them.'

'Well, if you're sure you don't mind.'

Diana unfurled like a cat and bounded from the room. Leslie waited for the sound of her on the stairs, then she opened the pad of paper. She counted the roughly torn edges: nine. What might Gwen's automatic writing produce that was worth dying for? Leslie could hear Diana's footsteps above her and the thudding of luggage being rearranged, so she got up and went to the bookshelves. 'God bless you, Gwendolyn,' Leslie whispered as her fingers moved through the alphabetized titles almost immediately to a slender spine of dark cloth printed in white: *Automatic Writing: The Subconscious Speaks*. Leslie pulled the book, slipped it in her pocket, and hurried back to where she'd been sitting.

A few minutes later, Diana returned with a sheaf of folded paper and a wine bottle. She handed the pages to Leslie. 'Keep them as long as you like.'

'Okay.'

Diana filled a glass almost to the brim, caught an errant drop on her finger, and licked it off. 'Oh, I almost forgot. The reason I wanted to see you is that I've had this tremendous idea. Want to hear it?'

Leslie smiled as she tightened her grasp on the paper. 'All right.'

'How would you like to work with me on Five Mile? Greg keeps telling Harry and me about all the research you've been doing on the place. You'd kind of be like my historical – thingie – consultant. What Gwen was.'

'Diana, that's not the sort of research I've been doing.'

'Oh, come on. It will be fun. This town is one fucking snoozeville, and with Harry so busy and your husband so busy, we could be decorating buddies.'

'You haven't seen my house, have you?'

Diana drained half the glass. 'It's just that, really, I just hate being alone.'

'You have Jack with you.'

'You know what I mean.' And she drained the rest of the glass.

Leslie did know what Diana meant, and that unnerved her, although *alone* wasn't Leslie's word for it. 'What if we make a deal? I'll help you with your project if you help me with mine.'

'What's yours?'

'Let's start with one question. The day Gwen . . . died, I came across a bit of information, and I was wondering if it might mean anything to you. Have you ever heard of something called the *Analecta Seriatus*?'

Diana grinned and poured more wine. 'Tons. Gwennie wrote her doctoral thing on it.'

Leslie sat back and considered the inebriated woman before her. 'How long did you know Gwen?'

'Just about forever. We met here in Wellington when I was going through my Wicca thing.'

Leslie rubbed her forehead. 'Is there anyone in this town who is not involved with the coven?'

'Oh yeah, absolutely. Take a look at your Historical Society directory thing. If you're in there, damn good bet they have nothing to do with the Rubble Witches. It's been that way since William Wellington came up with the idea of the Society.'

'It goes back that far?'

'Isabel didn't have kids, so William founded a trust to take ownership of the lake house after he died. The bad blood between the witches and the Wellingtons started before the Historical Society, though.'

'Yeah, huh? What sort of bad blood?'

Diana shrugged. 'Some old land fight. Historical Society's main job is to keep the Rubble coven from accessing certain pieces of land.'

'Five Mile can't be on that list. I saw one of the concrete recycling trucks up on the hill.'

'Sure. The coven can bring stuff in, but they're not allowed to haul stuff out.'

Leslie pressed her fingers deeper into her forehead where the smoke and conversation had become a diffuse ache. 'What sort of stuff can't they haul out?'

'You know, I didn't pay attention. I really didn't care about the coven and their legacy crap. Joining the Rubble Bitches was just a cool and easy way to freak out my family. That's what I thought. Turns out that real Wicca is a fucking lot of study, and Christ, they have all these holidays that take forever to get ready for, not to mention that there's a damned full moon every single month. Gwen had already been there a long time when I joined. She was a priestess or whatever the boss witch is called, I forget. Anyway, once they found out she was doing a Ph.D. in psych, of all things, the coven – make that Delores – felt like she might be going over to the dark side of science, and they tossed her. The whole Wicca thing fell apart for me after that. But I hear they still get together for the major feasts and shit.'

'What were you doing in Wellington?'

'Besides hunting down a rich husband?' Diana giggled. 'I'm not into the scholarly thing. I'd already flunked out of two schools, and my parents have this "degree or die" deal. They told me if I didn't stay in school, they'd stop sending the checks. State U at Rutherford was about the only place that would take me. They're not very – how do you say it? – selective. But as it turned out, I never had to finish because I met Harry and his wife had just died and well, now I send my parents money.'

'And you lived happily ever after.'

'It is sort of like a fairy-tale thing, isn't it?'

'You were going to tell me about the *Analecta*?'

'No, I wasn't. You said one question and I answered it. To get the rest, you have to help me with Five Mile.'

'Diana – '

'Please. It's so important to Harry that the thing gets done right, and like I said, I'm not into doing all the studying and stuff.'

'I don't know.'

'Our kids can play together every day. Look at how happy they are playing together. You'd get to spend more time with your husband.'

And we'll all live happily ever after, Leslie thought. 'All right. For a couple of weeks maybe. And I don't want my kids – or Jack – spending too much time up at that house.'

Diana yawned, her eyelids drooping. 'It will be fun. You'll see.'

Leslie stood. 'Would you like me to take Jack over to our place to play for a while?'

'No, no. Jack stays with me. Always. I'm just sleepy. It's nap time. Jack and I always take a nap together. Just send him in. Tell him Mommy said nap time.' Diana drifted off to sleep, her face slack with hazy contentment.

'Fun,' said Leslie to herself, and settled back in the chair. She pulled the book out of her pocket. So much for the intrigue of secreting it out of the house. The text only underscored Gwen's explanation of the two differing sects of faithful with regard to the phenomenon of automatic writing. First were the practitioners of the mantic arts who believed that one might converse with the spirit plane through a medium whose hand held a pen to paper. The second sect, of which the book's author was a devout member, held that it was the living human subconscious controlling the planchette. This by no means invalidated the writing; it only made clear its beneficial applications for those in the psychical study of obstructed minds.

Leslie closed the book and considered the pad of paper, the varnished wood and felt-tipped feet of the planchette. 'What did you see, Gwen?' She unfolded the pages Diana had given her. The edges were, as Leslie had expected, smooth, crisp. Gwen had removed them with the same care she had given to the other little details of her life. Leslie spread the pages on the table in front of her. She couldn't fault Diana for feeling perplexed; there was little on any one sheet that made much sense. The handwriting was very large, looping, and erratic. There was an occasional word of typical mystical bearing: beware; loss; sorrow. 'Five Mile' appeared frequently, written numerically: *5 mile*. There were, in fact, a lot of numbers, sequences that appeared to be counting sets of one to nine. Like in nine missing pages? Or was it nine as in the months of pregnancy? Leslie had to wonder if Gwen might have recognized these numbers as cries of her own mind, a warning of how deeply the miscarriage had scarred her. Perhaps she had been suicidal, but on a level beyond surface detection. Perhaps she had given these pleas for intervention to Diana, hoping Diana would see, understand, and intervene.

Leslie looked up at the slumped and snoring woman. 'Fat chance there.' But why Diana? Because she was an old friend from an old life? Or maybe the recurring references to Five Mile led Gwen to believe the writings were, in fact, intended for Diana. And what could possibly have appeared in that final session, the one Leslie believed to have been ripped jaggedly from the pad?

Leslie refolded Diana's pages, and then not believing what she was about to do, she opened the pad. She laid her right hand on the planchette so that the pen felt snug between her index and middle fingers. She took a deep breath, closed her eyes. She felt ridiculous. She sat there, still, in self-imposed darkness waiting for – whom? Gwen? Herself? Something to manifest itself in comprehensible symbols. Her hand moved, trembled and jerked a couple of short, erratic steps, but she was certain she'd done that on purpose. Leslie waited, kept waiting, felt the waiting start to draw her downward into the center of her breathing. She could hear her heart beating and Diana snoring and the children outside playing freeze tag.

'Screw this,' she said, laughing, squinting herself back into daylight. She looked at her page half-hoping, half-dreading it would be filled with copious writings she had been unaware of producing. Except for the little lines she'd drawn consciously, the page was blank. She ran her fingers over her work, slipped her hand under the paper and found the indentation on the page beneath. Then she flattened the top sheet back into place and she brought her head eye-level with the paper. She ran her hand across it, looking, feeling for impressions Gwen might have left behind. The page was as smooth as it was empty. Whatever had been taken away from here had been taken away completely.

Seventeen

IN RESOLUTE SILENCE, I withstood the invasion of Five Mile House. Those heavy-booted men stomped through my hallways, *my* rooms, swearing and laughing, oblivious to the fact they were uninvited. My days and nights rang with the high-pitched whines of machines designed to cut and pierce. Dust clouds clotted the air, settling over the floorboards in ever deepening drifts of white. The men hammered and hammered, pulling back up and reinforcing what I had so long hoped would come down. For over a century I have watched as the water rotted and the mildew ate and the sun parched the bones of this creature. And now I watched as it was methodically resurrected. They built it new bones of new pine and restored its flaked, failing hide with a thick coat of fresh plaster. Above the noisy vanity of their efforts they could not hear, day by day, the growing roar. Had I warned them, attempted to warn them, had they heard my voice over the racket of their work, it would have only served to spur them onward. They held that book, the story of it, as a prize. They did not understand that the book was no more than bait, the intriguing morsel meant to draw them, by means of their own hunger, into the bile, the bowel, the dark dissolving juices of Five Mile House.

I spent my days waiting by my window, in my tower, caged anew by the arrogant scaffolding erected to preserve my prison. I waited by my window, because I knew Leslie would return. She had not climbed the hill since that morning months earlier when her own ghosts had usurped my intent to speak. Still, I knew she would return; everything that belongs to Five Mile comes back to Five Mile, eventually. I waited. And I planned.

I was waiting by my window, my mind full with imaginings

of darkness and rest, when Leslie came back to Five Mile. She climbed out of the truck and held open the door for her children, Jack Wellington, and his mother. The five of them stood looking at the house, faces upturned in the hot, bright morning sun, an island of placid curiosity amidst the hurly-burly rush of workmen hoisting planks and mixing mortar. Their eyes were set on the tower; they were seeing but not seeing me. Diana's expression was that of childlike delight; the children themselves looked bored. Leslie regarded the tower with that same singular defiance, her jaw set, shoulders squared. She was refusing to participate from the beginning. I realized then, in a crush of despair, that even if I could make myself heard, she might choose not to listen. I might have only one word before she shut out my voice. I might have only one word, to set her on the path toward salvation for us both.

The women and their children approached the front steps, and I grappled with my limited language. I heard them enter, the little ones clambering on the staircase; their mothers scolding them to slow, to take care. Up. They were coming up. At that moment I decided what I must say, the single syllable that might fasten in Leslie's waking mind and root there. A word Leslie would understand.

'I am not going to tell you again, Emma Stone. Stop running.' Leslie raised her voice to send it to the top of the stairs.

'I want to see the tower.'

'We are going to see the tower. Molly, would you please hold your sister's hand.' Leslie groaned. 'This is why I don't want these guys up here. Diana, can I help you with some of that?'

Diana, who was carrying both Jack and a large leather portfolio she had qualified as being 'full of idea things,' declined. 'You go on ahead and make sure your girls are all right.' Leslie climbed, two slanting risers with each step, round the landings in the narrow stairwell until she caught up with Molly and Emma, who had been stopped by the closed tower door.

'It's locked,' said Emma.

'It's not locked,' said Leslie, trying to catch her breath. 'It's just stuck. Push. Push harder. Let me.' She leaned against the door and shoved. The door jumped open. A warm, sawdust-scented wind blew past them. 'Okay. Let's see the tower.'

'Cool,' said Molly, stepping into the room.

'Actually, it's suffocating,' said Diana, coming up behind them. 'Jack, sweetie, Mommy's going to put you down now. What was this supposed to be?'

'Don't you know?'

'No idea.'

'It couldn't have been living space. At least, I don't think so.' Leslie moved further inside the room, which she guessed to be barely nine feet wide. Plastic sheeting at the window snapped in the hot breeze. Flies buzzed in the heights of the pitched ceiling. The framing of the walls had been rebuilt, the new wood giving the effect of prison bars. 'Maybe it was an attic, some sort of storage space. I'll see if I can find out.'

'Mommy, it's hot up here. Can we go now?'

'Good idea, Emma,' said Leslie, wiping away the perspiration running down her temples.

'Not yet,' said Diana. She reached in her portfolio and pulled out the planchette just far enough for Leslie to see and comprehend.

Leslie smiled a hard, meaningful smile. 'No way.'

'Come on. We have to try.'

'No, we don't.'

Diana ignored the protest. 'Molly, why don't you take the little guys down to the truck? There's a cooler with sodas and all sorts of goodies in the back.'

Leslie started toward the door. 'I could use a cold drink.'

Diana caught her by the arm. 'Go ahead, guys. We'll be down in just a minute.' The little ones were already halfway down the first flight. Molly followed, calling after them, insisting they wait.

When the children were echoing far beneath them, Diana released Leslie's arm. She giggled. 'Sometimes I get a little carried away. Sorry.' Then she sat on the floor and went about setting up the pad and pen.

'We have to get something straight, Diana. You want to go ghost hunting? Fine. That's not what I'm here for, and I do not want my daughters even in the same room as the subject. Their lives are haunted enough.'

'Boy, I've really offended you, haven't I?' Diana looked up at Leslie, her eyes full of sulky chagrin. She put the pad back in the portfolio. 'I didn't know you took this thing so seriously. I just thought we were going to have a laugh or two.' She zipped up the case. 'We'd better get to work,' she said, and started down the stairs.

Leslie covered her eyes with her hands. Great. Now, Diana would complain to Harry and then Harry would complain to Greg and then Greg would lecture her on the necessity of humility when dealing with one's employer. She uncovered her eyes and straightened her posture, trying to check her wavering, translucent reflection in the plastic. She couldn't focus. The heat took on a sudden density like a vital energy coalescing about her, hemming her in. Her heart sped. I'm going to pass out, she thought, and turned for the door in hopes of getting down to cooler air.

The door, however, was closed. Who had done that? Surely, Diana, no matter how angered, wouldn't have shut her in here? Leslie yanked on the door, but it wouldn't give. She pounded at the door with her fists and shouted. Who was she kidding? No one was going to hear her over the circular saws and nail guns.

Leslie turned back toward the window. She could make out the shapes of her children and Diana in the drive. She'd call to them. They'd see her. They'd come. She crossed the room and reached to pull the plastic aside when someone, something grabbed her wrist.

I took hold of Leslie, and she looked at me. I can't be certain of what she saw, but her eyes shut down to slits and then grew quite large, as if in recognition. The heat flush in her face was sucked away. She faltered. I had only a moment. I held on tightly and leaned in close to her ear.

'War,' I said. 'It was war. War.' I said it until I could see she'd slipped into unconsciousness. I eased her limp, fevered body into a sitting position against the new wood of the new wall, and then I reopened the door.

'I am all right. I'm fine,' Leslie said, brushing Greg's arm away and with it the iced cloth he held to the back of her neck.

'Would you please cooperate for once.' He placed the cloth on her forehead. 'You're burning up.'

They were in the small, air-conditioned trailer that served as the site office. Leslie was sitting in Greg's swivel chair because she refused to lie down. Greg crouched next to her, fighting to keep the ice in place with one hand and plucking pieces of sawdust from her hair with the other. Diana paced back and forth in front of them.

'I thought you were right behind me, Leslie. I thought she was right behind me, Greg.'

'Then why did you shut the freakin' door on me?'

'But I didn't. Why would I do that?'

'Les, if Diana says she didn't shut the door – '

'Just drop it. I'm okay. I just fainted, that's all. I don't do real well when it gets hot.' Greg lifted the cloth for a second to look at her. Leslie pulled the cloth back to her head.

'New rule,' said Greg. 'Everybody stays out of the tower. Leslie, you were damn lucky. If you had fainted in the other direction you'd have gone right out that window.'

'You know, maybe *that's* what happened to Eleanor. Her suicide thing? Maybe she just sorta fainted in the wrong direction.'

'Good theory, but' – Greg hastened to amend his flattery with fact – 'back then there would have been glass in the windows.'

'The windows might have been open.'

'True. True.'

'No,' said Leslie. 'It wasn't like that. The windows didn't open. It wasn't an accident.'

'No one has any clue what really happened up there,' said Greg.

'It wasn't an accident,' Leslie repeated.

Diana stopped pacing. 'How can you be sure of that?'

'I just am.'

When Leslie convinced him that she had regained her strength, Greg went back to work. Leslie decided she'd had enough of the interior of Five Mile for one day. A tour of the grounds was in order then, or so Diana announced. Children in tow, they began to walk the laborious circuit that was the perimeter of the additions. The children quickly grasped the opportunity for a game of hide-and-go-seek. They hid and their wandering mothers would, by chance, discover them in a corner here or a nook there.

Leslie pretended to listen as Diana proposed impossible gardens and waterfalls and alcoves. In reality, Leslie was considering the structure itself, the foundation of stones bound by heavily mortared seams. The exterior walls rose at least twelve feet above the foundation. Not one wall had either door or window. It was a fortress, Leslie thought. Joshua Bly was building a fortress. Against what?

It was war.

Leslie stopped. She looked down at her right wrist where a ring of purple bruises was beginning to form. 'Diana?'

Diana glanced over her shoulder. 'You don't think the arbor thing would work here?'

'Was Five Mile House involved in a war of some sort?'

'Got me. I think a nice shady arbor would be great here.'

'Couldn't be the Civil War,' Leslie continued aloud. 'The house was built a good twenty years after it ended. Maybe it's the hill itself, something about this land?'

'Leslie, I really don't care about the hill or the land right now. I'm trying to see this as pretty. See pretty with me, huh?'

'No. We need to talk about the *Analecta* for a minute. We had a deal.'

Diana slinked back, her head bowed, a wicked smile on her lips.

'Okay. What? Like I told you, I'm not big on the student stuff.'

'Don't pull that innocent bimbo crap with me, Diana. Gwen told me the main reason for this whole Five Mile thing is that Harry is trying to find some part of the *Analecta Seriatus*. You do know that.'

She bit her lower lip and shrugged. 'Really, I don't know much about it, Leslie. I don't care about it. The *Analecta* is one of Harry's hobbies. It's like his polo ponies and the stock market. All I ever really knew about it was that he goes all gaga on the subject. That's why he hung out with Gwen. She was the major expert.'

'And you joined the coven to get in good with Gwen so you could meet Harry Wellington – '

'Exactly.'

'Well, you must have learned something about it, overheard Gwen and Harry talking.'

'I've learned enough to warn you that you don't want to be asking this many questions.'

Leslie cocked her head to the side. 'Are you threatening me?'

'No, silly. It's that there are a bunch of competing – what do you call them – interest groups involved. Everybody thinks everybody else is spying. You ask the wrong questions and it gets back to Harry, he's going to go all paranoid and take Greg off the job.'

'You are threatening me.'

'Just telling you the way things work around here.'

'I see.'

'So now I suppose you're going to quit on our deal, and I'll have to do this thing all by myself.'

Leslie raised her face into the midday sun. The shadow of the tower was beginning to lengthen in their direction. 'No, Diana. I'm not quitting. Not now.'

Eighteen

TUESDAY MORNING WAS OVERCAST and hot. Thunder grumbled in the distance, but moved no closer. Leslie loaded the girls into the van and headed out on her weekly errands. At the post office she chatted with Maggie, the counter clerk, about the awful humidity. Then she bought stamps and mailed off the mortgage payment. She stopped next at the pharmacy on Hawthorne Street, an establishment so old it announced its business as being that of apothecary, notions, and sundries. While waiting for her prescriptions to be refilled, she shopped for cosmetics she wouldn't use. The girls looked at the souvenirs with the new and official WITCHES OF WELLINGTON emblem. Leslie encountered prim, polite Mrs Widmark, her neighbor from up the street, and they both agreed that the day was already a scorcher. The pharmacist handed Leslie her white bag full of brown bottles, laughing as he predicted snow.

Lunch was next. They filed into the tiny diner on Main and took counter seats. Emma and Molly twisted on the chrome-plated stools. They dined on grilled cheese sandwiches and potato chips and chocolate milk shakes. As they were paying the bill, Susanna, their waitress, downed a full glass of ice water and wiped her brow. 'Why doesn't it just go ahead and rain?' she asked Leslie, as though Leslie might know. Leslie left her a generous tip.

Wellington's town square lay directly across the street from the diner. Century-old oak trees shaded the walkways that crisscrossed the space, corner to corner. A fountain spouted in the center of the square, and on sultry days like this, it was not unusual to see children wading through the waters in the fountain's wide, tile-lined base. This afternoon the waders were gathered to the far side of the fountain watching the Wellington Volunteer Fire Department run its regular monthly test of the emergency equipment: ladders were raised and lowered; safety nets were stretched and checked for tears; hoses were hooked to hydrants to gush as they were inspected for leaks. Sirens cried as the children hooted and covered their ears.

'Can we go play in the water?' shouted Emma over the careening wail from the fire truck.

'Not today,' Leslie shouted back as she scanned the square for the gray-haired hulk of Yancy Galleghar. Wherever he was, she and her girls were headed in the opposite direction.

'Please.'

'No,' said Leslie, taking Emma's hand as she spotted Yancy in his blue WVFD tee-shirt. He was showing some gauges on the truck to a couple of waders who had ventured from the fountain. Leslie wanted to make use of his distraction to get out of his line of sight. 'Come on, you two. We have to get to the grocery store,' she said, as she tugged Emma along until they reached the parking lot. Leslie risked a quick glance over her shoulder, and wished she hadn't. Yancy was looking right at them, his hand shading his eyes. She hurried her daughters into the van.

Leslie did whatever she could to avoid Yancy Galleghar, not for fear of what he might say but for the certainty that one of these days she was going to risk the broken bones and slug him. He was a retired cop out of Rutherford who had talked his way into the job of Wellington's town manager. On their first meeting, outside the apothecary at the beginning of summer, Yancy had waved her down and shouted, from across the street, 'Good shooting, baby girl!' He came over and introduced himself as being 'from that generation of cops who had the good sense to recognize the emotional limitations of the female mind.'

'And what you did only goes to prove my point,' Yancy said. 'I don't mean anything discriminatory by it, but normally you ladies just ain't cut from the chain-mail it takes to do the job. You got too much, what they call, inherent nurturing instinct. Too much heart. But whoa, honey, did you prove me wrong.'

Taken aback, Leslie had laughed and excused herself without comment. In a town full of witches and ghosts, a cyclops such as Yancy Galleghar was hardly out of place, but as later meetings brought forth more soulful musings on the mistake of burdening maternal nature with the realities of enforcing law and order, Leslie's patience with the man became so tautly strained that she felt it wiser for all concerned to keep Yancy and his slab of a skull out of striking distance.

She pulled out of the parking lot and checked the rearview mirror. Yancy was still watching them, watching her. Leslie wheeled the van on to the first side street to get out of his gaze.

They stopped at the grocery on the other side of town. Molly and Emma argued over who would push the cart until Leslie cut in and sent them to find their father's favorite cookies, a box of breakfast cereal, bread, and bologna. She knew the exercise in organizing this collective effort would occupy them for more time than she required to complete her shopping. She steered the cart along the aisles. The store was a small, rundown outlet, poorly stocked and staffed by pimply adolescents who hated their lives and therefore everyone else. Mrs Widmark was here, but having exhausted their conversation at the previous meeting, she and Leslie only smiled at each other as they passed in the aisle. In frozen foods, she encountered Mitch Ward loading his brother Dan's arms with bags of precooked chicken pieces.

'Party?' she asked them.

'No,' said Dan. 'Good price.'

Mitch nodded. 'My wife and I bought one of them chest freezers. Big enough for a whole deer.' He threw another sack into his brother's arms. 'These'll last us until hunting season.'

'We need to get a freezer,' said Leslie.

'Oh, yeah,' said Dan. 'Can't survive in Wellington without a freezer.'

Mitch glared at his brother. 'You don't have one.'

'I'm borrowing yours.'

'How about instead of borrowing, I rent you a corner?'

'How about I rent you a corner of this?' Dan extended his middle finger at Mitch and then dumped the bags of chicken back into the bin. 'Carry your own damn birds.' He strode toward the door.

Leslie laughed. 'What was that about?'

'You'll have to forgive Dan. He's just a lonely old cuss. He gets it in his head sometimes that I think I'm better 'cos I have Maureen. I can't mention getting new tires without him thinking

I'm rubbing his nose in the fact he's never found a woman who'd have him.'

'I get 'cha,' said Leslie, suddenly eager to continue on her way. 'How's the family?'

'Oh, we're all good. Speaking of which, I'd better locate Molly and Emma before they start helping themselves to the candy – '

'Shame about Gwen Garrett. That woman gave me the willies, but you hate to see that happen to anyone.'

'Yes. It is a shame.' Leslie moved her cart forward and then stopped. 'Mitch? You said there were stories about Gwen. The day you delivered our stuff. Remember?'

He looked off through the big windows in the front of the store, through which Dan was visible as he strode the length of their truck, talking vigorously to himself. Mitch said, 'My grandma held it was unlucky to pass along rumors concerning those who died in unsettled ways.'

'I'm just trying to understand why she did it.'

'And I'm just trying to outrun any more bad luck.'

'Come on, Mitch. Don't tell me you are a sucker for all those country superstitions.'

'There's superstition, and then there's common sense.'

'Okay, forget it. But how about this? I know Five Mile House is named for Five Mile Hill, right? Thing is, no one can tell me or seems to remember what the hill is five miles from.'

He chuckled. 'Hell, you've been asking the question the wrong way. It was called Five Mile Hill because if you lit a fire at the top of the hill you could see it for five miles all around. It was used as signal light, a beacon.'

'For what?'

'Couldn't really say.'

'Because of superstition or common sense?'

He didn't respond.

'Did it have to do with a war?'

'Gwen Garrett is dead, Missus Stone. Take my advice, and let it go.'

'Mitch? Why can't you talk about this?'

'Sorry, Missus Stone, Dan looks like he's 'bout ready to blow a gasket. I'd better go calm him down.'

'Mitch?'

When they returned home, Leslie put Molly to work unpacking the grocery bags. Leslie shut herself in the bedroom and pulled out her notebook. Try as she might, the little word *war* could not be stopped. It had echoed in her head like a half-remembered song, and Leslie was determined to find out why. If there had been a war, or even a battle in this region, record of it must be somewhere and surely Leslie must have already seen it – how else could she account for her current fixation?

She lay on the bed and read over the notes she had taken from Gwen's writings on the *Analecta*. The only wars mentioned were those already accounted for by history, none of which came close to Wellington. Perhaps it wasn't a real war. Gwen had held the *Analecta Seriatus* as nothing more than the illusory center for a labyrinth of story. Maybe this unnamed war was another of these tales. In the conclusion of her thesis Gwen had written:

Unable to rest easy in nature's equitable indifference to our insecurities, we look for gods fashioned in our image, deities that prove their divinity by humbling themselves to our will; gods who exist solely to love, serve, and protect us from our most formidable enemy – ourselves. It is this childlike craving for absolute certainties that has driven the centuries-old quest for the *Analecta Seriatus*. And yet, as this research has demonstrated, there is not an iota of physical evidence to support even the argument that such a document ever existed outside the stories told of it. Does this, therefore, relegate the *Analecta* to the realms of chimera? No, quite the contrary: the search for it is real, and that search has driven many individuals to exercises of extreme, if not demented, self-interest. The *Analecta Seriatus* is made real by the desire for its reality. It is an archetype of the activity humans turn to when we can no longer bear the mystery of being. We prefer these rational, predictable, and perfected truths we create and thereby control to this imperfect, unpredictable, and random world that implies unimaginable godliness in every molecule of its existence.

Leslie had copied this passage into her notes because it came closest to the words Gwen had used in her warning that the intent to find the *Analecta* made it real enough. Now as Leslie reread it, she had to wonder if she had fallen prey to the same trap. Had she not allowed her mind to get tangled up in Eleanor Bly and Five Mile House, and lately the *Analecta,* to the point of obsession? Did she seek the solution to the mystery of the hill and the house, or was it just the mystery itself she wanted? Was the illusion of answers in someone else's past a balm to the ache of the unanswerable questions in her present?

Either way, Gwen was still gone. It was getting far too difficult to deny the suicide. Greg and Joe and everyone else was right. Who would want to hurt Gwen? The hard-and-getting-harder part was that Leslie knew she should have seen Gwen's pain, that she would have seen it if not for fear of seeing the already too familiar shape of inexplicable disaster. She had chosen to keep her distance, and Gwen was gone. And Amy was gone. And the man who may or may not have been responsible for Amy's death. And Eleanor and her children. What house, what book, what human endeavor could give adequate reason to these mysterious sorrows? The answers would change nothing.

Leslie read the passage again: *We prefer these rational, predictable, and perfected truths we create and thereby control to this imperfect, unpredictable, and random world that implies unimaginable godliness in every molecule of its existence.* Poor Gwen – she had finally reached the limits of her tolerance for the imperfect. The last miscarriage had taken not only the woman's child but her sense of purpose. Gwen had gone from this embracing acknowledgment of the unknowable to that hospital bed speech about inevitabilities and lack of choices. Every life fulfills itself.

'And what about every death, Gwen?'

It was time to put this nonsense away. What did any of it have to do with Leslie Stone? Her only connection, a tenuous one at best, was a ring of bruises now fading on her wrist and the slightest memory of a voice as she slid into darkness, a voice belonging to a face so much like her own. She had explained it to herself a dozen times already: it was her reflection in the plastic she had seen; it was her own voice calling for assistance; it was the shock of Gwen's death finding its way to the surface. Nothing more than a trick of the mind. And the bruises with their precise fingertip alignment? Her own fingers, perhaps, or maybe Diana's when she had tried to rouse Leslie. All in all it meant nothing, it was a wisp of a moment, and she was driving herself into blind alleys of speculation so as to drive away her other troubles.

Leslie flipped through the notebook to the last page. *It was war.* She had filled this entire page with doodles and scribbling of the phrase. She reconsidered it, tracing it with the nail of her little finger, thinking about Gwen, thinking about the passivity Gwen had adopted toward the end, thinking about the fierce determination she had worn like a mask in Leslie's presence, the contradiction between inner and outer beings. *It was war.* Words in a book. But which being was the mask, Gwen? *It was war.* Just stories on top of stories. What were you trying to tell me? *War.* And why, if you were leaving, if you knew you were leaving, would you tell me anything at all?

Leslie sat up. Because Gwen had not planned on going anywhere. Because Gwen had planned on seeing this through to the end. Proving the *Analecta* a myth had been her life's work, and that work was not yet complete. Five Mile House itself was a dare to keep going. Five Mile House was her baby, the only one she had left. The old angry drone rang in Leslie's head. Her heart thudded against her breastbone.

Gwen Garrett was no suicide. She was sure of it.

As a detective, Leslie had seen as many cases resolved by luck as by skill; she knew insight to be serendipitous, and yet, she'd almost allowed her intuition to be subsumed in the malleable comforts of rational logic. While she might be able to dismiss the source of the words, she could not ignore the implications of their content. *It was war.* The phrase was meant to convey something, most likely from the depths of Leslie's own roiling subconscious. She thought of Gwen's planchette and the ways of automatic writing. Leslie decided to accept the phrase as it stood. Somewhere in the history of the hill, the house, the town, its families and tragedies, there had been a war. It was still being fought, and Gwen Garrett had been its most recent casualty. But with Gwen's body cremated and the crime scene corrupted, Leslie knew she'd need more than hunches to get a full-scale investigation launched.

Her will retrained to the hunt, she spent the rest of that afternoon poring again through her research on Five Mile. She went over, again, specifications from the original carpentry: the four-by-eight inch sills, 'laid on the flat and halved together at angles; angle-posts and intermediate posts and girts' – whatever they might be – 'spiked to the posts and studs.' The slating for the roof was to be the 'best quality of purple slate, 16 in. long, laid 6 in. to the weather.' She had read this before, down to the instructions about details such as doorknobs, 'bronze metal on the first floor, white porcelain on the second, and dark mineral elsewhere throughout.' All of it to be set upon a foundation of 'cellar walls of good flat building stone twenty inches thick, laid in hydraulic ground lime and clean, sharp sand mortar.'

This was the house as ordered and paid for by the Wellingtons. The modifications ordered by Joshua Bly were so bizarre as to point to motives more intriguing than severe cost-cutting. The only source of heat in the structure was the wood-fueled stove in the kitchen. The windows did not open, but the glass in them had been thick and made of leaded crystal. Hardly an expression of frugality there. While the floorboards throughout the first floor were standard for the day, in the additions, Joshua had insisted on the highest quality African mahogany. The pieces had to be three inches thick, no more than five inches wide and free of all knots or other defects. That floor, heavy and tightly made as the hull of a ship, was one of the only elements in the house that did not need replacement and, Greg said, was probably the reason these additions had stood so long.

Crazy Joshua and his crazy house. She saw nothing new, no hint of what had taken place on that hill before the Blys had arrived. Leslie threw the notebook aside in frustration. She raked her fingers through her hair, yawned and rubbed her eyes. Then she reached for the notebook and began again.

Nineteen

THE NEXT MORNING, WEDNESDAY, was brighter but no more comfortable. It was the first of September. Leslie told the girls to collect their swimsuits and beach towels; they were going to the lake.

Wellington Park reverberated with the late-summer sounds of children yelling and lifeguard whistles, the pulse of adolescent music and the calliope of ice cream vendors. Leslie settled her daughters on the beach, leaving Molly with a bottle of sunscreen lotion, money for lunch, and stern directions concerning Emma. Leslie then headed for the museum.

In the musty heat of the museum's tiny library, she went through files of clippings, heavy books, and maps in search of a single word. Not only were the texts barren of the term *war*, but as described in the anecdotal histories and more scholarly references to the area, Wellington was wholly benign. The weather was reasonable. Fish – perch, bass, and trout – ran plentiful. The land was too rocky for expansive farming, but it was rich enough to easily support the needs of a given family. Autumn brought abundant fowl and game, enough to last through the admittedly long, snowbound winter.

She closed the last of the books and rested her chin in her hand. Out the window she could see, just barely through the trees, Emma run to the lake, fill her plastic bucket, and then run back to dump its contents into the moat Molly was digging around the sand castle they'd built. Of course, by the time Emma returned with the next bucket the previous infusion of water had been sucked into the sand. Emma, with the perseverance common to all five-year-olds, kept at her task despite its impossibility.

Leslie looked back at the book, its time-darkened cover, and then at the shelves and file cabinets around her. Of course it's not here, she admonished herself. This is the family library, the moat around the Wellingtons' sand castle version of their town. Like Emma, the Wellingtons were making efforts to protect their story and this must have, at some point, proven useless.

Leslie shored up her patience until tomorrow's trip to the university library. She was close; she felt the nearness of connections. It was as if the slowly rotating facts in her head had realigned in polarity; they were pulling together now, as if by their own volition. She relished this sensation, the first quavers in the emergence of order. Leslie, her heart racing with anticipation, reshelved the books and went out to gather her daughters.

Wednesday night brought rain, just enough to slick the pavement and raise a thin steamy fog Thursday morning. Leslie said goodbye to Molly and Emma, who waved in a split moment of distraction from the program on the television screen. She fumbled with her car keys and notebook as she pulled the front door shut behind her. She was not looking when Mitch Ward came up beside her and touched her shoulder.

'Don't do that.' She threw him off. 'Please.'

'I'm sorry, Missus Stone. Truly. I needed to talk to you. Can we talk?'

'About what?'

He sneaked a glance over his shoulder. 'We need to go inside.'

'Mitch, I'm busy. I'm on my way to an appointment – '

'It's about Five Mile Hill, Missus Stone. What you were asking me about a couple days ago.'

'Can't we do that here?'

He shook his head. 'Wellington's like a big old family. We got rules. We don't talk about Uncle Pete's philandering at Sunday dinner when Aunt Bess is at the table.'

'Excuse me?'

'Inside. Let's go inside.' He extended his arm as though indicating she had no option.

Leslie let him in and led him back to the kitchen. He sat, backward, in one of the chairs. Leslie stood. 'Okay. Go.'

'Wellington's real touchy about certain things. You can't bring those subjects up in public without, well, without getting yourself labeled an outsider. We get quite a few outsiders around here. I would guess that's going to get worse with all the changes they got planned. Everybody comes asking about Five Mile House, which is understandable; it's their reasons for asking that concern us. I don't want you thinking we had a town meeting and came to a unified decision – this ain't no big conspiracy – but over the years, we just stopped talking about it. We just left the Historical Society to paint the pictures that brought money into town. Those of us who do know have no choice about knowing, and those of you who don't have no need to.'

'Then why are you here, Mitch?'

'Because I can't help sensing that you, Missus Stone, are kinda like the fox kit the wolves leave in the coop for the farmer to find. What took place here has nothing to do with you, but you are involved all the same. You need to know, so I decided I'd set about telling you.'

Leslie shifted on her hip, impatient. 'So?'

'I can only give you a little bit of it.'

'I'm listening.'

'Remember how I said Five Mile Hill came by its name?'

'Yeah. If you light a fire on top of the hill – '

'That's right, but of all the fires been lit on that hill, it's the last one we have a problem with. I'm referring to a particular fire on a particular night. The question you should be asking is as much about what was burning as why it was being burned. I should say who was burning.'

Leslie leaned against the counter. 'You're kidding.'

'It wasn't some church folk running round on some crazed witch hunt. It was the other ones.'

'The other ones?'

'That's all I feel right in telling you myself, but there's someone who can help you, if you decide you want to pursue it. She's what you might call another kinda historian. Her name is Delores Jacobi.'

'Wait a minute. Gwen mentioned her.'

'I'm sure Gwen Garrett did. I'm not promising anything. Delores has to take a liking to you. Hell, she may decide not to talk to you at all.' Mitch reached in his shirt pocket and handed Leslie a business card with a number written in red ink. 'If there's a purpose to your knowing more, she'll see that purpose and tell you whatever she thinks is necessary. Go talk to Delores, Missus Stone. I didn't inform her that I was planning on having this little conversation with you, but that doesn't mean she ain't expecting your call, if you catch my drift.' He stood. 'I won't be keeping you any longer.'

'Thank you.' Leslie considered the seven digits on the card. 'I think.'

'If you need to know, Delores will tell you. If she tells you nothing, then walk away. Make yourself a good life here, but ask no more questions.' He ducked his head in a curt farewell and saw himself out the front door.

Leslie picked up the telephone receiver. She heard the dial tone and hung it up. She picked up again. 'What are you afraid of?' As if to answer her own question, she punched in the numbers Mitch had given her.

The other end rang two, three, four times and then a young female voice came on the line: 'Hello, Wellington Concrete Recycling Center. How may I direct your call?'

Twenty

L ESLIE WHEELED HER VAN through the chain-link gate at the Wellington Concrete Recycling plant and parked beside a heap of bent, rusted reinforcement rods. Even before she opened the van door she could hear the sharp grate and growl of the grinding machinery at work. There were other vehicles in the lot, each layered with a fine gray dust, which, as she stepped out onto the pavement, Leslie saw was already applying itself, in drift and settle, to the dark chassis of her van.

The WCR offices were in a low, flat-roofed building on the other side of the yard. The plant itself was at the far end of the property. White silo-like structures towered over the rolling dunes of crushed asphalt and concrete. Leslie paused to allow a pair of dump trucks to pass and then made her way across the hot, rock-strewn yard.

On the window of the office door hung a sign: WELCOME TO WELLINGTON CONCRETE RECYCLING, INC. HOME OF THE RUBBLE WITCHES. Leslie frowned as she went inside. A pert and solicitous young woman rose from behind the receptionist's desk. Leslie stated her business, declining, in the process, offers of refreshment, tours, brochures. The receptionist poked her long, red-nailed fingers over the telephone keypad. She grinned at Leslie, then turned her back as she spoke, a hushed voice, into the receiver. After a few moments, and a slight giggle, she hung up the telephone. 'Delores will see you now.'

The young woman ushered Leslie into an office at the rear of the building. She announced Leslie with a dinner-is-served formality and then swished out the door.

Delores Jacobi was at her desk and coughing, mighty, racking coughs that began deep within the massive rounds of her body.

She raised a fat, ring-spangled finger, a gesture pleading – or ordering – pause. With the other hand she adjusted the knob on the oxygen canister next to her chair. A slender green tube ran from the canister to a device fitted into her nostrils. Whatever she had done to the canister seemed to bring her relief, and the coughing quieted. She smoothed her red, poodle-tight curls and tugged at the shoulders of the floral dress that barely contained what Leslie guessed to be over 400 pounds of flesh. Delores motioned to a chair, and Leslie sat as the woman she had come to see swiveled her head, camera-like, to focus around the cataract hazing her left eye.

Leslie glanced down at the name plate: DELORES JACOBI, PRESIDENT, WELLINGTON CONCRETE RECYCLING. There was a veil of dust over it, as there was over everything in the small, oak-paneled office. The air was refrigerator cold. Leslie could see the steamy trails of her own breath.

'Well, sister?' Delores's soft, rasping voice pulled Leslie's attention upward. 'You wanted to see me?'

'Yes.' This was not a woman who would indulge roundabouts or prologues. 'I want to know about the *Analecta Seriatus*,' she said.

Delores's head dropped sideways as though Leslie's words had physical sensation. 'And I want to know' – she placed her hands on her desk, heaved her mountainous self upward, and, panting voraciously from this effort, leaned hard toward Leslie – 'about Big Foot.' She fell back in her chair and brayed with laughter until the laughter set off another coughing jag. She gagged and retched until slowly she calmed herself enough to say, 'Apologies, sister, but you just looked so fucking serious.' She calibrated the dials on her oxygen tank again. 'I dare say Mitchell Ward knows better than to send just another tourist out here to try my good nature. So, I'm assuming you have more on your mind than the friggin' *Analecta*, sister.'

Leslie nodded. 'Mitch said you would tell me what happened on Five Mile Hill.'

'I might.' Delores rearranged her bulk. 'You are aware already that we in this valley have a relationship with practices often called witchcraft?'

'I'm starting to think I'm the only woman in town who isn't practicing.'

Delores pursed her lips. 'Don't be so certain, sister. Are you familiar with a work called *Macbeth* – of course you, an educated sister such as yourself, would be. Recall the witches good brother William invented; "Bubble, bubble, toil and trouble." He understood, good William did. Recall their magic? Quite right, there is none. Save for a questionable soup they make no magic; they only plant a seed in Macbeth's cerebellum. They give him an "if." His extant ambitions are fertile ground enough for tragedy's rooting.'

'Yeah, but it's his wife that sets everything in motion,' said Leslie, thinking of Diana.

'Wasn't good William insinuating that destiny is the faith of cowards?'

'Or maybe he was saying there are two kinds of witches.'

Delores raised an overplucked eyebrow. 'I wasn't paying attention when you came in, child. Are you wearing ruby slippers?'

'I do feel like I'm on a yellow brick road to nowhere. Can we get back to Five Mile Hill?'

'We never leave Five Mile Hill,' Delores said, and then grew silent as she leaned back in the chair, twiddling her thick thumbs, thoughtful. 'There are always two kinds of witches. We are one kind. We have yet to determine if you, sister, are friend or enemy.'

'Enemies? There was a war?'

'There is always and only one war, sister. What do you know of concrete?'

'Concrete?' Leslie dug her nails into her palms to control the frustration in her voice. 'I don't know. In a fair fight, it always wins?'

This response seemed to delight Delores. She applauded loudly and laughed, coughed, laughed. She opened a desk drawer and pulled out a tarnished silver flask along with two glasses. She poured into each a generous amount of a cloudy amber liquid. Delores pushed a glass in Leslie's direction. Leslie lifted the tumbler and sniffed the viscous brown liquid. It smelled like an old lunch box.

'I make it myself,' said Delores. 'The French call it calvados, but that's just a highfalutin way of saying applejack. I use it to toast meaningful events.' She lifted her glass in Leslie's direction. 'Don't sip.' She downed it in a single swallow.

Following the example, Leslie swallowed hers, closing her eyes against the flaming spear coursing down her gullet. 'Does this mean I'm a friend?' Her words sputtered and her voice, to her own ears, sounded stripped of pretense.

Delores moved her head side to side and her jowls wagged. 'Hardly. But you are entertaining, sister. While you are recovering from our little libation, I'll entertain you with a useful primer on what it is we do here at Wellington Concrete.'

Delores placed on her desk a rectangular wooden box with a glass panel in front. The box was divided into five sections, and each section held a different colored powder. Starting from Leslie's left, Delores tapped the lid over each section. 'Hydraulic lime. Silica. Alumina. Iron oxide. Gypsum. The first four are heated and then crushed – that's when the gypsum goes in. Add the right amount of water, a process called hydration, and a chemical reaction occurs that causes the compound to harden. That's cement, the modern portland version. Mix this with an aggregate, anything from plastic pellets to gravel to steel balls, depending on the strength you need, and you have concrete. Technological rock. It actually gets harder over time. Thousands of years and look at what's still left of Rome. The whole of humanity's time and impact on this planet can be mapped in the history of concrete.'

The applejack was worming its way to Leslie's head, where it whorled about, making concentration difficult. 'What about Five Mile?'

Delores ignored the interruption. 'But there are times when the coliseum or the cathedral just has to come down. What to do with all that unwanted rubble? It's damn folly to throw it away; you only end up wasting space in a landfill. That's where we come in. We grind it up and recycle it for use as an aggregate or as road bed, whatever.' Delores sat back and fixed Leslie with an expression of expectation.

Leslie knotted her brow and tried to look enlightened. 'Oh.'

'Oh? That's the best you can do, Stone? Oh?'

'Golly, gosh, swell. Is that better?'

Delores clicked her tongue. 'You were here to ask questions. Am I incorrect?'

'All right. Who buys your recycled rock?'

'Wrong question.'

'Where do you get the concrete you recycle?'

'Wrong question. You haven't been listening.'

Leslie exhaled hard; Delores was right. She was reaching the extremity of her limits to manage, with any sort of compassion or grace, all the hocus-pocus and fal-de-ral of witches and their covens. 'You're a witch.'

'I think we've covered that.'

'This facility is owned by the Wellington coven?'

'Owned and operated. Still, however, not the correct question.'

'What the fuck are a bunch of witches doing in the concrete biz?'

'There you go. What indeed, sister? What indeed?'

Leslie glanced at her watch. It was almost half past two. She had no way to contact Phillip to tell him she would be late. 'Look, I came here to learn what happened on Five Mile Hill.' She stood up. 'I'm not interested in the business ventures of your ladies' club.'

Delores grinned. 'Were you aware, sister, that according to those who believe in its existence, the first entry in the *Analecta Seriatus* is a recipe for cement?'

Leslie sat down again.

'A specific cement, one created to last the ages. It was supposedly meant to be used as the foundation material for a temple that would house the reunited *Analecta*.'

'And you witch people are doing your damnedest to grind all that foundation material back to dust.'

'Heard tell you were quick. The *Analecta* cement is one specific to Roman construction from, say, three hundred years before the birth of the rabbi Jesus to about five hundred years after. One of the ingredients was ash from dear old Mount Vesuvius. It's known as Pozzuoli ash. The volcanic ash was mixed with lime and sand. To strengthen the final product, the Romans, as we do today, relied on admixtures. Whereas now we use things like plastic fiber, the ancients had only organic materials to work with.'

'What did they use?'

'Fat and milk. Blood. Mostly that of goats and horses, animals that had worn out their other uses or newborns too frail to survive.'

'Oh no.' Leslie closed her eyes.

'But that was for the everyday sort of constructions; sacred construction necessitated sacred ingredients. As you may be aware, materials are made sacred through the sacrifice required to obtain them.'

'I can see where this is going. You don't really think – '

'And when the construction is meant to be the earthly home of a text said to generate gods, the sacrifice must be spectacular, wouldn't you say? The *Analecta* instructs that it must be mother and child, and the child young enough to be nursing. Nevertheless, in these modern times, one's civilized options are limited. Who better than one who's already been banished?'

'I don't believe this.'

'In the dead of January 1889, the coven took in a Rutherford girl after she was exiled from her father's home for making quite disturbing statements as to the source of the seed growing in her belly. The coven cared for her, midwifed the birth, a son. Several weeks after the birth, Isabel Wellington offered our charge a position in her household as a servant. The girl and her child moved, with our approval, into that lake house. They lived less than a month.'

Leslie opened her eyes. 'You've got to be kidding.'

'Oh, sister, if only I were. On top of that hill on the night of the autumnal equinox in 1889, while Della Rosa Benevista and her minions self-destructed in celebration, Isabel Bly Wellington and her brother Joshua slaughtered that girl and her infant boy. They burned the bodies, and as the bodies flamed, Isabel and Joshua mixed Pozzuoli ash, lime, blood, milk, and fat in sufficient quantities to fashion the cornerstone of that house. And we have been at war with the Wellingtons ever since.'

Twenty-one

I SABEL WAS OLDER THAN I, but only by a few months, and
when we first met I confess I found her energy and intellect
invigorating. Never had I encountered another woman who seemed
so interested in my very ordinary life. Isabel asked so many
questions of me. Who would not be flattered?

In the early days of my marriage to Joshua, Isabel would take
the train up from Wellington several times each week. We would
sit for hours over tea, and she would interrogate me. She insisted
on knowing every bit of my family's history. How did the James
Bitterfords end up on American shores. How did my father earn
his living? And his father before him? What did such work entail?
What sort of people engaged such services? I could not tire her.
Each new bit of trivia fanned the glow of fascination in her eyes,
so dark, so like Joshua's, like charred embers. Her gaze radiated
heat. Vanity obstructed my better sense, my childhood lessons
concerning fire. It was far too late when at last I realized that
for all the information Isabel had rendered from me, she had not
offered the most general of facts about herself, her brother, their
family.

She possessed other qualities that, in the unforgiving illumina-
tion of hindsight, I should have read with greater seriousness.
Isabel's attention to me was single-minded to an extreme. If
she discovered Joshua and I seated together, she would wedge
herself between us, flouncing her skirts and fussing until Joshua
moved to make room. On days when my duties prevented idle
indulgences, Isabel followed me about the house, in and out of
any room, questioning both my work and my state of mind. Was
I not bored? Was I not tired? She did not, to my knowledge, rest

during the daylight hours, and I am confident in assuming she slept little at night. When she was not asking her litany of questions, she was reading. She paced the halls, her neck bent so far over her book that once I teased that she surely must have another set of eyes atop her head. Isabel did not laugh at my jest. Never once did I hear Isabel laugh. Oh, she smiled. In fact, she was almost always smiling in that private fashion, as when one catches children in deep imaginative play. Isabel smiled at meals, at Sunday services, at me. Even then it unnerved me, but I held it as another mark of her girlish vitality.

I wanted not to doubt Isabel. Instead, I doubted myself. I, who had lost my only sibling in such a lengthy, agonizing attrition, was quite reveling in the sisterly affection that appeared to be growing between us. I wanted not to surrender it to the subtle warning twinges inching along my spine. Besides, as I would argue with that cautionary impulse, no matter what her mildly disturbing behavior, she was obviously devoted to me. Perhaps it was her maternal desires, long stifled by her inability to bear a child. Whatever its source, I held to that devotion, suckled at it like an opium pipe, until the cautions ceased altogether and cell by cell Isabel took over my being.

By such time, Joshua, except to give form to his dynastic ambitions, had removed himself from my bed and set up accounts with the house of Della Rosa Benevista. When I informed him of our first expectancy, he kissed me eagerly and then left for Della Rosa's. The next day, after the onslaught of my complaints, he suggested that we send for Isabel to live with us as a companion to me. Thus, much to her own husband's objections, barren Isabel moved to the city. She tended to me better than any nurse. It was Isabel who held my hand during all those harrowing months when I was sick and sleepless and weeping for my husband. Joshua would be at Della Rosa's nightly, coming home only in the darkest hour of early morning.

I was always waiting for him. I huddled, on my heels, at the door of my chambers and listened to Joshua coming in. Isabel met him; they would argue, their voices soft flares of anger. Occasionally, Joshua would bring a guest, and the visitor did more to intensify the arguments than dilute them. Each night, every night, voices simmered in my ear, but never clearly enough for me to discern their words. I was certain that Isabel in her earnest worry for my well-being was informing Joshua of the hurtful, hateful course of his abandonment. I envied her directness, her steady sense of purpose in what I imagined was Joshua's responding parries of sarcasm and self-righteousness. I had not one fraction of Isabel's will. Had I, at that time, the strength of heart to creep down the stairs, to listen more closely, I might have spared so many so much. But I was afraid of being found eavesdropping. I was afraid of losing the good opinion of the two persons I loved most in the world.

This is how I was to spend the next twelve years, huddled by my bedroom door, listening in the dark for some intelligible meaning in the sounds that spiraled upward and into one another: Joshua arguing with Isabel, his coming up the stair for me, coming for my body, for my emptied womb to fill it once more; the sound of my own labor-borne cries giving way to the cries of newborn infants; the sound of children running through the hall, demanding me, hushed by Isabel; the sound of night when the house was still and sleeping; the sounds of doors downstairs and sharp voices. I listened so intently. I heard it all. I understood nothing.

I remember my life in the city as one long night of listening, wrapped up tight in my quilt, squatting hard by the hinges, the band of light at the bottom of the door, how cool and smooth the wood felt against my ear. It is so odd, this thing called remembering. Some memories like those of the quilt, the light, the wood, solidify in an instant, a drop of molten glass hitting ice. Other memories are accumulated through simple repetition of the unexceptional, as in the endless routines of maternal duty. I remember my children's infancy not through separate incidents but as an inseparable whole. I cannot, for all my trying, remember putting any one of them to breast any one single time, but I remember absolutely the warm, sweet scent of their baby skin, the tickle of their cold fingers on my ribs, the pull of their suck as the milk began to flow.

There is another sort of remembering that might more accurately be termed the will to forget. These are the memories we refuse. These are the memories which, like hungry orphans, become devious and self-serving, vengeful, and determined. By trick or by bribe or by force, they eventually get through our barriers against them. Once in the waking mind, they demand acknowledgment, leaving us no recourse but claim them – to our shame and their rage – products of our careless living.

It was this third sort of memory that lay siege to my resistance when news of what had taken place at Della Rosa's reached my doorstep. Cook brought in the first edition papers after breakfast, and I had taken the front pages to the garden, where the children were already at play, trying to raise a kite on the accelerating breeze. The newspaper whiplashed in my hands as I read and reread the opening article: HORRORS AT NOTORIOUS BORDELLO. A large picture of Della Rosa Benevista, in full flamenco costume, appeared beneath the banner. I read the story a third time and a fourth, each time trying to balance the salacious information against what I held as the greatest dread of my heart. Joshua had been there, was supposed to have been there. Where else would he have gone? He must surely then be among the dead.

I dropped the paper. It scattered about the garden like so many failed kites. I ran into the house, calling for Isabel. She was nowhere to be found. She must, I thought, have heard what transpired and rushed off to discover her brother's fate. I sent one of the children's nurses and the cook to find her, to assist her by whatever means they could.

They returned many hours later, near nightfall, having been unable to locate Isabel. The cook did relay rumors of a single survivor at Della Rosa's, but as to his or her identity, there was no word. Isabel did not return that evening or night. The next morning I ran out to the curb and grabbed a paper from the boy's hands. I stood there in the cold, the soot of the coal fires falling on the paper as I read it. The city coroner had proclaimed the murders an incident of mass poisoning beyond the likes of anything he had encountered. Listed were the toxins he had so far been able to identify in the supper served that weekend. Again there was a portrait of Della Rosa in dance costume, a different one in which she was not alone. In the same photo, his arm about her waist, was my Joshua. The caption read LONE SURVIVOR HELD ON SUSPICION. Della Rosa had her arm lifted, poised like that of a matador preparing the final strike.

I was struck. As irrevocable as a brand on my flesh, I remembered Joshua and Isabel's nightly arguments and that sometimes third voice. It had been a woman's voice, a voice that leaped between imperfect English and an imperious foreign tongue. Della Rosa had been in my home.

Now Della Rosa was dead. My husband was being held on the most awful of speculations. Isabel had fairly disappeared. And still, I did not doubt.

'Where have you been?' Phillip pulls his mouth off Leslie's long enough to ask the question, but does not wait for the answer. He holds her against the hotel room door, tugging her shirt free from the waist band of her skirt and sliding his hands up to her breasts all in one motion.

It is Leslie's turn to pull her mouth away. 'I'm sorry. I got waylaid.'

He has buried his mouth in the sloping intersection of her shoulder and neck. He lifts his head and, staring hard into her eyes, drags his fingers, hard, through her hair. 'Waylaid. Now there's a term you don't hear much anymore.' He slides his hands down to her shoulders, easing them under the fabric of her shirt collar and with the most gentle insisting pressure, compels Leslie downward. She doesn't resist.

Afterward, they lay in the entry to the room, Phillip propped against the door, Leslie with her head in his lap. 'I should make you worry more often,' she says with a laugh.

'I do worry about you, Leslie.'

'There's a club for that, you know.'

'What do you tell Greg?'

'About what?'

Phillip sighs. 'You know what. How do you explain this Thursday thing?'

'Hmmm.' Leslie has worried about this moment more than she worried about Greg's questioning her activities. She has yet to confide in her lover any but the most rudimentary aspects of her interest in the Wellington family he represents.

'Has he even asked?'

'What if I said I preferred not to discuss Greg with you? I certainly don't discuss you with Greg.'

Phillip counters. 'What if he did ask?'

'I'd lie.'

'Would you lie to me?'

'If I felt it necessary, sure.'

'What makes lying necessary?'

'I don't know. Protecting myself. Protecting the ones I love.'

He laughs. 'She loves me.'

Leslie sits up. 'She loves you not. She loves no one.'

'She does lie.' He tries to pull her back to him, but this she resists.

'I should be going.'

'You just got here. You never leave first.'

'All the same . . .' Leslie begins to button her blouse.

'You still haven't told me how you came to be – what was your term? – waylaid.'

'It was nothing. I got caught up back in Wellington. You know, one of those appointments that you just can't walk out on.'

'So what time did you leave Wellington?'

'Why the interrogation, Mr Hogarth?'

'Somebody is in a bad mood.' He works his way to standing. 'Tell you what. I'll leave the beer and the food and you alone in the room. Maybe next week, my Leslie will come back.'

'Why is what I did today so important to you?'

'Because you're important to me.'

'But not important enough to do a simple favor.'

'You're holding me responsible for Joe Garrett's decision to include Gwen's note in the cremation?'

'I'm holding you responsible for not telling me the truth about that house.'

'Now I'm lying?'

She unknots the laces of her shoe. 'What is it about this town? Two women, a hundred years apart, go to all the trouble to lay out on paper the sad reasons for their self-termination, and before those of us who want to understand get a chance to see those reasons, some helpful family member tosses their efforts in an incinerator.'

Phillip covers his eyes in comprehension. 'You think there's some connection between Gwen Garrett and Eleanor Bly? Are you investigating this?'

Leslie didn't answer.

'Then it's a damn good thing I didn't get a copy of that letter. The last thing you need – '

'Do not protect me.'

'Protect you? Leslie, I have no idea who you are. I know every inch of your body; I know almost nothing about you, about Leslie, the person who lives in that body. What little I do know frightens me – let me finish, damn it. I am frightened for you. But ask you one simple question, damn it, and suddenly I'm standing alone holding my severed balls. Each and every Thursday afternoon you make a point of telling me, one way or another, that all I'm worthy of is your cunt.'

'Well, you probably aren't going to get any more than this cunt. If it isn't enough, you know the way out.'

'Fine,' he says, tucking his shirt tail into his trousers. 'I guess we're pretty clear then.' He turns and strides out of the room, slamming the door behind him.

She waits, watching the door. A minute passes. Then another. A small smile creeps across her face at the sound of the key turning in the lock. He is letting me win this one, thinks Leslie. They always let you win the first couple of rounds. They want you to trust them.

'Is he here?' Amy's voice is insistent, frightened. It seems to resonate from behind the mirror.

'Yeah,' Leslie whispers as the door slowly opens. 'But this time, I'm here too.'

Leslie sped home, accelerator jammed to the floor, windows open, the wind ripping through her hair. The last light of day lay limp and pale on the horizon; the clouds above blocking whatever moon, stars, or sun might still be about. The occasional light of oncoming headlights flashed in passing, catching the gold of her wedding ring as her hands worked the steering wheel.

Greg had not asked, nor would he. That didn't mean he had not already guessed. Such were the politics of long-term marriage, what Leslie knew of marriage, her own, those of her friends and her parents. There were public fronts and private realities, and sometimes real commitment meant an unquestioning respect of the line between the two. If Greg were to ask or she were to tell, then they might have to admit to larger truths that could not be managed: that they missed their old selves horribly, that they didn't know how to fix things, that they felt obligated to each other in ways that made words like *love* sound laughable. What they had been was gone. What they'd become was impossible but had to be maintained all the same. If they started to tell, sooner or later, one of them would ask why. Why are we doing this to ourselves, to each other? Leslie was certain what terrified him, her, both of them most was having to admit to having no answer.

By the time she arrived in Wellington, full night had fallen. The last few miles to her home were down residential streets lined by mostly abandoned houses, although here and there windows glowed dim or bright. Leslie felt an old loneliness sink into her; she wanted nothing more than solitude and sleep. On pulling into her driveway, she saw that too would be impossible.

Diana's BMW was slanted across the drive, as though she'd slammed on her brakes, as though she had been in a great hurry to get to the Stones' house. The implications registered immediately. The children. Leslie parked on the street and ran to the door. Before she was even inside, she was calling, 'What's wrong? Is everything okay?'

She opened the door, to find Jack Wellington, wide-eyed and frozen in surprise, coming down the stairs. He was bundled up in footed pajamas, far too warm for the time of year. His yellow hair stuck in places to the perspiration running down his thin little face. Recovering himself, he raised a finger to his lips. 'We're playing hide-and-go-seek. I'm It.'

'Oh,' Leslie mouthed, and she tiptoed, relieved, into the front room, where Diana, voice low, hands gesturing fiercely, was explaining something to Greg. Greg lifted his eyes and, seeing Leslie, made an expression of supplication for release.

'Hey, Diana,' Leslie said. 'What's up?'

'Oh my God, Leslie. Oh my God. You have to come with me. You have to see this.'

'See what?'

'Gwen. Gwen's automatic writing. I mean, I talked to Gwen with the thing, or she talked to me. No, that's how it started, I mean. Leslie, you have to come see this.'

'Yes, Leslie,' Greg said. 'Please go see it.'

Leslie sat on the couch. 'Diana, calm down. What do you want me to see?'

'Gwen had a message for you.'

'For me? Why didn't you just bring the sheet of paper?'

'I couldn't. I mean, it's not on paper.' Diana dropped to her knees and laced her fingers as though in prayer. 'Please.'

'Have you been drinking?'

'Just some wine, and you know.' She mimed inhaling.

'I'll come over for a few minutes and I'm driving. Jack can spend the night here.'

'No. Jack stays with me at night. Jack always stays with me.'

'All right. We'll pick up your things and you both can spend the night here.'

Diana was already halfway out the door. Leslie turned and waved to Greg. 'We won't be long, and get Jack out of that damn polar bear suit before the poor kid suffocates.'

Twenty-two

'SLOW DOWN, DIANA. TELL me again.' Leslie was sitting on the floor of Gwen's study and looking at the writing on the ceiling. 'Everything you remember. From the beginning.'

Diana paced, hugging herself. 'Okay. I'd just put a video on the TV for Jack, and I came in here to try the planchette thing. I sat there, close to where you are now, and I held my hand on it, just like Gwen did. I waited a long time. Nothing happened. Not even a scribble. I smoked a joint. Thought it might help if I loosened up a bit. But nothing. I got bored, and maybe, well, the thing is I got kind of silly. I started talking to Gwen or more sort of just calling to her like "Gwennie? Oh, Gwennie," you know, real creepy like "Speak to me, Gwennie," that sort of thing.'

'And nothing showed up on the pad.'

'Zilch. By then it was time to give Jack a bath and get him ready for bed. I turned out the light.'

'How long were you out of the room?'

'No more than an hour. And I probably wouldn't have come back in tonight except I remembered I'd left my wineglass in here.'

'Hmmm,' said Leslie as she ran her hands over the carpet.

'What are you looking for?'

'Signs of a ladder.'

Diana pouted. 'You think somebody came in here and did this?'

'Come on, Diana. How else would that have gotten up there?'

'Gwen, of course.'

'Gwen Garrett came back from the dead to write "Tell Leslie to watch the children" on the ceiling?'

154

'She didn't come *back* from the dead. She never left here, remember? And that is Gwen's handwriting.'

'That looks like Gwen's handwriting, but it wasn't written by Gwen.'

'How can you be so sure?'

They went on like this until Leslie, if only to end the debate, relented on the possibility the message may have come through Diana's attempt to contact Gwen. Thus satisfied, Diana went upstairs to pack an overnight bag for Jack and herself. In Diana's absence, Leslie moved about the room reading the words from different angles. She was certain Diana had done it as part of some bizarre attempt to reinforce her own beliefs by winning over those of others. Leslie removed the pad from the coffee table and then took off her shoes. She stood on the table, and now closer, could see that the strokes were not made in pencil as she had assumed, but in something soft that flaked away at her touch. She put a fingertip of the substance to her tongue.

Diana returned with an unnecessarily large suitcase in her hand. 'What is it?'

'Ash of some sort, I think.'

'Gwen was cremated.'

'Enough, Diana. I've had enough.'

'Admit it. You don't know, do you, Leslie? Not about the spirit thing, not for certain.'

Leslie put her hands on her hips. 'If I'm admitting stuff, Mrs Wellington, I have to admit I'm not certain your relationship with your son is very healthy. I have to admit I'm not certain about the idea of your moving him into Five Mile. And as for Gwen, I have to admit that the only way I can accept that she wrote those words is if she is not really dead.' Standing close to the ceiling as she was, Leslie's words were amplified. She heard herself, heard the question she hadn't asked. She jumped down from the table. 'After all, I never saw the body.'

Diana narrowed her eyes. 'I think you are very upset by what's happened here, and that's why I'm going to ignore everything you just said.' She turned off the light. 'Grab that for me.' She pointed to the suitcase, either assuming or reminding Leslie of her station, and then she left. But Leslie didn't follow. She stood in the darkened room, considering the words she could no longer see and realizing,

155

once more, that just because a thing could not be seen did not mean it was gone.

Diana quickly recovered her conspiratorial glee, and throughout the ride back to Leslie's she compounded one theory upon another: it was Gwen; it wasn't Gwen; it was Eleanor; it wasn't Eleanor; it was Gwen and Eleanor working in tandem; it was . . . Leslie eventually set her mind to register Diana's voice with the same significance she allowed to toddler talk and drunken prattle. She simply nodded and agreed at regular intervals, hoping the source would soon exhaust itself and fall asleep.

Diana was still theorizing when Greg, a set of bed linens in his hand, met them at the door. Jack was awaiting his mother's good-nights in the girls' room where all three of them – and the dog – were camping out on the floor.

'I really don't like the idea of Jack being on the floor,' Diana said to no one in particular on her way up the stairs.

Greg and Leslie watched her disappear.

'Criminy,' Leslie said, as she took Diana's suitcase into the front room.

Greg followed. 'How long does she think she's staying?' he asked in a whisper.

'Diana thinks?' Leslie made no attempt to soften her tone. 'Thank God. At least the world has a bitch more twisted than me.'

'You are not twisted.'

Leslie unfolded the mattress from the base of the sleeper sofa. 'What am I then?'

'If you're any thing like me, you're tired, Les.' He shook out the linens, letting them billow and fall over the bed. 'Just plain old fucking tired.'

'Yeah.' Leslie smoothed the sheets and tucked in the corners. She sat on the edge of the mattress. 'Can I ask you something? About Five Mile House, the work you're doing?'

Greg sat down next to her. 'What do you want to know?'

'I heard a rather juicy little tale about Isabel and Joshua Bly, about the cornerstone and ritual sacrifice.'

'I wondered how long it would take you to get around to the Witch War stories.'

'You could have told me up front.'

'What? Deny you the fun of digging it up and then being pissed at me for not passing along another happy little rumor of ritual murder? I figured you'd hear about it eventually.'

'How much of it's true?'

Greg laughed. 'How much of anything is true? It's a good story, and it explains how Five Mile got its name. I'm willing to bet that what really happened is that a hunter killed a deer or a boar up there, built a fire, and cooked his kill. There's your blood and fire, add to that the sudden local appearance of authentic murder suspect Joshua Bly, and you've got plenty of grist for your story-making mill.'

'So then what's behind this supposed war between the witches and the Wellingtons? And if it's not true, why aren't the Rubble Witches permitted to take anything off the hill?'

'Would you want to do business with someone who was telling those sort of stories about you? I almost got my ass canned for purchasing gravel bedding from them before I knew the rules. It's just traditional ill will between the rich and those they step on. The Wellingtons moved in here, bought up all the land, and displaced the locals from homes that were generations old – what?'

'Has Harry or Diana or anybody up there mentioned something called the *Analecta Seriatus*?'

'Damn, you have been at the library, haven't you? They're looking for it, yeah. I'll save you the trouble of asking: yes, that's why Mansfield Custom is up there, why every wall has to be unmade and then remade, every floorboard lifted, every fucking mortar joint chiseled out so that every fucking stone can be looked under. There's no way we'll get it done by October, no matter how loud Harry Wellington yells.'

'But finishing the house isn't what he wants, Greg. He wants to find the *Analecta*. That's why he wants to renovate the other houses. Nothing's turned up at Five Mile, and he's sure it's here somewhere in town.'

'And if he doesn't find it in Wellington?'

'Then tomorrow the world.'

'Just what I need, another fucking nutcase.' Greg looked at her and then buried his face in his hands. 'I'm sorry, Les.'

157

'There's no apology like a knee-jerk apology.' Leslie stood. 'I'd better go see what's keeping Diana.'

Leslie went upstairs to Molly and Emma's room. It was difficult to walk for all the pillows, blankets, sleeping bags, and sleeping bodies. Diana had moved Jack to Emma's bed, where she slept with him, her child pressed like armor to her chest. Jack's mouth was softly dropped, his fist held a fraction of an inch from his lips the way children who were thumb suckers sleep after they've been weaned from their habit. Diana and her son breathed in syncopation as though one exhaled so the other might draw his or her next breath.

He was protecting her as much as she was protecting him, thought Leslie. Diana knew the stories: what had happened to Eleanor and Eleanor's children. Reality, for Diana, was moot because being a member of the Wellington family put her in the center of the story. Diana had no choice but to believe, and as Gwen had said, it's the believing that matters. Still, as Leslie stood there watching them sleep, she had to wonder if Diana's beliefs were not stitched together from a fabric more substantial than the ephemeral veil of the family ghost stories.

Twenty-three

WELLINGTON'S CITY BUSINESS WAS conducted in a set of small offices on the second floor of the post office. Leslie rang the chrome service bell on the tall, laminated counter that divided public space from city space. 'With you in a sec,' called a female voice from behind a bulwark of file cabinets.

Leslie could hear the raucous laughter coming from Yancy Galleghar's office; Wellington's local government was in session. There hadn't been much in town on which to apply what administrative ambition Yancy possessed, and his office had been little more than the daily forum for minds like his own. With Wellington now on the brink of economic reinvention, that daily forum had taken a turn toward serious considerations of individual positioning for the greatest possible gain. When it came to the nitty-gritty of city business, unless town clerk Betty Myers did it, it did not get done.

'No hurry, Betty,' Leslie said. A burst of hilarity rang from the backroom. The fragrance of cinnamon rolls and coffee floated about in the lazy circulation of an overhead fan. A small clock radio on Betty's desk was tuned to a country music station, and sweet fiddle sounds waltzed about the room. Next to the radio was a coffee mug on which there was a stylized graphic of a woman with rock grinders for teeth, and the words RUBBLE WITCH were printed beneath it. Another one, thought Leslie.

'Too damn hot in here,' said Betty as she dumped an armload of files on the counter. 'I don't know why it always has to be so damn hot. How are you, hon'?'

Betty Myers called everyone 'hon.' She was a plump woman in her midfifties who moved through life like the whirl-a-gig ride at a county fair; she was everywhere, doing everything at once. Betty wore polyester suits in pastel colors, nylon stockings, and running shoes. Leslie had never once seen the woman in any other costume. Around her neck, on three separate cords, she wore a pair of reading glasses, a pen, and a set of keys.

'All righty!' Betty folded her hands on the counter. 'What may the fair township of Wellington do for you today, Leslie Stone?'

'I was hoping I might talk to Yancy for a few minutes.'

Betty leaned over the counter and said, 'That's a rotten thing to do to a perfectly good morning. Are you sure there isn't something I can do, hon'?'

'It's kind of a cop thing.'

'You looking for a job, hon'?'

'You got it, Betty. I'm here to audition for Yancy Galleghar's all-girl-cop revue.' She made a little curtsy.

'Hon', you're a hoot. Wait here. Let me see if old Great and Powerful is taking visitors.' Betty went down the hall, tapped on the door, and let herself in. The voices quieted and then erupted again in laughter. Leslie could hear Betty scolding them. The door opened and out came Betty with Yancy in tow.

'He's all yours, hon'.'

Yancy leaned against the wall, making it clear Leslie was going to have to go to him.

'Morning, Yancy.' She extended her hand expecting him to return the gesture. Instead he threw his hands in the air and bellowed.

'Don't shoot!' From behind the door came suppressed snickers.

Leslie withdrew her hand and clenched her fingers into a fist. She swallowed. 'Been waiting a long time for that one?'

'Just a joke, Leslie. Just a joke. What's a little joke between a couple retired cops – oh, but that's right, you didn't exactly retire, did you?'

'No.'

'What can I do for you, killer?'

'This was a mistake.' She turned to go, and then turned back. 'Look, I'm not certain what you do around here, but you sure as hell must have been shit awful on the job.'

'Now you wait one second, young lady. I was a damn fine officer.'

She had him. 'As damn fine as your piss stupid jokes? And speaking of piss stupid, I was out at the Garrett place less than twenty-four hours after Gwen died. There was no sign of any crime scene investigation. Not one freaking inch of yellow tape. Nothing. Who you hiring for police work around here? Your relatives?'

'It was a fucking suicide.'

'How do you know that?'

'Because of the note.'

'The note? The note? How hard is it to fake a suicide note?'

Yancy blinked his watery blue eyes fast and stammered. 'Well, who would have wanted Gwen Garrett dead? Why?'

'Hmmm. Suspect and motive.' She tapped her finger to her temple. 'That would be the point of an investigation now, wouldn't it?'

'It was suicide.'

'How can you be sure?'

Yancy threw open the door behind him. 'Hey, Mark, get out here.'

Mark Humphrey appeared in the door as though he had been yanked forward on a string. Short, densely freckled and gap-toothed, Mark was the cheery, hand-grabbing president of the Wellington Chamber of Commerce, the Wellington representative to the state tourist commission, Wellington's only mortician and, therefore, its local coroner.

'Hiya, Leslie.' He grabbed her hand.

'This isn't a fucking tea party, Mark. Leslie here thinks we botched the Garrett suicide.'

'I think *you* fucked up the investigation, Yancy. Just because something looks like a suicide doesn't mean it is.'

Mark's smile melted into an expression of sympathy both practiced and sincere. 'Leslie, sometimes when loved ones or friends take such drastic action it becomes difficult, if not impossible, to accept they were capable of such things. This was a suicide, Leslie. I did the initial postmortem.'

'Did anybody not involved with the Wellingtons see her?'

'What the hell is that supposed to mean?' Yancy crossed his arms and made himself taller.

Mark pursed his lips. 'It's a good question, Yance. Yeah, you're right, Leslie; I'm not a medical examiner. Because Gwen Garrett was an employee of Mansfield Custom, they insisted, for insurance reasons, that the county coroner do a formal PM – an autopsy. They arranged transportation of the body to Rutherford. From there, she went home with her husband. That's the last I heard.'

Leslie nodded. 'Was she cremated there in Rutherford?'

'No. Joe wanted to take the body back to her family. Let them say goodbye.'

Yancy said, 'See. Suicide.'

'That doesn't mean it wasn't handled sloppily. Thanks, Mark. You're right, it's hard to lose a friend.'

Yancy relaxed his stance. 'Now, Leslie. I believe you wanted to talk to me about something.'

'Yancy,' said Leslie, 'I've had about all the talking to you I can stomach for one day.' She strode down the hall, silently giving thanks that someone outside of Wellington's open-air asylum – thank God, thank God – had seen Gwen Garrett's dead body. It didn't exactly explain who had been writing on the Garretts' ceiling, but it did eliminate the first logical suspect. It wasn't Gwen.

'You take care, Leslie,' said Betty from behind her.

'You too.' Leslie looked back. 'By the way, can I borrow a paper clip?'

Twenty-four

Leslie drove slowly past Gwen's house. No sign of Diana and Jack's return. She pictured them fused together, mother and child, in that strange symbiotic sleep, and for the first time Leslie was glad they had spent last night with her. She parked and made her way around to the rear of the house. The lock on the back door was old and could be opened as easily with a kind word as with a key. She took the paper clip from her pocket, straightened it, and fit it into the lock. Within seconds she was inside.

The kitchen was dimly lit by the sunlight seeping beneath the shades. Leslie opened them in hopes that better light might make evident something she had missed. The counters were bare except for a single wineglass and a plate. The floors were swept. There were no faint trails of ash or any other material.

She went from the kitchen to the front room. The fireplace was closed off for the summer. A black metal sheet covered the opening, and that was fronted by a decorative fire screen. Leslie moved them aside in less than a minute, but was disappointed to find the hearth and grate vacuumed bare of ashes. It was then Leslie thought of Diana's comment that she had been smoking. She returned the fireplace to its original state and went in search of ashtrays.

She found two, both containing ash and the paper stubs of Diana's marijuana cigarettes She took one of the ashtrays into Gwen's study. In the desk, she found a sheet of white paper. With paper in hand, Leslie climbed up on the coffee table and pressed the page against the script on the ceiling, tapping gently, carefully so as not to smudge it. She pulled the paper away. Satisfied with the sample, she climbed down. Back at the desk, she dipped a fingertip in the ashtray and drew a line of ash next to what she had taken from the ceiling. The marijuana ash was far lighter in coloring than that used on the ceiling.

She sat down at Gwen's desk. This was ridiculous. What was she trying to prove anyway? If Diana had written these words on the ceiling, what would Leslie do with the information? Confront her and get Greg fired? Because that's how that equation would work. Whatever Diana's convoluted reasoning for this childish trick, it had nothing to do with Gwen's death. If Gwen was indeed dead.

Stop it, Leslie ordered herself. You start down that path and you're going to end up back at a hospital. Still strong was Leslie's gut-level certainty that Gwen wasn't the pure and simple suicide advertised. It was murder. But who would want to kill Gwen? That would be the first question and Leslie could not answer it. Yes, Gwen knew about the *Analecta*, but hell, the woman didn't believe it existed. How could that have been a threat?

Maybe you want her to be a murder victim. Leslie closed her eyes before the self-accusation. Maybe you want that because it's the only chance you have left to help her. Maybe Gwen had been nothing more than a sad, troubled woman. Who could say how much the miscarriage had cost her? Certainly not Leslie. Gwen had held on for six weeks, but held on to what? Postpartum depressions were bad enough when everything turned out well, but to have nothing to hold on to as your body completed its chemical and physical transformation would be brutal. How horrible to have the milk come in and no one to take it. Leslie thought of Yancy and his proclamation of how it was the inherent need to nurture that drove women to destruction. Who, other than Gwen herself, would want Gwen dead?

Leslie looked again at the ash on the paper, then the ash on the ceiling. She got up and went to the table, this time not to examine what was above her, but what was below. The rust-tinged blush of the stain she had tried to remove. Ash and blood and milk. A mother with a nursing child. But there was no child here. Unless . . .

She went upstairs to what had been Joe and Gwen's bedroom. She opened the closet door. It was filled with Diana's clothes. Leslie rummaged around the top shelf, but found only boxes of receipts, a couple of old hats, and some blankets. The bottom of the closet held only Diana's shoes and suitcases.

Leslie checked the bathroom. The clothes hamper was there, but it had been emptied. She stopped to think, if it were my baby, my baby . . . of course. She went to the door at the top of the stairs. Behind it lay what was to have been the nursery. Leslie opened the door. The room was bare. Joe had packed away most of the furnishings almost immediately, but a rocking chair remained.

She entered the room, trying to be quiet as though fearful of disturbing another's slumber. Leslie knew that Gwen would have hidden the surrogate because she would have been ashamed and afraid of what it told her about the depths of her needs. Except for even more of Diana's suitcases, the closet here was empty as well. Leslie stretched up on her toes and felt around the shelves. Nothing on the first, but then Gwen had been taller than Leslie. Leslie stretched even further. In the far corner of the top shelf, her fingers brushed something soft. She pulled it down. It was a stuffed monkey made from socks. It looked old – one of its black button eyes was missing – and well loved, as though it were from Gwen's own childhood. Its lower limbs were pliable, but as she worked her hands up the body, the stuffing grew stiff. The sour smell coming off it was pronounced, wholly recognizable.

Leslie hugged the toy against her, against the ache of understanding. She hugged the toy once more and then put it back where she had found it. She went downstairs, retrieved her sample of ash, and then headed out for the Concrete Recycling plant to see if Delores would verify Leslie's solidifying suspicions.

'Why, yes, it is Pozzuoli ash. Where did you get this, sister?'

'Before I answer your question, you are going to answer mine.'

Delores squinted at Leslie. 'My applejack must have soaked into your bones.'

'Why was Gwen Garrett asked to leave the Wellington coven?'

'She wasn't "asked." We closed the circle against her when her interests became contradictory to ours.'

'Diana Wellington said it was because of Gwen's research, her studying of the *Analecta Seriatus*.'

'Diana Wellington is not to be trusted on distinguishing her mouth from her cunny.' Delores laughed. 'Wiccans, which we are, pride ourselves on our scholarship. We are hardly going to renounce a sister because she seeks wisdom.'

'And Gwen?'

'Was not seeking wisdom. Every war has its mercenaries.'

'Witch for hire, huh?'

'Gwen rented herself out to the Wellingtons. Perhaps her loyalties never changed. Perhaps Sister Gwen sought the *Analecta* for the right reason, to make certain it would never be reconstituted.'

'But it's not real.'

'Precisely why we must continue to obliterate all pretenders.'

'And Gwen was a pretender?'

'Nonbelievers are always the truest.' Delores played with the dials on her oxygen tank. 'It is the ardent atheist who must most fully concede the existence of a god. If not, his nonbelief has no meaning. That's why he's always seeking to prove there is no deity.'

Leslie leaned forward. 'Was Gwen's nonbelief a threat to you or the Wellingtons?'

'Yes.'

'Yes to which one?'

Delores laughed from deep in her chest. 'Gwen was her own assassin, sister. She understood how determined the Wellingtons are to have an *Analecta* they can hold in their hands. She was equally determined to prove it unattainable. Either way, she was bound to fail those who have no tolerance for failure. Gwen signed her extermination orders the day she signed on with Mansfield Custom.'

'Why?'

'Dear child, didn't you know? The Wellington family owns Mansfield Custom. Mansfield Custom's sole purpose is to search for the *Analecta Seriatus*. It's the true nature of what they do, and they are liable to do anything.'

'Like kill Gwen Garrett for failing to produce their sacrificial child?'

'Kill Gwen Garrett and then serve tea over her corpse, if it suited them.'

'If this was a Mansfield project from the get-go, why the hell do they need Greg up there?'

Delores sat back and laced her thick fingers over her immense belly. 'You already know it is not your husband they are interested in, sister.'

'Me? Because I look like Eleanor?'

Delores nodded slowly. 'They need you, but they fear you too. Sister Eleanor, whether she knew it or not, found a way to stop them, for a little while.'

'It was war,' Leslie said, wrapping her left hand around the faint circle of bruises on her right wrist.

'It is war.'

'You told me how the *Analecta* began, the concrete. How does it end?'

Delores closed her eyes and sighed heavily. 'Dear sister – Leslie – watch your children.'

Twenty-five

THAT DIANA'S BMW WAS gone from the Stones' driveway told Leslie more than she wanted to know. She ran into her house, calling her daughters' names, receiving nothing but silence in return. She checked the bedrooms and tore back downstairs. In the kitchen she found a note from Diana: *Taken kids to 5M. Join us when you can. We've got work to do.* Leslie bit down on her panic and raced back to the van.

The harder she pressed the accelerator, the slower she seemed to move. The road was sliding backward, an unraveling of time that made it impossible to get anywhere but farther away from where she needed to be. She beat the steering wheel with her fist until the illusion dissolved.

She rounded a curve and came to find the shoulders of the road lined with parked cars, each bearing the Mansfield Custom decal on its rear window. She reached, at last, the entrance to Five Mile House. The drive had been graded and a layer of gravel laid down to provide traction for the construction vehicles. It was still steep. Leslie wheeled sharply into the turn, sending the rear of her van into a precarious skid. She recovered control and stomped again at the accelerator. The tires spat gravel as they tried to answer her demand for uphill momentum. A couple of workers in dusty coveralls came running toward her waving their arms.

'Hey! Missus Stone!' One of them pounded on her window. 'Hey! You can't get up there in this – '

She jammed the accelerator to the floor. The van swerved, struggling. The two Mansfield Custom workers jumped aside. Finally, she threw the transmission into Park, swung the door wide open, and started to run up the hill.

'Christ! Missus Stone? What's the problem?'

Leslie didn't look back. She only ran. A couple times she slipped, cutting her hands on the sharp-edged gravel, bloodying her knees. She ran by several crew members, who watched her pass with expressions of confusion and concern. A few asked if she needed help. She didn't answer. She only ran and ran, and in doing so nearly ran down Molly and Emma, who were standing at the top of the hill, watching her. Seeing them staring at her, Leslie stopped, and, smiling, bent forward, palms on thighs, to recover her breath.

'Hi, Mommy,' Emma said.

'Yeah, hi,' echoed Molly. 'Some guy at the bottom of the hill called Dad and said you were coming up. Are you okay?'

Leslie waved off her concern and nodded. 'Am now.'

'Mommy? You skinned your knees.'

'Sure looks that way.'

'Does it hurt?'

'Naw.' Leslie looked up to see Greg rushing toward her.

'What's going on?' he asked gently, putting his arm about her and helping her to hobble up to more level ground. 'The guys at the bottom of the hill said you seemed pretty upset.'

'Mommy, are you mad about something?'

'Mommy's fine.' Greg turned to Molly. 'Take your sister and go play some – '

'They stay with me.' Leslie grabbed Greg's arm. 'They don't leave my sight until we get out of here.'

'Fine. I'll take you three home right now.'

'No. Out of here. Out of Wellington. I'm taking the girls and I'm leaving. Now.'

'But I don't want to leave Wellington.' Emma broke into sobs.

'Leslie' – Greg drew a deep breath – 'you are upsetting – Molly, take your sister – wait, Les – Molly, take Emma to my office, lock the door, and stay there until I come to get you. Understand?'

Molly nodded and dragged the weeping Emma off toward the small trailer. Leslie tried to follow, but Greg held her back. 'You're scaring the shit out of those kids. What the hell is going on?'

'It's starting again. Children are going to die, quite possibly ours.'

'This is why I didn't want you reading all the crap about Five

Mile. Nobody's kids are going to die.' Greg glanced about and, seeing their gathering audience, said, 'Now, come over here and sit down.' He led her to the shade at the edge of the wood.

Leslie sat, facing the trees. She wouldn't look at him. 'You are working for a bunch of lunatics.'

Greg said nothing. He just sat beside her, picking at the spikes of dead pine needles at his feet.

Leslie said, 'Whether you come with us or not, I'm taking the girls and getting out of here.'

'Maybe that would be good. If you go away, I mean. Maybe you need to be away. But you can't take the girls. You're not . . . if you try to take them, I'll . . .'

'You'll what?'

'Do whatever is necessary to make sure they're safe.' He looked at her hard. 'I promise you that, Leslie. I will always put their safety above anything else.'

'Then leave here, now.'

'I can't. I won't. There's no reason – ' His voice was cut short by a sudden, keening wail. Both Greg and Leslie turned around to see Diana, standing in the weedy center of the drive. She was swaying, hugging herself. Leslie leapt to her feet and ran.

'Diana?'

Diana, wild-eyed, screamed. 'I can't find Jack.'

'What do you mean, you can't find him?' Greg had caught up. 'He's got to be around here somewhere.'

Leslie took Diana's face in her hands, steadying her. 'Where did you see him last?'

Diana, crying now, said, 'He was playing with Molly and Emma. I was out back with them. I must have fallen asleep or something. I've looked everywhere.' She collapsed into Leslie's shoulder.

Greg ran to his trailer and pounded on the door. Molly opened it, and he motioned her out into the sun. She listened and then pointed toward Leslie and then toward the back of the house. Greg made a large gesture of anger with his arms and Molly, head down, went inside the trailer. He jogged back.

'Molly says they were playing hide-and-go-seek. When I sent the girls to wait for Leslie, Jack was still hiding. Molly says they called to him, but he probably didn't hear because, although they've been told a thousand times not to, they were playing in the house. He's probably in there waiting to be found.'

Leslie raised her eyes and stared up at the tower. 'Well, we'd better go find him.'

Greg patted Diana's arm. 'Don't worry. Let me round up a few guys and we'll find him in no time.' He looked at Leslie as if to forbid her assumptions. Leslie returned his gaze to let him know it was too late.

Diana headed for the front steps, calling out her son's name. Leslie placed herself in the woman's path. 'You know, Diana, I bet he's looking for you. Why don't we wait out here so it's easier for him to find – '

'No. No. You don't understand. He can't be left alone.'

'Why not, Diana? What's going to happen if you leave him alone?'

Diana screamed again, flailing her arms, clawing at Leslie, until she had knocked Leslie down. Diana scrambled away to run up the steps, shouting Jack's name.

Leslie went after her, but by the time Leslie was inside the house, Diana was nowhere to be seen. Leslie listened to the growing number of voices calling for Jack, but Diana's did not seem to be among them. Outside she heard Greg instructing the search party to quiet down; the additions were so convoluted that if the kid heard all these people yelling for him he'd get even more lost. Leslie hoped that Diana's silence meant she had realized the same.

It occurred to Leslie, briefly, that Jack might have gone back up to the tower, but she dismissed that as unlikely. It was too hot up there and the door was too swollen for a slight child like Jack to manage. She looked at the yellow-green ghosts of bruises on her wrist. Nope, she thought, not the tower.

Leslie chose the corridor that led off the room to her left. The additions were, outside the fact of their simple existence, an ordinary meandering of narrow hallways and occasional intersections. There was a vague scent of mildew from the bare earthen cellars under the thick mahogany floorboards. The mildew was offset by that Christmasy clove aroma that she had smelled months earlier. Leslie's footsteps reverberated, drum-like, over the hollow cellar space.

She wandered, peeking into dead ends and checking around

corners. She was deeply grateful for the electric lighting Greg had installed. If Jack was alone, at least he wasn't alone in the dark. Every so often, her path would cross that of another searcher. Leslie would ask if he'd seen Diana or heard her. The encounter would end with a shrug or a shake of the head. Sometimes Leslie would turn a corner and find herself exiting into one of the rooms of the main house. She'd go back the way she came until she felt sufficiently disoriented. Then she'd begin again. She had no idea how long she had been walking around like this. It might have been ten minutes or two hours; the structure had a numbing effect on her mind. As such, she nearly cried out in fright, when just after passing through an intersection, she heard Molly's voice behind her.

'Any luck, Mom?'

Leslie whipped around. 'What are you doing here?'

'I'm trying to help. I was supposed to be watching them. Dad's all mad at me.'

'Don't worry about your dad. Where's Em?'

'Back in the trailer. She's coloring. The door's locked.'

'I don't want her alone, Molly. Come on, I'll take you back. I think it's this way.'

'Mom?' Molly took her mother's hand. 'Is everything all right?'

She led Molly to the left. 'We go down here – you want the truth?'

'I just want to know if everything is going to be all right?'

'If you mean is it going to be easy, I don't think so – look, there's one of the front rooms – it won't be easy, but we'll get through it.' Leslie put her arm around Molly's shoulder and squeezed. They went through the plastic drapery into the bright, dust-sparked light in one of the main rooms. Leslie kept her arm about Molly as they made their way out of the house. Molly trudged along, resting her head against her mother's shoulder, until they turned the corner of the house and saw the door to Greg's little trailer swinging back and forth, wide open.

'Emma!' Molly yelled, and ran forward.

Leslie stood unmoving, her hand clamped over her mouth. Molly leapt up the steps into the office.

'Look who I found!' Molly shouted, as she came out of the trailer, pulling Jack Wellington behind her. She lugged him forward. 'Look, Mom. Jack's just fine. Hey Jack, where'd Emma go?'

Twenty-six

W<small>E LIVED WITH ISABEL</small> and her husband William for almost six months. William had built the house for her after it became clear there would be no children. Not meant for a brood the size of mine, the walls of the little lake house fairly bulged. I longed for privacy, but the children seemed happy enough. They spent their free hours in the fresh air, chasing one another through the woods, swimming and boating on the lake. They grew rugged looking. Their faces shone with health. Country living, if you would call it such, agreed with them.

As for me, I was contending with the first real tremors of wariness about Isabel. While she was with us in the city, I had indulged her peculiarity as an endearment. Now, I found myself watching her ever more closely. It was her love for the children that troubled me. Her great devotion to her nieces and nephews I had, at first, attributed to her own lack of children. Yet, from daybreak of the morning we arrived in Wellington, I caught myself questioning inane details like the manner in which she embraced the children. Isabel did not hold or embrace or caress. She threw her arms about the children and engulfed them. Isabel consumed.

The weeks passed. I grew daily more nervous and tired on account of the double vigil I was keeping: one on Isabel and one on my children.

I never left the children alone. Never.

In equal measure to my nervousness, Joshua became bitter and withdrawn. Perhaps he had always been so, and I was seeing him plainly for the first time. The infamy of the events at Della Rosa's clung to him like a smoky odor that could not be washed away. He kept his distance and I kept mine. He busied himself in the minutiae of Five Mile House, poring over drawings and specifications for craftsmen. His evenings were spent in close counsel with Isabel and William – more quiet voices behind closed doors – while I bathed the children, fluffed their pillows, read to them. I listened to their prayers, kissed their cheeks, sang lullabies. Long after they slept, long after Isabel and William and Joshua had retired for the night, I wandered from child to child, making certain, making sure.

I never left the children alone.

My health began to fail. I grew thin and weak. Even Joshua, from the depths of his distraction, could sense my increasing frailty. It evoked, unexpectedly, a consideration in him that I had not seen in months. He asked if perhaps I had not undertaken too much, the care and tutoring of seven children. Would I not allow Isabel's help?

No, I insisted, not after her great kindness of providing us shelter.

Then, would I not want some help, a girl from town or from Rutherford?

No, again I insisted, it was not necessary. The children themselves were a great help to me, the older ones tending after the younger. I would look after the children.

A day or two later, he proposed another solution. The Wellingtons kept a cottage only a few miles down the road. It was where Isabel had stayed during her betrothal to William. The place was small for a family of ten but comfortable enough. We might install the children and myself there, giving us all a bit more room. The only disadvantage, to Joshua's mind, was that Isabel would not be immediately present to offer assistance should I need or desire it. I, disguising my relief as acquiescence, agreed to the plan. By the afternoon of that same day, I and my children were setting up household in the same cottage where now hangs a well-loved photograph of Leslie, Greg, Molly, and Emma Stone.

Leslie sits on the floor of the trailer that is Greg's office and looks up at Jack. The little boy swivels in the chair, his legs rocking slightly to and fro. Diana stands behind him, her hands on his shoulders. His body trembles slightly; he's been crying.

'Jack, listen to me,' Leslie says quietly, 'no one is angry with you. You haven't done anything wrong.'

'You called the police. You called the police because I went in the house.'

'That's not why the police are here, sweetie.' She waits until her voice has steadied. 'We called the police because we need help finding Emma.'

'We were playing hide-n-seek. Maybe she's still hiding. Emma's good at hiding.'

'So are you, I hear. Did you know we were all looking for you?'

He nods. 'Mommy told me.'

Diana kisses the top of his head. 'He heard us calling for him and he thought he'd get yelled at for being in the house, so he sneaked out.'

'Diana,' Leslie says, 'it would be better if Jack tells it. What happened when you heard everybody calling for you?'

'I thought you'd be mad, so I tried to get out as quick as I could, but first I got kinda lost.'

'There were a lot of people in the house. Did you see anyone? Anyone at all?'

He thinks a moment. 'I saw people, but they didn't see me.'

'What do you mean, sweetheart?'

'I saw a lot of workers, but I hid before they could catch me. I didn't want to get in trouble.'

Leslie nods. She picks up a scrap of paper from the floor and twists it between her fingers. 'What happened when you finally got out?'

'I went here. Home. The place you go in the game.'

'And what did you see when you got here?'

'I already told you. The door was open. I came in to see if Molly and Emma were here. But they weren't.'

Leslie twists the scrap of paper until it tears apart. 'Jack, think real hard. When you were in the house, who did you see?'

'I don't know. I saw Mister Stone and a bunch of the builder guys, and once I saw Molly. I don't know the names of everybody. I saw a lady that looks like you.'

'You saw me. I was looking for you, too.'

'No. She was wearing a dress, a long, old-fashioned dress. On the tower stairs.'

'What?' Diana rotates the chair so she can look at her son.

Jack begins to sob. 'She had black hair like Missus Stone and she was far away from me, but I know it wasn't Missus Stone. She was scary.'

Diana glares meaningfully at Leslie, who tilts her head in a gesture of warning: *Don't you dare.* Leslie then turns the seat of the chair back so that Jack can see her face. 'Jack, when people get scared, they can see things that aren't really there. It happens all the time.'

'Yeah?'

'Yeah. Has anyone ever told you scary stories about this place?'

'Maybe. A couple.' He looks up at his mother.

'Your mind was playing tricks on you, sweetheart. You saw me, and because you were scared you thought you saw something or somebody else. Okay?'

'Okay.'

Leslie stands. 'Jack, I bet some of the policemen outside are going to want to ask you a lot of the same questions. It might get a little boring. Or it might get a little scary – like they don't believe you. Just tell them the truth, and everything will be all right.'

'Okay. I'll tell them my mind was tricking me.'

Leslie leans forward and brushes the tears from his cheek. 'We'll find her,' she says for both their benefit. She turns to go, quickly before he can see her fear.

Outside the trailer waits Yancy Galleghar, the three squad-car force of the Wellington police, as well as the entire Wellington Volunteer Fire Department. Rutherford has been contacted, and they are sending reinforcements. Emma has been missing for nearly four hours.

'Anything?' Yancy asks.

Leslie shakes her head.

'She's probably still in the house.'

Again Leslie shakes her head.

'You don't know that.'

Leslie looks up at him. 'I walked right into it.'

'Into what?' Yancy's usual arrogance has softened.

'Bait and switch. I walked right into it. Where's Molly?'

He points to the egg-like shape, knees hugged to chest and head tucked, balanced on the edge of the old stone wall at the back of the property. 'She's in a bad way.'

'I know,' Leslie says. 'Come get me if you find – if you hear anything at all.' She crosses the distance and sits next to Molly, stroking her daughter's hair. The sun falls hot on their backs.

'It's not your fault,' Leslie whispers.

'I'm not stupid,' Molly says without raising her head. 'If I'd stayed with Emma then . . .'

'Then something might have happened to both of you.'

'Or maybe just me and that would have been better.'

'Don't, Molly. Please.'

'I want to look in the house again.'

'We've spent hours looking in the house. If she were in there we would have found her.'

Molly turns her head. 'Then where is she?'

'I don't know. I think somebody took her.'

'Who would take her? Why?'

'I think somebody's trying to scare me.'

Molly's face darkens with understanding. She straightens her limbs and pushes herself off the wall. 'I wish you'd never come back,' she says to Leslie before running off toward the front of the house.

Leslie sits with the sting of her daughter's words until it fades and is absorbed by the heat and the nonsensical buzzing of mosquitoes, bees, and hand-held transmitters. Far inside herself, in a place of absolute and private emptiness, Leslie is screaming. It is all she can do to maintain the barrier between those screams and the methodical thinking process she knows she must manage. She puts her hands over her ears and closes her eyes. Still, what she hears is the barrier cracking.

'No,' she says aloud. No. She plants her feet on the ground and stands up. Her hands fall to her side. Breathe, she tells herself. Breathe. She turns and looks out over the hillside below her. The sun is bright, glaring. She shields her eyes against it and blinks. There is someone down the hill, in an open stand of birch. A woman. The sun is shining, yellow-white on the woman's hair. She is looking up at the house, looking up at Leslie.

'Gwen?' Leslie says, quietly at first. 'Gwen!' Then she is running, yelling, the cracks in the barrier giving way, her voice flooding the silence, as she stumbles toward the trees. 'Gwen!' The woman doesn't move. Leslie gets closer and closer until her foot hits an exposed root and she is sent tumbling, over and over. As rapidly as possible, Leslie regains her footing, but runs no further because the woman has gone.

The commotion, however, has brought Yancy, his men and some of the newly arrived Rutherford officers galloping down the hill to where Leslie is now examining the birch trees and the grasses.

'What is it, Leslie?' Yancy calls before he's reached her location.

'It's Gwen Garrett,' Leslie answers. 'Gwen Garrett has Emma.'

Twenty-seven

GREG HAD LESLIE BY the shoulders, his fingers digging into her until he hit bone. 'Gwen Garrett is dead.'

'So everybody keeps telling me. But I know what I saw, Greg.'

'Do you? Do you? First you think Gwen was murdered. Now, you think she's not only still alive but she's kidnapped Emma?'

Leslie wrenched herself away from him. The Wellington and Rutherford police officers were standing a short distance away, watching. 'Greg, please listen to me. I saw Gwen Garrett.'

'You think you saw Gwen.'

Leslie glanced again at the officers. 'Okay. I think I saw Gwen, but – '

'Leslie, we have to concentrate on Emma right now.'

'What the hell do you think I'm doing?'

'I don't know, Les. Right now, all I can do is go back in that house and rip out every fucking wall until we find her. If you can't help, then stay out of the way.' He turned, head down, and motioned to some of the crew. They followed him up the steps.

'She's not in the house, Greg,' Leslie yelled after him. He did not respond.

Yancy walked over and stood beside her. 'Is there anyone we can call for you, Leslie? A doctor or somebody.'

She narrowed her eyes.

'I know I've been giving you a hard time since you got to Wellington, but I want you to know we're going to do everything we can.'

'It's starting to get cold,' Leslie said, as she turned around and began to walk toward the drive down the hill.

'You going somewhere?' Yancy called after her.

'I'm going home for a few minutes to get some warmer clothes for Jack and Molly – and Emma. I'll be right back.'

'Diana Wellington and the boy left about ten minutes ago. I'll have an officer drive you to your place.'

'I have my van.'

'Under the circumstances, Leslie, I think it's probably best if you're not by yourself.'

Leslie stopped and looked back. 'What are you trying to say?'

Yancy spread his knob-knuckled hands before him. 'I think you know.'

'Yeah, I do. I also need to get home for my medicine.' Leslie smiled hard. 'If you think I'm crazy now, wait until you see me without my meds.'

'Why do you have to make this difficult? I'm trying to be nice here. Truth is, in a couple of hours, if we haven't found her, we're going to have to sit you and your husband down for a polygraph.'

'I remember the law, Yancy.'

'So, what happens if I let you take off, and you don't come back?'

'There's only one reason I would do that.'

'Fact is, I can think of several, and ain't one of them that's good.'

Leslie folded her arms against her middle and stared up into the dimming sky. 'It's going to be dark soon. They're not going to find her, not up here. I need to get a photograph of Emma to put out on the wire. Every minute we wait is a minute we don't get back. Please, Yancy.'

'One hour,' Yancy said. 'I'll give you one hour to get back up here.'

'One hour,' Leslie said and then continued on her way down the hill.

She locked her hands on the steering wheel. The secret of holding herself together was to hold on to something else, to connect her solid being to the solidity of the world, and to move, like a mountain climber, from handhold to handhold. As she drove, Leslie fused her attention on each jostle and bump of the van as it took the frost heaves and pot holes in the asphalt. She had left logic back at Five Mile with Greg and Yancy and their orderly approach. She was not going home.

The parking lot at the concrete recycling yard was deserted, the chain-link fence closed and locked. Leslie pulled off the road, easing the van into the shadowy overhang of roadside pines. She turned off the engine and waited, waited to see if her arrival had attracted attention, to see if Yancy had had her followed, to see if somehow a saner solution might reveal itself, miracle-like.

But no. It was war. Leslie had to declare her loyalties, and there were – God help you, Gwen – no choices. Emma was all that mattered. To that end, Leslie had come to the recycling plant to enlist the Rubble Witches, allies by means of a shared threat. If anyone was going to believe Leslie, let alone second-guess Gwen's next move, it would be Delores.

Leslie exited the car and crossed the road. Although she could see lights on in the office building, the front gate was locked for the night. She didn't want to risk discovery by using the intercom. So, she scrambled over the chain-link fence and jumped, graceless and heavy, landing hard on the parking lot. No alarm sounded, but she hadn't expected one at this point. She surveyed the moonscape scenery of broken rock and crumbled concrete slabs in silhouette against the twilight. From the far end of the yard came a rhythmic pounding, loud and mechanical. The crushing machines were working overtime.

With a sudden synchronized flicker, the exterior security lights came on, bathing the rock and concrete in white. Leslie hurried to the corner of the building that held Delores's office. She leaned against the wall, feeling the vibrations of the crushing machine every time it struck, the footsteps of a giant in approach.

Her plan was simple. Leslie was going to march into Delores's office and demand the solid piece of something that would point infallibly to Emma's location. Then it was a mere matter of retrieving her daughter. Simple. That the situation might be more complex and its resolution less direct was achingly clear. Leslie, however, pretended not to feel the ratty little teeth of doubt. She checked behind her to make certain she was still alone, then she went to the door at the front of the building. The rectangular window in the door showed the reception area to be dark, but she could see light coming from Delores's office. A dead-bolt lock was fitted above the knob, and, given the late hour, she expected it to be locked; she'd have to break in. Leslie tested the door's resistance by turning the knob and leaning into it with her shoulder. The door opened.

'Hello?' Leslie called into the darkness. 'Delores?' There was no answer.

Not good, thought Leslie. This is not good. She went inside. The outer rooms were in order. The door to Delores's office was partially ajar, and from behind it Leslie could hear a faint hissing. She sniffed at the air; it held a bright, almost invigorating quality that contradicted the other odors Leslie recognized too well, the flat metallic scents of blood and fear. A curving band of fat red drops wound its way from Delores's office and out the door.

Leslie trained her ear toward the hissing and moved closer. She nudged open the door to Delores's office, and the hissing instantly increased in loudness. It was, Leslie realized, Delores's oxygen tank. She stepped inside the room. The office was in complete disarray. File cabinets had been overturned and their contents thrown about. Frames were smashed, and the photographs taken from them and torn. The drawers in the desk had been yanked completely free and dumped. Leslie was aware of a new smell, the potent alcoholic aroma of applejack, mixed with – what was that? – fingernail polish remover, which appeared to have been spilled over much of the paper.

Oxygen, thought Leslie, plus fuel. Where's the ignition? She scanned the walls to the ceiling and down again and around the office until she caught the shimmer of glass. The carafe from a coffeemaker lay broken on the floor, its jagged side edged in blood. It took her only a moment then to locate the coffeemaker on the paper-cluttered credenza behind the desk. She shifted acetone-soaked papers, hot to the touch, aside and found the Off/On switch, the beady red operational light glowing. Leslie shut it off.

Whoever did this had left only minutes before Leslie arrived. From what little she recalled of her arson training, she knew the place was meant to be in full flame shortly. But the ransacking of this office would not be hidden by fire; such an obvious arson was meant to be interpreted as a message, a punishment or warning for Delores, if not the entire Wellington coven. If it were up to Leslie, she'd cordon off the area and have it searched for long, white-blond strands of female hair. This was Gwen's work. Leslie was certain of it. But to call in anyone on even a hint of that suspicion would be her guarantee of a no-return fare back to Muzak and art therapy.

No one is going to believe me; the inevitable truth of that beat against her sternum in a low-level ache that kept pace with the repetitive pounding of the crushing machine. Leslie put her hand to her chest, physically holding the panic down. She looked around the office once more, looking at the blood droplets scattered over the papers on Delores's desk: memos, letters, invoices, yellowed newspaper clippings, a newspaper clipping with Leslie's photo. She pushed the other papers away. It was titled VIGILANTE OFFICER NOT GUILTY. Leslie shoved it aside. Beneath was another from the same time, and beneath that a stapled set of articles about the suspect's death, the suicide watch, her release from the hospital. All of it collected in a manila folder.

'Christ. Christ. Christ.' Leslie went through page after page. Her entire ridiculous history was sitting there atop Delores's desk. Which meant what? That Delores had researched Leslie, and this was mere information. Or had Gwen and her doctorate in psychology surmised that this would be the first place Leslie would turn for confirmation? Had the fire been intended, or had Leslie been so thoroughly fathomed as to assume she would arrive here in time to stop it? That was it, she thought. That's what Gwen is trying to tell me. She knows who I am. She knows what I'll do. Because I have no choice. Leslie picked up the file folder and threw it against the wall. Remnants of her life floated to the floor.

There was a piece of paper beneath the folder. It was a photocopy of Gwen Garrett's death certificate. Leslie saw everything that Mike Humphrey had told her would be there. His postmortem comments, the estimated time of death, Mansfield Custom's request for the body to be sent to Rutherford. It would have seemed to Leslie a bad practical joke, except she was reading now the form attached concerning the Mansfield request. Gwen's body was to be picked up by and accompanied to the county hospital by the undersigned, who was accepting all responsibility for its safe and timely delivery. The signature was in a brisk, practical style, well formed and unforgivably legible. Phillip Hogarth.

Leslie rang the doorbell a third time and doubled-checked the crumpled bit of phone book page in her hand. Finally, there was a gruff command for her to hold on a second. The door opened and Mitch Ward, sleepy and beer-scented, stood before her.

'Hell, Missus Stone. What are you doing all the way out here?'

'Mitch, I need a favor.'

Dan appeared behind his brother. 'What's up?'

'Come on in.' Mitch waved her forward. He led her to a den where the television showed soundless pictures of a baseball game. A woman, as large as the men, looked up at Leslie. She was in a housecoat and curlers. 'Maureen, this is Leslie Stone. Missus Stone, this here's my wife.'

'You'll have to pardon us,' said Maureen, patting her head. 'We weren't expecting – '

'I'm sorry,' Leslie cut her off. 'I need help, Mitch. I need a gun.'

Mitch sat down. 'This about our talk of the other day?'

'It's better if you don't ask questions. And if any one else should ask . . . later, if anyone has cause to ask, you tell them the weapon was stolen.'

'My husband doesn't lie, Missus Stone. And what makes you think we've got a gun to give you?'

'You hunt, right? I thought Mitch might be able to . . . it was all I could think of. Somebody's taken my daughter. If I'm going to get her back I'm going to have to – never mind, you wouldn't believe me.'

'Wouldn't believe what?' said Dan.

Mitch stood up and walked from the room. He returned a minute later with a burnished wood box. 'I have this old thirty-eight. It belonged to my grandpa. I use it for target shooting every now and then, so it's oiled and working good. Don't have many bullets left, though I suppose there's enough to do the job.' He handed her the box.

'I don't want to use it, but if I do . . .'

'It was stolen.' Mitch gave her a taut smile. 'Just remember, Missus Stone. I did try to warn you.'

Twenty-eight

O NCE WE WERE IN the cottage and away from Isabel, my nerves quieted. My appetite returned. I slept dreamlessly the full night. Oh, she still visited, daily, to inquire after all the tiniest details of our happiness and health. Isabel felt that her duty, she explained, what with Joshua so caught up in other matters. Her persistence now struck me more as annoying and pathetic than menacing; I could dismiss her by merely kissing her cheek and closing the door. This is what I believed. This was my first mistake.

Perhaps I might not have been as easily fooled had it not been for the sudden distraction of my son Samuel's illness. For weeks, I had pretended not to hear his coughing, pretended not to see him decline invitations to play. The attacks began in earnest in the depths of one particularly stormy night. I was awakened that night not by the raging wind nor booming thunder, but by the ghostly echo of a sound I knew too well. Confused by the lightning and the crazed shadows of the storm-bent trees, I must admit that for more than a few minutes I believed myself back in my childhood home listening – trying not to listen – to my brother's gasping, hacking, laborious existence. In what I would then naïvely term the most frightening realization of my life, I remembered where I was and that the sound I so dreaded must have lodged itself in one of my children.

I ran from room to room and found storm-startled but quiet children. And still I heard the cough. I made my way down the stairs to the kitchen where I found Joshua and our son, who was sitting bent over a soup tureen with a towel tenting his head. The air was sharp with menthol, a sickroom scent.

I was not brave. I collapsed against the doorjamb and wept. Not again. I could not watch this happen again. Joshua looked up at me, his face was drawn, as sad and helpless as ever I had seen him. By the following week, Samuel had been seen by the doctor and we had been told, officially, what I already knew. It was decided that Isabel should set about locating the very finest sanitarium, and when I decided that Samuel's care was more than I could manage, we would have him moved.

She undertook her research with typical zeal. Isabel wrote not only to the hospitals but to the families that had entrusted their loved ones to such prescriptive care. She'd read each of these lengthy missives to me aloud so that I might approve or disapprove her wording of Samuel's current condition, which seemed to be degenerating rapidly. At first I was grateful for Isabel's interventions on our behalf, and I allowed myself to second-guess my hesitancy toward her demand for unconditional intimacy.

My second mistake. The results of her solicitations became an instrument of daily torture and nightly terrors. Isabel brought me articles, tales, rumors of institutional horrors. Secret experimental treatments on children, the use of an invalid child as a toy for perverse pleasure, babies left to nurses who, to public scrutiny, were the jolliest and most loving of creatures but, when alone with their charges, became sadistic fiends. Burnings, beatings, starvation. One can never be certain, Isabel would impart with sympathetic earnestness over the bone china lip of a tea cup, one can never be certain. And with that she would leave me the next on her list of possible doctors, houses, and retreats.

Shamed by my own cowardice as a mother, I would thank her for her efforts and then resolve, in secret, to find whatever strength necessary to see Samuel through to the end of his journey, a resolve that crumbled beneath the very next breaking wave of a coughing seizure. With each wave, a little more of my heart eroded until there was too little left there for anyone. I ceased trying to love Samuel or any of the others. I knew myself a failed soul. They were all lost to me.

At last, we sent Samuel to a hospital far to the West. It was warm year-round, and the dry air was believed an aid to comfort and healing. I did not accompany him to the train. Once at the hospital, Samuel wrote me letters and cards, sometimes twice a day, for a while, until it became evident to him I was not going to answer. I have no idea how long he lived.

My personal habits changed. I was as vain as any woman, but in a short time I found myself too exhausted to dress or arrange my hair. I began to lust for my sister-in-law's visits, eagerly eliciting the new, scandalous details of brutality she'd uncovered. I invited her veiled denouncements of me, happy in my shame. I was, with Isabel's kind encouragement, quite plainly going mad.

Joshua lived with us and abided me without remark. We ate at the same table and shared the same bed, although my appetites at both had exploded into insatiable demons. I craved meat, raw and bloody, the fat and bone. I ate potatoes and huge onions ripped directly from the earth. I then took to eating earth itself, great handfuls of soil. In bed, I allowed Joshua no rest. I bucked and begged for degradations which he indulged if only to silence me. The mornings would find him bruised and bitten, yet he would rise, dress, and depart without comment. I would writhe in my bed, digging my fingers into my womb, and await Isabel.

In the lobby of the hospital at Rutherford, Leslie faced the bank of pay telephones and counted the change in her palm one last time. Stalling, she accused herself, you're stalling. 'Please, let me be wrong.' She plugged the coins into the slot. After the dial tone she punched in the numbers on Phillip's business card. In a moment the message service came on. Leslie left the number of the pay phone and a single word: 'Pastrami.' She hung up and waited. Three, five, ten minutes passed. Nurses helped a pregnant woman into a wheelchair while her husband filled in forms. A smooth female voice spoke from the public address system. She informed them that visiting hours were now over. The elevators to Leslie's right responded with bells as the doors slid open to disgorge families, spouses, children. She had caught the eye of a toddler who was being pulled along by the hand. Leslie smiled. The child yawned.

She grabbed the receiver on the first ring. 'Phillip?'

'I couldn't call on my cell phone. They're monitoring the air-waves. Where are you?'

'Can't tell you that.'

'Well,' he said softly. 'I'm at Diana's. She's in the other room.

Leslie, you need to come back here. They haven't found Emma yet.'

'And they won't.' She gripped the phone tighter. 'Gwen Garrett is alive,' she said. 'Gwen has Emma.'

'Leslie. Oh, Leslie, sweetheart. You are under a lot of strain right now. There's no way – '

'Okay, then you prove me wrong. Get your attorney ass to work and bring me proof that she's dead. I'll be at the usual place.'

'What do you want? Certificate of death? Coroner findings?'

'I want proof.'

'All right. All right. It may take a while.'

'I'll wait.' She hung up the receiver and joined the final stragglers, the very worried and the very reluctant, on their way out of the hospital.

In the parking lot, she veered away from the well-lit spaces allocated for visitors and walked toward a dim corner beyond the area restricted to emergency room patients. She reached her van and stopped. On the rear window, drawn in what looked to be soap, was a small five-pointed star enclosed in a circle. From behind her came soft footsteps. Leslie fingered her car keys until they protruded from her fist like claws. She cocked her elbow, ready to strike upward. She pivoted around to find Betty Myers standing with her arms raised to her face for protection.

'What the hell?' Leslie said, breathless.

'Blessed be, hon,' said Betty, equally breathless. She pointed to the symbol on Leslie's window. 'Delores sent me. Says she owes you one. She wanted you to know you go with the Goddess's goodwill.'

'I cannot handle anymore of this witch crap.'

'You need to know that they won't hurt her, hon'. They won't hurt your daughter. It's you they want.'

'But why? I'm not Eleanor. I'm not related to her. It's a freaking coincidence.'

'Precisely, hon'. That's what they want. I know this is hard, but if you're going to help your little girl you're going to have to accept the situation for how it is.' Betty lowered her eyes.

'Fight your own fucking war.' Leslie rubbed at the symbol on the rear window until the soap smeared. 'What if I told you I don't think it's the Wellingtons who are involved in this at all. I think Gwen Garrett is still alive and that she has Emma.'

Betty cocked her head and sighed. 'I wouldn't be all that surprised. It's the *Analecta*. She's trying to prove to them it doesn't exist. She's found out how to do it, or she thinks she has. That would be why she needs you. That's why we closed the circle against her, hon'. Gwen was studying the *Analecta*, thinking she could touch the stories without the stories touching her. The *Analecta* is seductive that way, gets you believing that it ain't nothing more to the world than the proper arrangement of a few dozen words, nothing more to people than a few lines of genetic gobbledegook.'

'So you believe me?'

Betty took a step forward and touched Leslie's shoulder. 'Well, hon', where would not believing get me?'

Twenty-nine

ISABEL USED MY MADNESS, or rather the madness she had so carefully cultivated in me, as her opportunity to ensnare my children. It was so plain, she'd say, that I was not up to the task of caring for my babies. I must allow her assistance. She did so love them all, each and every one, as though they were her very own. I suppose I was grateful, at first, because I found the chores and routines so dreadfully tiring. Nevertheless, the few moments of peace I did know were fostered by my children. One would bring flowers to my bedside. Another would pester me to read. My older daughter insisted I consult on her choice of costume for the country dance she was to attend. It was as if my children anchored me into a semblance of reason by reasonably refusing to see me as anything other than their mother.

Their withdrawal was imperceptible at first, much like the first petal's fall from a spent rose. More and more often, I was left alone. Isabel would say that she had tended to the children's wants so as not to disturb me. When I complained that their visits were not a disturbance, Isabel grew stern. She said that my behavior was frightening to them and that until I was 'more serene,' it would be best for the children to rely on her.

Rely they did. I would hear them in the garden calling 'Auntie Isabel! Auntie Isabel! Watch me!' I spied out the window and saw them, held rapt, gathered about her skirts as she read. They, the children and Isabel, giggled together in controlled voices outside my door. When she'd march them in for formal good-nights there would be all sorts of stolen and secretive glances.

Once, I attempted to follow them to their beds, to make myself present again in the pattern of their lives. I waited until Isabel had departed and the house was still and Joshua slept. Then I padded, quiet as snow, across the bedroom floor. Ever so carefully, I turned the knob – only to find it locked!

I roared. I shook Joshua; I wept and pleaded for my babies. Awakened and furious, he instructed me to adapt a more appropriate attitude and thank the good Lord that I was fortunate to have such a kindly sister in Isabel, for surely this was not an easy time for her. My jealousy, my suspicious nature, he said, was as much to blame for my current state of nerves as was my refusal to rest. He took a key from his dressing gown and left the chamber to sleep, God knows where, in our crowded little house. The withholding of his body, compounded upon Isabel's withholding of my children, sent me into fits not unlike the agonies of a morphine addict denied his relief. I sat on my bed and I screamed.

I suppose I believed that should they know the vastness of my suffering, I might touch their hearts, elicit some pity. When the screaming did not work, I tried to be good. I dressed well and fixed my hair. Still, the door stayed locked. The children came no more at all. It was as if I were dead to them. No, more than that. It was as if I had never existed. The most I saw of them was from my window. Even if I called, they never looked up, not one. Except Isabel. Isabel would raise her bright, hungry face and smile at me, her bright, hungry smile. There was a word for her. Succubus.

And at last I understood. This was war.

Leslie sits in the motel room waiting for Phillip. He will bring her proof of Gwen's death. She knows that. He will bring her everything he can find, and she will be convinced. She is sitting cross-legged in the middle of the bed with the gun box open before her. The red felt lining is stained with oil. She picks up the revolver and snaps open the barrel. One by one, she slides bullets into the six chambers and then snaps the barrel shut. She reaches over, lifts the bedspread, and shoves the gun beneath the mattress.

Across from the bed, a mirror is bolted to the wall through an ornate, Mediterranean-style frame. Leslie considers her reflection, stiffening her posture to strike a pose. So, Eleanor, she thinks, how much alike do they want us to be? She laughs, but not with amusement, then she closes the gun box. Then she opens it. Leslie runs her fingers over the depression in the top and bottom, the symmetrical spaces created for holding the weapon. She closes the box and opens it. Closes, then opens it. She jumps up from the bed and goes to the desk beneath the mirror. She rummages through the drawers until she finds a piece of motel stationery and a pen. Quickly, without concern for precision, she sketches the floor plan of Five Mile House, ignoring the additions. Then she folds the paper, matching up the lines, knowing they will match. Leslie looks at her reflection again and, for a second, sees what they see: facing leaves in a book with mirrors for pages.

'It's not in the house,' she says to her Eleanor self. 'It *is* the house. Five Mile House is the *Analecta*.'

My first view of Five Mile House came near dusk from the rear of a wagon we'd hired to haul our furnishings. The children and Joshua had gone up earlier in the day with Isabel, of course, to picnic on the lawn. And now I approached, in a wagonload of boxes and crates of other unnecessary things. Not that I was demoralized, not in the least, for I held a secret in my belly, a living secret I had kept hidden for nearly four months. I had determined that this was a new beginning. I had a power Isabel did not, and in proclaiming my motherhood, I would reclaim my children.

As such, that first sight of Five Mile House filled me with a brilliant joy, an almost holy sense of hope. It was, I thought, a fine house. Sensible, like Joshua, in its lines and proportions. Generous in size without being ostentatious. It sat atop the hill as if it belonged there, a natural fact of the local geology. In the half-dark of evening, the windows, except for that in the tower, shone gold. Tendrils of smoke trailed upward from the rear of the house. The air was sultry with smoldering wood smells. I felt indeed like I was coming home.

Isabel met me with hugs and kisses at the door, asking after my journey as though I had come from abroad. She took my case and, with her hand at my elbow, led me down the front hall and then we started up stairs. I asked if I might see the children before dinner, and Isabel clucked; surely I would want to rest before descending into the chaos that was their table. Up we went. I asked about the arrangements. Having lived for so long like too many peas in a single pod, did the children have enough room, were they pleased with their chambers? Oh yes, said Isabel, as up we climbed, she had seen to everyone's comfort and all seemed satisfied. Up we continued through many turns and landings until we reached an equally narrow door. Isabel opened the door, urging me into the room.

I understood at once that this was to be my chamber, this little room in the tower. It was furnished with a cot, a table, a washstand, and a single lamp. Isabel assured me it was only temporary, that for the sake of my health she thought it best that I have a private place away from the clutter and noise. She had me sit on the bed, as she gently pulled the pins from my hair. Then she knelt in front of me to unbutton and remove my shoes. Isabel picked up the lamp and bade me rest. She left upon promises she would return shortly with my dinner. The door shut. I heard the sharp snap of the lock.

I suppose she was expecting, if not outright desiring, a show of surprise in my realization that I was being imprisoned once again. But how could I be surprised at anything? I know she waited outside the door, listening for some indication of my fury. Instead, I laughed. I fell off the cot onto the floor of my dark little room and I kicked my heels and yelled for the comedy of it all. Isabel believed, genuinely believed that something so vain as a single locked door was going to hold me?

The knock at the door is hurried, light. Leslie refolds the drawing of the house, puts it in the gun box, and then quickly puts the box in one of the dresser drawers. She goes to the door. Phillip looks at her and his shoulders droop.

'Oh, Leslie,' he says, and opens his arms. She falls into his embrace and lets herself be held. 'I was so worried about you.'

'I'm afraid to ask,' she says. The words are muffled against his chest. 'Emma?'

'Nothing yet. We need to get you back there. Your running off like this is making it harder on everyone.'

She pushes herself away. 'What did you find on Gwen?'

'Nothing. I didn't look.'

'Why not?'

He tries to pull her close once more. She resists. 'You've already made up your mind about what you believe, Leslie. If I tried to prove you wrong, I'd start looking like the enemy.' He laces his fingers through hers and kisses her cheek. 'I am not the enemy.'

She turns her head so that her mouth meets his. She kisses him, trying to give impression to, to imprint on his skin the sorrows for which she has no words. She allows him to undress her, each layer coming away like a bandage from an old wound. He lays her down on the bed, runs his fingers across her collarbone, over her breasts, down her belly and pubic mound. He kisses her neck, her eyes, her shoulders. And then he is inside.

Splinters stabbed my cuticles and my fingers bled where my nails had ripped away. Yet, I had succeeded in sufficiently loosening the screws on the plate to budge it from the door. The knob was already off on my side and I'd pushed the spindle through to the other, taking a moment to dance in celebration at the sound of the heavy stone knob bouncing down the stairs. What a ruckus I was making! I'd then settled in to work on the tiny escutcheon screws, which was difficult as it was dark. I cursed myself for having bitten my nails so ferociously over the previous weeks. I was not patient with myself, and several times attempted to claw my way through the door, a silly exercise as it tore off what little nail I still possessed. Not to mention that such outbursts would only serve to justify Joshua and Isabel's actions. I resolved to think more clearly. Slowly, the little screws came undone.

At last the top edge of the plate came free. It swung, with a minor clatter, on the bottom screw. I hurried to quiet it. The house was asleep, and I feared the slightest sound would awaken my jailer. Carefully, I finished with the lower screw. In triumph, I lifted the iron plate to the heavens. Assured of blessings, I held the plate in my hand like a knife and began to hack at the wood between me and the lock.

Phillip takes the keys from her hand. 'Let me drive you back. There's an all-points bulletin out on your car, and the last thing you need right now is a run-in with the local yahoos.'

Leslie finishes tying her shoe. 'That's a good idea. I'm going to call Greg and tell him I'm on my way.'

Phillip nods.

'Um, I'd rather you not be here when I do. It would seem kind of – you know.'

'Of course,' he says. 'I'll wait for you outside.'

'Thanks.' She picks up the phone, but when the door closes, she puts it down. She reaches beneath the mattress and pulls out the gun. She faces herself in the mirror – 'now that I've been thoroughly frisked' – and tucks the revolver beneath her shirt into the waistband of her jeans at the small of her back.

Thirty

I HAD THE MORTISE lock in my hands, wrenching the heavy mechanism back and forth in the hole I had cut through the door. My hands were slick with blood and sweat, so it was difficult to maintain my grasp. My strength, however, seemed to increase multifold with each fraction of an inch I came closer to freedom. I have no idea how long I had been working, but time seemed to be arcing in a pendulum fashion, for as I had arrived just as dusk slipped into darkness, darkness was slipping now back into dusk. It may have been only a single night or several days. The hollow in my middle only made certain Isabel's intention to starve me into my grave. Was anyone other than Isabel aware I was in the house? Outrage fueled my physical being with a purity and grace I had never before experienced. It was with the image of Isabel's throat clenched in my bloodied hands that I at last pulled the mortise free. The door swung open, and I made my way, barefoot, down the dark of the stairs.

The night speeds past them. Leslie rests her head on the passenger window and watches the headlights tick off the white lines down the center of the road. Phillip drives, from the time they leave the motel, in silence. Leslie can sense him watching her.

'Just ask,' she finally says.

Phillip clears his throat. 'You truly believe Gwen faked her death?'

'Yep.'

'But why would she do that? Why take Emma?'

Leslie laughs and shifts to better feel the gun dig into the small of her back. 'Because she's, uh, insane?'

Phillip sighs. 'I'm not saying I don't believe you, Leslie. I'm just saying I don't understand.'

'That's more vindication than I've gotten elsewhere, so thanks, I guess. Gwen lost so much. There's only so much of pain you can take. Trust me, I know about that.'

He is quiet for a while. 'Maybe it's better if I don't take you straight to Five Mile. When I left, the press was starting to arrive, and you've gotta know what they're going to do with your theory. I'll take you to Diana's. You can call Greg, and he can meet you there.'

'Where will you be?'

'Where would you like me?'

'Don't leave me alone.' Leslie put her head on his shoulder, closed her eyes, and bit down on her tongue until she tasted blood.

Even in my distracted state, I sensed there was an intrinsic oddness to the house. At once orderly, yet confusing, the children's sleeping chambers were laid out like a warren, nests of little rooms. The first door I tried led to a playroom which held in its center a box-like closet. Therein, I found my youngest son, asleep on a spartan pallet similar to a monastery cell. My curiosity for the architecture abated immediately upon seeing the long-denied reality of my child. I dropped to my knees beside him, and in one greedy swoop gathered him to me, his rough blanket and pillow in my arms. He awoke in an instant and his sleepy eyes grew wide in horror and fear.

'Auntie Isabel!' he cried, 'Auntie Isabel!'

I wanted only to quiet him, to show him he was safe, safer than he'd been in ages. I held him close, tightly to my chest, whispering, 'It's Mother, angel, it's Mother,' until his screams and his fighting ceased.

Diana is startled to see them. 'Harry is on the way,' she says as if they've come to see her husband. Jack peeks out from behind her. Phillip apologizes and then explains that it will be easier on everyone if they can figure out a way to get Leslie up to Five Mile without having to make a big entrance. Diana relents and lets them in. She requests a few moments alone with Phillip, and taking Jack by the hand, leads Phillip toward the back of the house. Leslie hears them arguing in harsh, low voices. Jack begins to cry.

Phillip returns to the foyer alone. 'Diana is worried that by bringing you here, I've endangered her and Jack. You don't even need to say it, Leslie. I tried to explain that if Jack was the intended – if, as you say, Gwen, or whoever, wanted Jack – they had their opportunity earlier today.'

'She's not convinced, huh?'

Phillip shakes his head. 'You know how she is. She says we can call Greg, make whatever arrangements we need to, but then she wants us out.'

'You mean, she wants me out.'

'As far as I'm concerned it's the same thing.'

I rocked him, not a long time, until Isabel burst into the room. He was whimpering still when Isabel prised him from me. I didn't resist too forcefully, for I didn't want to hurt him in struggling with her. His little face turned toward mine, his eyes softly shut. He was sleeping again. My baby.

What have you done? Isabel shouted. What have you done?

I did not comprehend her question. I had done nothing but hold my child. Perhaps she misread the traces of blood on his flesh. I showed her my hands. It's mine, I said, it's mine. It is then she struck me. With my child in her arms, she kicked and punched and shrieked at me, landing blows upon my face until I, weakened from shock and hunger, collapsed before my quickly receding consciousness. The last thing I recall is Isabel standing over me, her panting breath, her incandescent smile.

Ask me what I am certain of and I will say little. The path of the sun, the turn of the tide, the coming and going of seasons are, all of them, amendable within my mind. Even more mutable is God and His compassion; His nature is fickle at best. What I hold as unchangeable and inalienable is a mere bit of knowing: when Isabel took him from my arms, my son was alive.

They are in Gwen's study. Leslie is lowering the blinds, shutting the curtains.

Phillip sits at Gwen's desk and studies the writing on the ceiling. 'I'm starting to believe Diana needs serious help,' he says.

'You'd better call Greg.' He lifts the telephone receiver and offers it to her.

'I don't want to call Greg,' says Leslie.

Phillip drops the receiver back in its cradle. 'Okay.'

'It's better if Gwen has no idea where I am.'

Phillip rests his chin in his hand and gazes at Leslie. 'When are you going to tell me what's going on? If – big if – you're right, why would Gwen want to pretend to be dead?'

Leslie sank into a chair. 'Has Harry Wellington ever mentioned a book or a scroll, something like that, he hoped to find up at Five Mile?'

Phillip made a sound of disgust. 'Not that *Analecta* shit again.'

'So, you've heard of it.'

'Christ, yeah. It's what? – directions on how to build your own personal Allah out of stuff you may already have at home? Let me give you a basic truism, Les: never sign on as sole counsel for any single family. They tell you things they wouldn't dare tell their shrinks.'

'Gwen Garrett wrote her doctorate on the *Analecta*.'

'And the connection between Gwen, the book, and Emma would be?'

'Me.'

He stands. 'Leslie, we need to get you back up that hill. I don't want to tell you some of the theorizing going on up there. Forgive me for saying this out loud, but if they find Emma and anything has happened to her – '

'Emma is safe,' Leslie says. 'It's not Emma she wants.'

'Then what's the point of taking your daughter?'

'Gwen wants me to do something. Emma's her guarantee.'

'What does she want you to do?'

'Don't know yet. It doesn't matter. Gwen has my daughter. I'll do anything I'm asked.'

Thirty-one

I AWOKE IN SEMIDARKNESS on my cot in the tower room, my mind an aching whorl of images as if from a shattered nightmare. When that ache seemed to center itself in my hands, I raised them before my face to see the flaking brown streaks of dried blood. I sat up, certain now of my reality, beyond the hope of attributing any of my pain to a bad dream. My dress and stockings had been removed; I was clothed only in my undergarments. The door to the tower was shut. I, much to my abhorrence to confess, reacted to this sight with an unrelieved rage.

Even in the midst of my raving, the throwing of my furniture, the overturning of my bed, a small part of me retained composure enough to know such behavior would only prolong my banishment. For all the common sense of this pronouncement, the larger part of me did not care. I hefted the washstand and swung it against the window glass, shattering the panes and breaking out the mullions.

I hefted the stand again and this time swung it with all my might against the door, which bounced open. The sight of the freely swinging door chilled my rage. Whoever returned me here had neglected to barricade me in – or so she wanted me to surmise. Isabel would not have made such an oversight. It could only mean she wanted me to venture down into the lower levels where I might find what? My sweet sister-in-law awaiting my arrival with an unsheathed blade? She would, after all, only be protecting the children from their madwoman mother.

I returned the washstand to its place and then went to sit, quieted and calm, on my cot. Mad I might be, but I was clever and growing more clever with each hour. Like those hot-house rarities of fly-traps or carnivorous orchids, I would bide my time until she mistook my patience for benign passivity.

'I finally got Jack to sleep.' Diana shambles into the study. She is swirling a full wineglass, and when she drops into the chair beside Leslie, a large portion slops over the side. 'Shit,' she says, and laughs, but makes no attempt to clean up the spill. 'You know, Leslie, I don't want to sound unsympathetic, but when I talked to Harry, God, was he pissed at your husband.'

'Oh yeah?'

'Yeah, apparently Greg's been going at Harry's precious house with a crowbar looking for your little girl.'

'There's no accounting for a guy's priorities, huh?' says Leslie.

'Diana – ' Phillip begins, but Leslie interrupts.

'You've been afraid it was supposed to be you from the beginning, haven't you?'

'I don't have any idea what you're talking about.'

'When the house was finished, or rather the additions, and it was time to test the fucker, you were terrified they'd ask you to choose between yourself and Jack. That's why you can't let him out of our sight.'

'Okay, Leslie.' Phillip comes and crouches beside her. 'I think it's time to stop.'

Leslie looks at Phillip. 'When Harry gets up to Five Mile, he's going to clear the building.'

'That would be my guess. He'll want to assess the damage. But a few holes in the walls aren't going to matter to him.'

'Because it's not the walls, the angles. It's in the length and turn of each hallway, or how each element of the addition relates to the absolute symmetry of the main house.'

Phillip sits back on his heels. 'The lady has done her homework.'

'And the tower, that tower room is what? The engine?'

'Nope,' says Diana, as she runs her finger along the rim of the wineglass and, in doing so, generates a low-pitched hum. 'It's more like the focal point of an array of lenses. That's what Harry says. When the *Analecta* thing is, like, activated, the power will be located there. But Gwen said that you can only turn it on by turning everything else off.' Diana spills more wine and laughs again.

Phillip, his voice uncertain, says, 'I don't know anything about lenses; what are you talking about, Diana?'

'Gwen didn't tell the Wellingtons everything she knew about the *Analecta*, did she?'

'Secrets.' Diana puts her finger to her lips. 'Only an idiot gives away all their secrets. That's also what Harry says. The Wellingtons didn't tell Gwen everything, either.'

Leslie closes her eyes and says, 'Okay, Phillip. Let's get this over with.'

The footsteps on the stairwell echoed like the sounding of an old bell. Slow and heavy, they climbed toward my room. I knew it was Joshua. Perhaps he had learned of my mistreatment and was coming to rescue me. That was wishful on my part, I already sensed as much, but as those solemn footsteps grew closer, I indulged the fantasy. Most likely, he was coming to scold, to lecture me on my churlishness and threaten, as he had before, to have me committed to one of those horried asylums. By the time he was on the last few steps, I knew I could not bear to look at him, or have him look at me, so I fixed my attention out my window, at the pretty flashes of light flickering on the points of broken glass.

I heard, distinctly, the door creak open. Still, I did not turn to greet him. His breath was labored and thick, as though he had been weeping. My Joshua weep? Was it for me? Had he at long last found some fragment of pity for me? My own eyes welled as I turned to face him. The sight that met me dissolved what ever solid bit of me remained. I was a thing made of tears.

Joshua carried our son, our youngest, the one to whom I'd revealed myself earlier that hateful night. The little form draped across his father's arms, flaccid, bulky like a bolt of wet flannel. I went to him. The eyelids had gone a deep purple against the pale blue of his cold body. When I moved to lay my hand on his cheek, Joshua clutched him away from me. Without speaking, he turned and went down the stairs, the slow echo of his footfall fading as he descended.

'You should have come to me earlier,' says Phillip, as he makes the turn that will take them to the lakeshore road and Five Mile Hill. 'Really, Leslie. The Wellingtons take this shit seriously.'

'You don't say.' She is looking at the moon. It's a couple days past full, but still large and bright. 'Tell me something I don't know.'

'All right. How about this? By the time we get up to the house, Harry will be evoking trespassing laws, and Yancy will be backing him up. They've been searching that place for hours. It doesn't mean they're going to stop searching, but without probable cause, Harry has every right to throw them out. So if, as you believe, Gwen has Emma, if she's up there, then none of us are going to be able to do a thing about it.'

'I'll be going in.'

Phillip shifts gears and steers around the bend. 'I don't want to be unkind, but if you insist on making a big scene about your Gwen theory, you're going to find yourself sedated in the psych ward at Rutherford General.'

Leslie laughs. 'Before this is over, I bet I look a lot worse than crazy.' She reaches behind her, pulls the gun, and shovels the point into Phillip's temple. 'Now, you are going to take me to my daughter.'

'Leslie? What the – '

'Shut up, Phillip.'

'Okay. Okay. Leslie, darling, you're really upset. I'm just – '

'I know what you are, Phillip. Shut up and drive.'

Sound travels strangely in this house; it is pulled upward, into the tower. All that afternoon Five Mile was full of terrible sounds, terrible voices: the voices of children crying in disbelief upon learning of their brother's death, the voices of Isabel and Joshua shouting in argument, my voice, which had somehow detached itself from my throat and was speaking to me from outside my head. *You know what you must do*, it instructed, *you know what you must do*.

From what I was able to discern of it, the subject of Isabel and Joshua's contention was whether or not I should be allowed to attend the funeral. Joshua was of the loud opinion that should I not be in attendance, suspicions about town would only increase. Isabel's response, even louder, was that she owned the larger portion of Wellington and could not have cared less for the town's opinion than she did for the flea bites on their hounds.

After much argument along this track, Joshua suddenly softened, or his voice did, and he offered a different point. Perhaps the ordeal of services and public scrutiny might prove too much for me? My resolve nearly melted at that small concession to pity, until I heard Isabel's agreement. Yes, said Isabel, such might prove too much and therefore an aid to their cause.

You know what you must do.

Nights passed. I lost count of them. Rain came in through the window, and it was cold. One morning, Isabel arrived and said it was time for the funeral. I did not resist as she worked to dress me. So much weight had fallen from my flesh that I did not fear her noticing the small swell below my waist. The black gown she brought me was mine, but it hung on my frame like so much drapery. At that thought, I asked if I might have some cloth to cover my broken window. Isabel, who was brushing my hair, said that perhaps, in a day or two, they would have someone come repair the glass. Still, it would serve me well to live with the weather as a reminder to take better care of my things.

I said yes, Isabel, I know what I must do.

They are still a mile away from the main gate.

'Stop here,' Leslie says.

He stops the car. 'Please talk to me, Leslie.'

'Get out. This side. We're going for a little walk in the woods.'

He struggles and stumbles his way out the passenger side, never taking his eyes off her. 'I thought you trusted me.'

'It's all right, Phillip, you can think I'm crazy. You won't be alone.' She pushes the gun into his ribs. 'You lead.'

'This isn't what you want to do,' he says, as he jumps the rain ditch.

'Hell no, it isn't.' She stays right with him.

'Think, Leslie. What are you going to do when we get up to the house? There's a lot of armed officers just roaming around waiting to be heroes. The press is up there. Cameras and shit all over the place. Do you want Greg to see you like this? Molly?'

'You're good' – She jabs the gun hard against his bones – 'but believe me, this is exactly what Greg and Molly are expecting to see.'

They start up the hill. The woods are milky blue dim in the

moonlight. Above, breaking through the trees, is the glow coming from the lights around Five Mile. Phillip stops and tries to turn around. 'We're going to get nowhere near the house, Leslie.'

'Then you die here.' She cocks the hammer.

'All right. Damn it. All right. There's another way into Five Mile.'

'You know, I thought there might be.'

Thirty-two

'IT'S NOT ON ANY of the blueprints,' Phillip says as he leads her further into the woods, but away from the house. 'Only the family knows about it.'

'And you. And Gwen.'

'Over here,' he says, pointing.

From that direction, Leslie hears water, a hollow drumming. Quickly, they come upon an outcropping of stone rising like a crooked finger out of the earth. They move around to the side where the waterfall sound grows louder. The moonlight is brighter here on the rock and she can see the many overlapping works of spray-painted graffiti. Leslie follows Phillip to a slender opening of equal height and breadth.

'The local kids play back here,' he says, 'even though they know they're not supposed to.' He wrestles his arm up into the crevice, swears under his breath. 'Sooner or later, someone's going to – got it,' he says. A few feet from where Leslie stands, a square of earth drops away. 'Ta-fucking-da,' he says.

She can make out the shape of a ladder braced against the top of the opening. 'Another one of Joshua's improvements?' Leslie asks, using the gun to motion Phillip toward the ladder.

'No, this was put in during the Wellingtons' bootlegging days,' he says, but doesn't move. 'Leslie, as I see it, we've got a problem here.'

'Oh yeah?'

'If I go down first, how do you know I won't take off without you? And if you go down first, how do you know – '

'That you haven't tricked me into a dead end? Because one way or the other, you've got to get me into that tower. That's your job, right? That's what we've always been about.'

He doesn't answer. He just shakes his head and starts down the ladder. Leslie keeps the gun trained on the downward slope of the rungs. She hears his feet thud against the bottom. She falls on her knees, steadying her finger on the trigger, ready to empty all six chambers into the place he should be, when the opening and the tunnel beyond it suddenly glow with soft yellow light. Phillip appears in the opening.

'You can put away the gun. If getting you into that tower will help you trust me again, then I'll take you to the goddamn tower.'

'I have never trusted you, Phillip,' Leslie says as she descends.

I recall little of my son's funeral. My mind was adrift, caught in the undertow of grief. I do remember an abundance of flowers, most brought in from the surrounding fields. Many dozens of columbines and daisies, woven into a blanket of greenery which covered his tiny coffin. I remember being led to the front of the chapel, Joshua on one arm and Isabel on the other. I felt oddly like a bride again in a terrible parody of my past. Bedecked head to foot in black, a translucent veil of black netting shielding my face from the wanton stares of those who know this night will usher me beyond innocence. And I, welcoming or fearful of such knowledge, had resigned all option to oppose. I had betrothed my destiny to another.

I recall candles about the altar, burning sharp, like pricks of moonlight on the eyes of a fleeing beast. The reverend, I don't remember his name, spoke like a sleepwalker, his eyes half-closed, his voice a drone, too soft and indistinct to compete with the eloquent mutineer who sought to commandeer my hapless thoughts.

You know what you must do.

Beside me, Isabel wept, or made weeping noises, I can't be certain. I was aware only of the handkerchief in her hand and its steady, flowing pace up and down from her lap to her eyes. Joshua held my arm throughout as though I, like an unbroken filly, might bolt my stall and in doing so kick in his skull with an errant hoof. He knew me too well. I had made the mistake of allowing him that knowledge.

The tunnel is earthen, cut through the hillside and supported by rough-hewn beams. A series of bare-bulb electrical lights connected by exposed cord runs down the low ceiling.

Phillip starts off down the tunnel as if he is no longer concerned with how Leslie might respond. 'The additions weren't Joshua's idea; they were Isabel's,' he says. 'After Eleanor went and screwed up all their perfectly set plans, there was no choice but to wait.'

'Wait for what?' Leslie walks behind with the gun raised and aimed.

He looks over his shoulder.

'For me? What is so fucking special about me?'

'With respect to the Wellingtons and this place? I have no idea. I have no idea what was so special about Eleanor, except the *Analecta* supposedly specifies her, ah, type.'

'What type?'

'The *Analecta* is supposedly a long string of code. DNA is a long string of code. Matching up one to the other, I guess, allows some sort of deciphering. A code key. That's Harry's favorite explanation.'

'Enough *Analecta*. Where's Gwen?'

Phillip stops. 'She's dead, Leslie.'

'Yeah, and I guess you would know as you were the one who took possession of her body.'

'What?'

'I saw the forms in Delores's office. I saw your signature on the release.'

'Leslie, darling, I have no idea what you are talking about.'

'Don't lie to me. Just keep moving.' She prods him forward with the gun.

They walk until they reach what looks to be a solid wall. Phillip reaches up, and yanking on a short rope suspended from the ceiling, pulls down a folding staircase. 'This takes us under the house,' he says, as he begins to climb.

Leslie steps up close behind him. She raises the gun and slams the butt of it into the back of his head. He falls to the side, landing in a heap at the foot of the staircase. 'Sorry, darling,' she says, as she continues up the stairs.

We walked behind the coffin, the sun bright on the flowers, bright on the wood. Everything was so bright, the cloudless blue horizon, the green of the fields, grasshoppers springing from the grasses like sparks. It was an arrogantly sumptuous day. Even when we entered the shaded drive to Isabel's house, the shadows offered no refuge from the brightness as millions of minor suns swirled and collided on the forest floor.

We buried my son in a small, gated yard behind the house. It was, Isabel said, a family grave site, but I saw only the single stone cross with my child's name engraved upon it. I did not recall noticing the gated yard before, which struck me, even then, as impossible, for when I looked back and away as they lowered my baby into his grave, I saw the window of the room in which I'd been caged.

When I looked back they were shoveling earth into the void, and I had a vision. The ground around me trembled and broke as a half-dozen more stone crosses sprouted at my feet, each cross bearing the name of another child.

I believe then I fainted, or fell into some sort of stupor, for my next memory was that of once more climbing the tower stairs, rather Joshua's climbing and my floating along beside him. He dropped me, not unkindly, upon my cot, and left me. The door had been repaired and the sound of the lock sliding home was mighty indeed. The thought of the lock did not trouble me, for I did not intend to leave this room again. I understood now that should I make an overture toward any of the children, Isabel would punish me by making certain that child would be removed from me by death.

I did not undress. I simply sat at my window and waited for night. I knew what I must do. How could I go on in this world when my very being was a threat to those I held most dear? And yet, how could I leave when leaving meant abandoning them to the creature that called herself my sister?

Leslie hauls up the staircase, making certain the rope pull is caught on her side. She unknots it quickly and then just as quickly ties the hinges on the folding mechanism, jamming it shut. Satisfied Phillip will not be able to follow her, she looks around. She is in another tunnel space. The walls here are rough natural stone mortared together at irregular intervals. Leslie realizes she is in the cellar of Five Mile House, under the additions.

The only light is what thin beams seep through the joists and floorboards above her. The strange spice aroma is stronger here than it was in the halls above. It reminds her of the clove-studded oranges her mother hung in closets, an oriental citrus smell, only denser and oily.

'What is that?' Leslie asks aloud, trying to place it.

'Preservative,' says a voice further ahead. 'Isabel's special blend. She found the recipe in a book about mummification.'

Leslie moves forward, steadying the gun. 'Gwen?'

A slight stirring at the end of the tunnel draws her attention. A large round of bright light hits her in the face, blinding her. A voice calls out quietly, 'Yes, Leslie, it's me.'

Leslie steadies her aim by gripping her right wrist in her left hand. 'I want Emma.'

'I know you do,' answers Gwen without moving.

Leslie pulls back the hammer on the revolver and sprints straight into the light.

Thirty-three

I SAT BY THE window, the night wind shearing cold through the broken glass. There was a sound in the stairwell, the bolt sliding back. Isabel came into the room. I know this not because I saw her – my eyes were fixed on a particular point of starless dark – but because of her voice as she spoke my name. She brought a lamp for me, she said, and some food. I must eat, she insisted, if I were ever to get well. She asked if I might like a change of clothing, or perhaps even a bath. I did not answer. She came to stand beside me and took my head in her hands, turning my face to meet hers. She bent low. If I required anything at all, I must not hesitate to seek her out, she said softly. Isabel then kissed me, but not with a sisterly kindness. She forced her mouth against mine, for only a moment, and then she smiled. You must, she whispered, forgive me. And then she was gone.

I awoke, slumped against the window frame, convinced at first that the scene I've just described was from a dream until I wakened sufficiently to notice the lamp glowing on the washstand. The supper tray was on my cot. I lifted each of the silver domes covering the plates. There was squab and potatoes and a bread pudding, all now cold. How long had I slept?

I reconsidered Isabel's visit, the invitation to seek her out. I recalled her leaving, but not the sound of the door locking after her. I understood, before I even attempted it, that it would open, that Isabel's solicitude was a perverted demand for a final confrontation. I took up the lamp and went to the door. Had I been less vain, less consumed by a desire for vengeance, I would have lifted that lamp and smashed it before me, immolating myself and this horrible house. The children might have escaped.

That is hindsight. At that moment, in the life I was given, I believed I had no choices. I knew what I must do.

As fast as Leslie runs, the light continues to recede before her, turning corners, until at last the tunnel spills into an open space lit by battery-run lanterns. Gwen, her white-blond hair hanging in a tangle, is laughing. She is wearing a loose and dirty blue maternity dress with large pockets on the skirt. She drops the flashlight into a pocket and leans against one of the timber posts that support the ceiling; she is trying to regain her breath.

'Damn,' she says between gasps. 'I haven't run like that since I was a kid.'

Leslie walks up to Gwen and puts the muzzle of the gun to the woman's sweat-dripping forehead. 'Emma.'

'She's sleeping. You know I wouldn't hurt her.'

'Emma. Now.'

'Over there.' Gwen points across the cellar floor. The packed earth is strewn with many large sheets of paper. In a dim corner, there is a makeshift camp. Leslie forgets Gwen. She walks slowly to the tumble of blankets and sleeping bags where quickly, mercifully, her eyes fall on Emma's sleep-balled figure.

'You can't keep that child covered to save her life.' Gwen laughs. 'Sorry. Poor choice of words.'

Leslie falls on her knees. Don't frighten her, she instructs herself sternly. 'Hey, Em?' She shakes the little shoulders softly. 'Hey, Em? Wake up, sweetie. It's Mommy. It's time to go home.' But Emma won't wake, won't even shift. Leslie lays her hand on Emma's backbone and nearly implodes with relief to feel its gentle rise and fall. She recovers her daughter for warmth. Then Leslie stands and walks back to Gwen. Gwen smiles. Leslie locks both hands around the gun grip and swings all her fury into Gwen's grinning jaw.

Gwen hits the ground with a thud and a cry more of surprise than pain. In an instant, Leslie is on top of her, the gun at Gwen's throat. 'What did you give her? What the hell did you give her?'

Five Mile was quiet. It was the quiet of emptiness more than the quiet of sleep. Still, I knew Isabel was about, awaiting me. I reached the second level. The doors were shut against intrusion, but surely I was no intruder.

I went into the first room, where my eldest daughter lay in deep slumber. I took it as an omen. It had been my hope to find the older children first, for I feared they would struggle and I felt my strength would be too taxed to leave them for late in the work. I sat beside her for a time, watching her dear face, so untroubled. I held no doubts about the necessity or propriety of my task; a short life happily lived is far better than what I was certain was fated to them in Isabel's care. When my farewells were completed, I kissed her eyes, and her forehead. I begged the Lord not to hold her mother's failings against her. Then I pulled the pillow from beneath her head and with the same laborious determination required to push her from my womb, I held the pillow over her beautiful face until her breathing stopped. I knew she was at peace.

She did not fight me, not at all.

Gwen turns her head and spits out a large amount of blood. 'She's all right, Leslie.'

'What did you give her?'

'A bit of syrup to help her sleep. Christ, Leslie, the child is terrified.'

'If you don't tell me this fucking instant –'

'I don't understand why you're so angry. I thought we were on the same path, that we wanted the same thing. We do want the same thing, an end to all these pathetic illusions.'

'All I want is to get my daughter to a doctor. Gwen, it's Emma. She's a little girl.'

'I know why you're worried. It's not the same preparation I used to make my exit. What Emma took doesn't require an antidote. Really, she's all right. I just needed to get you here.'

Leslie sits back on her heels. 'And you needed me to look crazy, too?'

Gwen coughs and spits more blood. 'I'm trying to prove it's all a bunch of crap, Leslie. There's only one way to do that, to prove it absolutely.'

'You're going to follow it all the way through, right? You think you're going to bring the *Analecta* to its grand finale. That's the only way to disprove it?'

'Well, what good is it to stand in the streets and shout that the emperor has no clothes, if the narcissistic bastard never goes public?'

'And when it's over, Phillip Hogarth spirits you out of here like he did at Mark Humphrey's funeral parlor?'

'That was Joe. He's waiting for me with the' – Gwen reaches up and pulls bloodied hair away from her mouth – ' oh, but you mean . . . Delores's office. Sorry, but I needed you to come alone. I really didn't enjoy doing that to you. Phillip seemed to make you – well, happy isn't the word – oh don't scrunch your face at me, Leslie Stone. Wellington is a teeny-tiny little town. Everybody knows. Don't be embarrassed. In the long run, it will help explain things.'

Leslie is thinking of Phillip lying unconscious. She realizes her attention has drifted and she refocuses, pushing the gun deeper into Gwen's flesh. 'It's over.' Leslie gets up on one knee, then the other, raises herself to standing, Gwen's head at her feet. 'Get up. You're going to lead us out of here.'

'But don't you want to see it?' Gwen says, lifting her chin to look at Leslie upside down. 'The ever-loving *Analecta Seriatus*?' Gwen raises a finger and points toward the ceiling.

'I'm not going in that house except to get out of here.'

'Don't have to go anywhere. Just look up.' She reaches for the flashlight in her pocket and then tosses it toward Leslie. 'Look.'

Leslie keeps the gun on Gwen and bends forward, picking up the light in her left hand. She trains the beam upward and glances at what it might have hit. She sees the underside of the floorboards, thick, red mahogany planks.

'I see nothing.'

'Of course you can't just see it. They were smarter than that. Press your hand against the wood.'

She hesitates and then stretches up on her toes. She pushes her fingertips into the wood and then withdraws them. They feel oily and carry the citrus-clove aroma.

'Now, quick,' says Gwen. 'Look at your skin.'

Leslie shines the flashlight on herself. Embossed on her flesh are several small numerals, some whole and some in part, none more than an eighth of an inch in size. She turns the light upward, running it over the planks, but looks down at Gwen. 'It's like this throughout the additions?'

Gwen shifts up on her elbow. 'I figured it out when I was

doing an autowrite session for Diana. It must have been in my unconscious for a long time, but finally just popped out. That's why Isabel called them "the additions." Get it?'

'Harry will be thrilled. Let's go tell him.'

'Do you know what that is up there?'

'Gwen, I don't want to know. I just want to take my daughter home. Get up.'

Gwen climbs to her feet. 'You are really disappointing me, Leslie. It's pi. You know, three-point-one-four-one-five-nine et cetera, et cetera, ad infinitum. That's what the main part of the *Analecta* is – it's the sequence of digits in pi. It's never been completed. It is supposedly infinite.'

'I don't care.' Leslie keeps the gun on Gwen and eases her way back toward Emma.

'How can you not care?' Gwen groans with frustration. 'We're talking about the secret of circles, the path to perfection, eternity defined. Geometry is everything, Leslie. Solve pi to its final digit and you have ultimate reality. Or so the believers would tell you.'

'Listen to me, Gwen. I don't care about your fucking numbers.'

'Not just any fucking number: the last fucking number. The *Analecta* tells us how to arrive at the last digit. Come to the tower with me, Leslie. Let's find out what's really real.'

'I'm going to pick up my daughter now, and you are going to lead us out of here.'

Gwen bites her lip. 'If you come to the tower with me, I'll give you a present.'

'I don't want anything from you.' Leslie stoops and – weapon never wavering from Gwen – hauls Emma into her arms.

'You may change your mind,' says Gwen. 'I've found your answers, Leslie. I have the pictures.'

Emma is very heavy, dead weight against Leslie's shoulder. 'What pictures?'

'From the hotel room, remember? I have the pictures of Amy.'

Their lives gave way to my will like stalks of spring wheat before a scythe. It was so quiet. As each one passed, I felt his or her being reabsorbed into mine. I was not stealing, only reclaiming what I had sent forth into a world that was not safe. This I believe they knew, for not one of them fought my regathering. It was with true rejoicing I lowered the pillow on the last little face, for it was done. They were mine once more. What happened now was unimportant. I had saved my children from Isabel. The victory was mine.

I closed the door on the last room. With the same stealth I had descended, I made my way back to my tower. The dull gray of first light was falling through the broken glass. I went to replace the lamp on the washstand but found it already occupied by a large amber bottle. Before the bottle, in a precise row, lay six silver spoons. The bowls of the spoons were sticky and hazed with residue. The bottle was unmarked. I pulled the cork and was met by an ever so slight aroma of bitter almond. I didn't understand. It was then I realized I was not alone. Isabel stood in the far corner, wringing her hands and watching me with bright, hungry animal eyes.

'I was there,' said Isabel. 'I was there first.'

They are in another tunnel, one that slants upward at a sharp degree. Gwen leads with the flashlight. Leslie follows close behind with Emma sleeping in her arms. The gun is readied, aimed at the base of Gwen's skull.

Gwen is playing tour guide, enthusiastically recounting the bootlegging days when these tunnels were full of whiskey barrels smuggled out of Canada, all the while the greatest treasure in history languished directly above their heads. Leslie hardly hears her. She listens to Emma's deep, slow breathing and tells herself that once the doorway is in sight, photographs or not, she will get her daughter to safety. Leslie repeats this promise over and over. Each time she says it, it sounds more like a lie.

Gwen is now explaining that Joshua and Isabel had been introduced to the *Analecta* quite young when they were sheltered for a month in the home of the newly arrived Della Rosa Benevista. Gwen is certain that Leslie must have read about the brother and sister's misadventure. It was Della Rosa who told them the stories, not realizing that Isabel's little head was a mite too predisposed to delusional obsession.

'It was all in place, but Eleanor broke with the very precise instructions of the *Analecta*. With their linchpin gone, they had to find a means of saving their work until the cycle began again. That's when Isabel came up with the idea for the additions,' said

Gwen, swinging the light over the structure above them. 'Once the boards were in, she inscribed the numerals, burnt them in using darning needles and a candle. She seared off her fingerprints in the process. She coated it all with her ancient Egyptian mummy juice. It took the rest of her life. Isabel died down here. They didn't find her for a couple weeks, but by then she'd soaked up so much of the preservative – well, she looked quite good.'

They reach a swinging panel. Gwen holds it open, and they pass through into the central hall of the main house. 'Could it get anymore Gothic than that?' She turns off the flashlight.

Leslie looks first to the front of the house and then the rear. Lights glare through the plastic coverings. Voices outside are clear and close. 'All right, Gwen. That way. Get your hands in the air. You're walking out first.'

'Don't you want to see the photographs?'

'You can give them to me outside.'

'Grant me a bit of foresight here. I don't have them with me. They're in the tower. You'll have to come all the way to the top to get what you want.'

'If the photographs even exist.'

'Well, then, Leslie dear, since you believe in choices . . .'

'Not here I don't,' says Leslie, hugging Emma tighter. The child stirs. Leslie stops. 'Emma?' Leslie shakes her softly. 'Em? Can you hear me?'

Emma yawns. Her eyelids quiver an instant and then open. The first thing her daughter sees is the gun.

'Mommy?' Emma says, as her eyes close once more.

'Wake up, Em. Stay awake.' Leslie lowers the gun. She is distracted just enough for Gwen to wrench the revolver from her hand.

Isabel grinned expectantly, as though I were winding the crank on a jack-in-the-box and she, she alone, knew on which note it would pop. I looked again at the spoons. My interior self began to shiver with a cold more intense than any winter I had known. The baby in my womb kicked hard in complaint. Wrong. Something was very wrong. The baby kicked again, fighting in primal conflict with my disregard. Fighting. None of them had fought, not one of them, not for a single breath.

Isabel must have seen the realization break on my face, because she clapped her hands over her mouth to suppress her delight.

The climb is hard. Round and round the stairs. Emma is heavy. Gwen behind them is chatting pleasantly, the gun pressed between Leslie's shoulders. Leslie kisses her sleeping daughter. She can barely breathe for the shame she feels. She should have taken Emma and run. She is as certain of this as she is that Gwen has lied to her. How could Gwen have found those photographs? I'm sorry, she says to Emma. I'm so sorry.

Isabel came out of the shadows. They were already gone, she said. They were gone before I brought your dinner.

I had accomplished nothing. Isabel had raped all the meaning from my last act of free will. She approached me without fear, for she sensed that I was, at last, no more than an extension of herself, that I would do as she wished, bend as obediently as her finger.

'Isabel killed Eleanor's kids, didn't she?' says Leslie on the tower stairs.

Gwen clucks her tongue in thought. 'I don't think Isabel wanted to kill the children; it was that Eleanor was so unyielding. The *Analecta* says that the final sacrifice has to be pure. Eleanor had to offer her life in compensation, and she had to want to do it. Isabel thought the massacre she'd orchestrated at Della Rosa's would be enough, but obviously it wasn't. When Isabel saw how Eleanor reacted to Samuel's contracting TB, well, that was all she needed.'

Poor Eleanor, Isabel said as she took me by the hand and led me to the window. Poor Eleanor. We stood there for a while, Isabel holding my hand. She laid her head on my shoulder and said, quite sadly, that there was no other way now. The children, she said, will be waiting for me, and we would all be together. Happy.

'I won't do it,' says Leslie, turning back to stare at Gwen. 'Whatever you're thinking, I won't do it.'

'Your choice,' says Gwen, as she uses the tip of the gun barrel to play with Emma's curls. Leslie knocks the gun away.

Gwen shakes her head. 'Don't you understand? I'd have to kill you both. I can just disappear. To the rest of the world I'm already dead. But before I go, I'd have to leave a story that makes sense. Human beings need things to make sense. I'd have to make it look as though you killed your daughter.'

She showed me where to step up onto the sill, allowing me to support my weight against her for balance. I would be guilty of a falsehood if I did not confess the sense of liberation I felt there on the ledge. The dawn air was so clear, so sharp against my skin and in my lungs that I was immediately charged with an energy I had not known in months.

Leslie says nothing more. Her energy now must go only toward finding a path of escape for herself and Emma. She rounds the final landing and halts. There, in front of the door, stands Amy. Her hair is in pigtails and pink ribbons that match her pink party dress. A scab mars the girl's left knee and her white socks are folded uneven at her ankles. Her black party shoes glimmer in the flashlight. She smiles. Her front teeth are missing. 'Is that him?' she asks brightly. 'Is he here?'

Isabel still held my hand. She was consoling me in my plight, reminding me how in but a few short seconds I would be forever at peace with my babies. Yes, I thought. Yes, it is only peace I want, an end to this confusion, this interminable stumbling of my mind. Peace.

And then the baby kicked.

I looked down; it was as if the rocks rose up, clutching for my child, greedy fingers full of pain. No. I turned, I tried to turn back. No, I said, but I cannot recall saying it aloud. No. I grabbed at Isabel's hands, but it was of little use, for she had pushed me over the ledge of the sill, and I was left nothing to stop my fall.

There was a large sound, like that of lightning striking close by, and then nothing. And then a darkness that faded gradually to reveal that I was back in the tower. I watched Isabel leave the tower room. I heard her scream in rage all the way down the stair. I have waited here for years. She never once returned to my prison.

Thirty-four

THAT IS MY STORY. I am appalled. I am guilty of the most heinous of crimes. I willed harm upon my children. Isabel's part does not abrogate my guilt; intent is of consequence. Yet, acknowledgment and condemnation are in themselves inadequate. Surely, there is more to my history than this awful sequence of awful events. It is, finally, not truth I seek but meaning. If what I knew would not save me, then perhaps I might save Leslie. It was with this desire to give meaning to my cursed existence that I allowed Leslie to open the tower door. I gathered myself. I waited for them inside and behind the shadows.

'Oh, don't be stubborn,' says Gwen, as she gives Leslie a nudge with the gun. 'It's almost done.'

Leslie forces herself to take the next step and Amy vanishes. They reach the door, and Gwen has Leslie open it, a difficult thing to do with Emma in her arms.

The walls and roof are still braced by a slanting phalanx of two-by-fours. The plastic curtaining makes a translucent filter for the red, blue, and yellow lights of the emergency vehicles below. The room is awash in swirling colors. Leslie can hear Yancy Galleghar down below. He is bellowing instructions over a fainter hum of voices and radios.

'All right,' says Leslie. 'I'm in the tower.'

Gwen reaches in the pocket of her dress. 'I kept it with me just in case we didn't get this far.' She winks at Leslie and pulls a brown paper envelope from her pocket.

Leslie's hands begin to tremble as she takes the envelope from Gwen. 'Shine the light over here.' Gwen obliges by directing the flashlight's beam parallel to the gun. Leslie hefts Emma higher on her shoulder and raises the envelope. She can see rectangular shapes silhouetted against the paper. 'How did you get these?'

'When I went away, after I lost the baby, I needed a project. I'm the research maven of the western world, Leslie. I haven't looked at those; what I saw in the process of locating them was enough for an entire lifetime.'

'I've seen enough, too.' Leslie throws the envelope at Gwen's feet. 'Now let's go home.'

'I'm afraid you have an appointment with larger concerns – unless, of course, you want Molly and Greg to have to spend the rest of their lives thinking you – '

'Gwen, you've suffered a terrible, terrible loss. The grief is making it hard for you to think clearly. We need to get you down from here.'

'We need to get to the truth. That's all.'

'The truth? Nothing's going to happen up here. There's the truth.'

Gwen shrugs. 'You're probably right. Still, we can only hypothesize that the outcome will be null. That's the great fail-safe of science, Leslie: we can't say we know anything until we perform the experiment.'

'The experiment was performed. Eleanor jumped. Nothing happened.' Emma shifts and coughs. Her skin feels clammy against Leslie's cheek.

'We don't know if the variables were under proper control,' Gwen says. 'We don't know if maybe Isabel – oh, how did you put it that night? – we don't know if Isabel physically *helped* Eleanor out the window. Let's face it, Isabel was probably the most uncontrollable variable in the bunch. Then again, maybe there was something about Eleanor that made her an invalid sacrifice.'

'Invalid?' Leslie feels herself blinking, as if her eyelids are mechanical.

'The *Analecta* is all math. If it isn't done absolutely right, it's wrong.'

'You're a fraud. You know that, Gwen? You're a liar and a fake,' Leslie says, stalling for time, time to think, time to remember how to think. 'You're not trying to disprove anything. You want something to happen. I step out that window and – what? The stars rearrange themselves into a giant number eight? God's going to do cartwheels for you? That's what you're truly hoping, isn't it? You, more than anyone, need there to be something, someone you can hold responsible for what you've had to go through.'

Gwen smiles, her old, sad smile. 'No, Leslie. Gods are not what I hope for. You could not begin to imagine what it is I truly hope.'

Leslie tries to focus on the emergency lights pirouetting on the plastic. She still hears Yancy shouting. Think. 'So, I guess that makes you Isabel, huh?'

Gwen starts. 'I am nothing like Isabel.'

'You don't look like her. But if I'm Eleanor and you want me out that window, you are Isabel.'

It is I who am now awakened to the truth. All these years I have watched, I have waited for the wheel to turn back round to me and gain my chance to reveal the full scale of Five Mile's treachery. What has arrived, at last, is not absolution. Leslie has not been sent for my redemption. She has brought Isabel to me. Isabel has returned to the tower.

'All right, I concede I am taking a rather Isabel-like stance. I won't push you, however. You have your choices. Simply understand that the only way Emma leaves here alive is if you go out that window.'

'That's not a choice.'

'What have I been trying to tell you?'

Leslie presses Emma tightly to her own body. The child's breath is shallow and hot against Leslie's neck. Leslie closes her eyes and prays that she is not choosing wrong. 'I'll do it on one condition. I want everyone down there to see that Emma is alive, so that if anything happens to her at least Greg and Molly will know it wasn't me.'

Gwen bobbed her head in thought. 'I suppose that's only fair. You get up there, give them a minute or so to see you two and then hand her back to me. I'm going to be right here with the gun pointing at her sweet little head. If you shout, speak, whisper, think even a single word, any single word – do you understand?'

Leslie nods. She lugs Emma onto her left hip. The child's head lolls back, her mouth falls open. Leslie struggles to manage Emma's weight as she rips the plastic curtain free from the frame. She tests the sturdiness of the sill, and then holding on to the frame with her right hand, pulls herself up to standing.

The sky is darkness made pale by moonlight. Leslie stands very still, breathing very hard. Her eyes are locked on the figure of Yancy Galleghar, striding about the drive. She waits. Emma is so heavy. Leslie's arms have grown numb from the weight. For a terrible moment, Leslie feels the child begin to slip and then just as quickly Emma is lifted up, secured, as though some second set of arms had added their effort. The air is cold and Leslie shivers. She feels as though she's been standing here for centuries, but it is only seconds before there are cries from below and a searchlight is swiveled up to the tower window where Leslie is standing, motionless and silent, Emma drooping in her arms.

The ground below her seethes with sudden activity. Greg is running toward the house, shouting at her. Molly stands in the drive and stares upward. Voices yell to her to stay calm, relax, not to move. Yancy is giving orders and the emergency lights flash. Gwen, crouching low by the window, whispers, 'That's long enough.'

Leslie pretends not to hear. She watches Yancy directing his crew.

'Now, Leslie. They'll be up here in a second. Leslie! Give Emma to me now. I hear one foot on the staircase and . . . that's right, turn around slowly, so they can see you put her down. That's right. Now drop her to me.'

Leslie has turned. She is looking down at Gwen. She moves Emma off her hip, but instead of sliding the heavy body into Gwen's arms, Leslie locks Emma hard against her chest.

'My choice,' she says to Gwen, and then steps backward, out into nothing.

There is a sudden snuffing out of sound and motion and then a soft thud of impact. I watch her creep forward until she can see over the rim of the sill, until she can look down. There, at the foot of the tower, Emma is being hurried into an ambulance. Leslie, cradling her arm, is being helped to her feet. She is struggling to free herself from the rescue net the Wellington Volunteer Fire Department had deployed, on Yancy Galleghar's orders, at first sight of Leslie in the window.

Realizing Leslie's survival, she rushes to the tower door, races down the stairs. She heads for the hidden panel in the front entrance, hoping to use the tunnels to flee. Isabel will not escape twice. I wrench a beam free from the ceiling and throw it to block her exit. Five Mile House roars at the wound. She runs then for the additions, tangling herself in the plastic curtain and nearly tumbling into the cellar. The floor is gone, for I am collapsing the floorboards. They fall into the pit like keys sliding from a satanic organ. The sound, the sound of the wood ripping and splitting, crashing to the earth: the sound is wonderful. Electric wires are severed, they flail and spark. She retreats and runs back for the stairs, up again, fast as I smash the risers behind her. She reaches the tower and shuts herself inside. It is with happiness beyond description that I twist and splinter the bones, snap the bracing, crush the supports. Slate shingles pour in on Isabel like razor-sharp rain. She covers her head with her hands, crying out. For more than one hundred years I have waited. In a span of moments, I bring Five Mile to its knees.

Thirty-five

A T THE HOSPITAL, THEY drew blood from Emma and concluded the most she'd been given was codeine. She was dehydrated and frightened, more by the IV needle than any event she remembered. They wanted to keep her overnight for observation, but she was expected to recover fully. The doctor convinced Leslie to leave Emma's side long enough to have her own arm examined. She would need a cast, she was told, as the injury turned out to be what the doctor termed 'a stress fracture.' This diagnosis sent Leslie into a fit of laughter.

She asked the nurse applying the plaster-embedded bandage about Gwen and was told that the woman was alive but the situation was not encouraging. Severe trauma to the head had resulted in a coma. Leslie asked if she might see Gwen. The nurse said it was not a good idea.

When they finished with her arm, Leslie went to check on Emma. Outside Emma's room, Greg was leaning against the wall and talking with Phillip, who was holding an ice pack to his head. They didn't see her, and as she drew closer she heard Greg explaining his theory of how the irregular seaming in foundation materials presented the weakness that had caused much of Five Mile's collapse.

'Fortunately we had enough of it reinforced that we didn't lose the whole house – and I still can't believe that those oils in the flooring didn't go up what with all the electrical sparking – hey, Les!' He straightened and opened his arms to her. She accepted the invitation and then whimpered and withdrew when the embrace hurt her arm. She stepped back and looked at Phillip.

'You okay?'

He nods.

'Phil was playing hero,' Greg said with a laugh. 'He was trying to get in through the old bootleggers' tunnels when the house came down on his head.'

'Oh,' said Leslie.

'Ouch,' said Phillip. 'I'm very glad you're all right. And Emma.' He laid his hand upon her bandaged arm. She didn't flinch. He smiled at her. 'I need – I need to look after some things.'

'I understand,' said Leslie, and watched him leave. She then turned back to Greg and saw that he understood as well. 'Where's Molly?'

Greg pointed to the door. Inside Molly was sitting on Emma's bed. They were playing rock-paper-scissors. Emma was giggling.

'Can you stay with them?' Leslie asked Greg. 'There's something I have to do.'

'Of course I'll stay with them.' Greg didn't look at her.

Leslie walked off down the corridor. She took the elevator to the main lobby and headed toward the emergency room where they'd come in. In the reception area, Yancy Galleghar and a couple members of the Wellington Volunteer Fire Department were chatting with a nurse as she went over their request for supplies. Yancy glanced up and saw Leslie. He gave her a two-finger salute. She returned it, and then went outside.

By the time Leslie had driven back to Wellington, it was nearing dawn. Everything from sky to street was the same shade of blue-gray. The town was dim and quiet. She passed through it without seeing as much as another vehicle. She drove a bit farther, rounded the now familiar bend, and parked the van on the shoulder of the road.

The wooded hillside was peaceful, still. She climbed steadily. The morning air was cold, swathed in mist. She reached the second gate and was certain she was alone on the hill. Five Mile House stood before her, stooped but unbroken. In some sections, the additions had caved completely, while the walls only leaned inward in others. The main house remained as upright as ever, although the roof line sagged in deep depressions. The tower roof had collapsed fully, but the tower itself appeared sound.

Leslie entered the house. The interior was thick with settling dust. The oily fragrance of oranges and cloves was stronger than ever, but unable to mask the incandescent singe of ozone, Leslie went straight to the tower stairs. She started up, carefully stepping around the fist-sized holes in the risers.

The door at the top was open, jammed into position by the broken frame. It looked to Leslie as though the door had been blasted outward. She thought about her first visit to this room and was grateful for this guarantee of exit. The room itself was heaped with broken wood and shingles. Above her, through the torn open tower, the day was brightening. She didn't have a lot of time. Leslie decided on the most likely spot and began to move the debris aside until she had cleared it to the floor. When that one didn't prove correct, she changed direction a bit. At one point, she found a small puddle of blood. She stopped and thought about Gwen, but then continued. With her left arm immobilized by the cast, the process took longer, was more arduous than she feared. She was now hurting badly. Her good hand cut and bleeding. It only made her work harder. She wanted to get this over with before she was discovered. Eventually, she saw a corner of brown paper protruding from the ruin. She moved the rest of the rubble away from the envelope, which was crumpled and dirty, but intact. Turning it in her hand, she felt the contents shift.

Leslie took the envelope downstairs, into the front room. I saw the match flicker to life, and I knew then, at last, I was free.

The fire was assumed to be the result of electrical malfunction, although Greg Stone would swear that he personally had made certain all power to Five Mile House had been shut off. Harry Wellington, surveying the smoldering remains, came close to tap dancing with joy. The events of the past few days had given Five Mile and its Hallowe'en-perfect history national exposure. He was already getting calls from parties interested in participating in the rebuilding of Five Mile House.

'Of course, we'll rebuild,' Diana said for the television cameras, as she stood on the other side of the padlocked gate, Jack hanging from her hand. 'Five Mile House is a national treasure.' On the subject of recent trespasses and vandalism, she said the family was most discouraged by the destruction of the original cornerstone. She hugged her son close and added that it wasn't anything that could not be replaced.

The Wellingtons pleaded, cajoled, and finally paid Greg Stone enough money to stay on to supervise the rebuilding. Greg's one stipulation was that his family live somewhere, anywhere other than Wellington. They agreed. He packed up his things, his daughters and the dog; he returned to the city without Leslie. Molly and Emma called daily, they sounded, to Leslie, happy. She missed them. Phillip Hogarth also called, from another city, a different direction.

Leslie lived in the cottage for a few weeks, raking autumn leaves and cutting back dead foliage. One afternoon, Joe Garrett called. His voice was soft, choked with regret. He wouldn't say where he was, but he apologized, and then told Leslie that he'd decided to turn off the machines, to let Gwen go. Leslie said nothing, she just hung up the phone. The next morning, hours before the first snowfall, there was in the front yard a FOR SALE sign. The van was gone. Leslie didn't come back. This was where Leslie's story became her own again.

There are three roads out of Wellington. I do not know which one she chose.

Five Mile House gone, I went to the earth, to the rock and the root of it; I remain here on the hill. I gather myself about the old foundations. I watched the witches come with their picks and hammers. I watched the cornerstone break. They sang as they carted the rubble away. They were neither joyful nor triumphant. They knew it would start again. It is war.

This is why I choose to stay. I will be here when Five Mile House returns. I anticipate intrusion. Even more, I anticipate escape.